THE SHUT EYE

BELINDA BAUER

LARGE
PRINT

First published in Great Britain 2015
by
Bantam Press
an imprint of Transworld Publishers

First Isis Edition
published 2015
by arrangement with
Transworld Publishers
Penguin Random House

*A catalogue record for this book is available
from the British Library.*

ISBN 978–1–78541–120–5 (hb)
ISBN 978–1–78541–126–7 (pb)

Published by
F. A. Thorpe (Publishing)
Anstey, Leicestershire

Set by Words & Graphics Ltd.
Anstey, Leicestershire
Printed and bound in Great Britain by
T. J. International Ltd., Padstow, Cornwall

This book is printed on acid-free paper

To Eve and Michael Williams-Jones, whose
generosity allowed me to become a writer

CHAPTER
ONE

Valentine's Day, 2000

John Marvel looked at his watch.

It was eight thirty-seven, and he'd done the same thing less than a minute earlier. He had promised Debbie he would be home by nine. Normally it wouldn't matter, but tonight it did, although he wasn't sure why.

He felt the cold invade his lungs as he stared up into the dome of light that masked the stars. Frost hung in an ethereal ring around the streetlamp, waiting to settle, and Marvel could feel it fingering his shins through the thin material of his trousers.

He didn't like to be outdoors. It was too . . . *fresh*. Even here, where London had sprawled south, overlapping the river and coating what used to be the Garden of England with its grime and its traffic and its smell of decay.

Marvel had started to sprawl with it: too much home cooking.

Too much home.

Comfort had always made him restless. He needed to be always moving on, moving up, otherwise he got frustrated.

Now he looked across the road to the King's Arms. It was filled with warmth and noise and booze. It had been more than a year since he'd been there — been drunk — and he still missed it like a lover, with a yearn in his chest and a dry lump in his throat. He wouldn't have gone in tonight. Or any night. It was a test — a game he played with himself. Driving past, slowing down, craning to look.

Not stopping.

But tonight he'd stopped. He didn't know why. He was no more thirsty than on any of the other four hundred days since he had had a drink.

And then he'd seen the woman.

And now it was hard to stand here, so near and yet so far. The pub's grubby stained-glass windows were lit from behind, like Christ in a cathedral, calling all sinners.

Marvel checked his watch.

It was eight thirty-eight. The second hand arced through the quadrant in a series of cheap jerks.

"Look," he sighed. "Are you going to jump or not?"

The woman on the ledge flinched and her fingers pressed more tightly against the brick parapet. In the cold amber glow, Marvel could see the goose-bumps stippling her skinny arms. She was wearing indoor clothes. A thin, strappy top and skinny jeans and those stupid little ballet shoes women wore nowadays instead of high heels.

But then, she didn't strike him as a high-heels kind of girl. She had a pinched, undernourished look to her face that made her cheekbones sharp and her eyes seem huge, but in a way that was less Audrey Hepburn, more eating disorder.

Marvel guessed she was in her early twenties, but she could have been seventeen. Or forty.

She glanced at him and shrugged one bony shoulder in apology. "I . . . I'm waiting for a train," she said. Then she looked back down between her shoes at the tracks.

"Interesting," said Marvel, with a sage nod of his head — as if she had explained everything.

He stepped towards her and leaned briefly over the parapet to look at the glimmering rails. While he did, she gripped harder and watched him warily — as if he might suddenly lunge at her, grab her, pull her backwards over the wall to safety.

Heroically save her life.

Despite his name, Marvel did no such thing.

Instead he gave a humourless grunt and said, "Then you're shit out of luck. The trains don't go through here after eight."

She said nothing for a long moment. Then, without raising her head, she said, "Wh — what time is it now?"

Marvel lifted his watch again — tilting it so that the face was illuminated by the streetlight. "Eight-forty."

The girl nodded slowly at the tracks, her straggly brown hair veiling everything but her brow and the red tip of her nose. She wrinkled the brow and wiped the nose on the back of her hand.

"Oh," she said, and Marvel could tell she was crying.

Crying was not his thing, so he decided against words of comfort or a pat on the back, which might open some kind of emotional floodgate. He just stood there while she sobbed quietly.

"I can't get anything right," she finally whispered.

"Join the club," he snorted.

She only shook her head slowly, apparently declining to join the ranks of any club that would have him as a member — even in her desperate state.

"What's your name?" he said.

She didn't tell him and he didn't care, but he had to pretend. It was expected.

Marvel wasn't going to keep the nine-o'clock promise. He was glad. Promises were traps; shackles to be broken.

I'll be home by nine.

I'm not in the pub.

I love you.

The girl was still crying a little.

He looked at his watch again. Eight forty-three. "Come on," he said brusquely. "Hop back over and I'll take you home."

She gave a long, shuddering sigh and nodded fractionally. "OK."

Marvel was a little surprised. That was easy.

Too easy.

His jaw clenched with annoyance. She'd probably never meant to jump at all. He'd stood here in the freezing February night for almost thirty bloody minutes in full tortuous view of the King's Arms, and the whole time she'd just been waiting for an opportunity to climb back over the wall.

Time-waster.

4

His life was full of them and they made him sick.

Still, it had given him a good excuse to be late. Not that he'd really needed one. He often lied to Debbie about where he'd been and what he'd done, and it didn't change a thing. What could she say? In his line of work you could make up any old bollocks and people had to believe you. Perk of the job.

He put out a hand to steady the girl as she swung her legs over the parapet, but she swayed away from him, so he left her to it. She slid awkwardly off the wall and dropped on to the road beside him. She was almost a foot shorter than he was, and Marvel was no giant.

She shivered and hugged her own arms for warmth.

Before either of them could say anything, the eight twenty from London Victoria shook the bridge.

They both stared down at the blurry black roof, blocking out the rails as it raced under their feet and through Bickley station.

In the silence that followed, the girl gave him an accusing look, but Detective Chief Inspector Marvel only shrugged.

CHAPTER
TWO

"*James!*"

James Buck was standing with a Golf GTi balanced on a single oily hand, like a waiter bringing a main course to a car-crusher. He looked round at his boss. He hadn't heard him coming because the garage was always loud with engines and echoes and the radio playing. And because he'd been thinking. Always thinking.

About Daniel, of course.

"What?" he said.

"James!" yelled Brian Pigeon again. "Ang! Turn that bloody thing down!"

Ang went over to the radio, sulkily dragging his broom, and James lowered his arm. The car stayed up without his support — floating on the hydraulic lift, with its wheels dangling from their arches, like a puppy that's just been scooped off the floor.

The music blared very slightly less loudly.

"You did the timing on Mr Knight's car!"

Mr Knight had a pristine Audi TT with a chrome Billy Boat exhaust. Last time they'd had it in, someone had scraped a wing, so if something else had gone wrong with the Audi, it was serious shit. James hadn't touched it on either occasion.

Not that that made any difference.

"What car?" he said blankly.

"That one!" Brian shouted, and jabbed a finger at the garage forecourt. "The one dripping oil all over my new cement."

James didn't look at the forecourt; he looked back up at the underside of the Golf and swallowed hard. He didn't trust himself to answer just yet. The cement wasn't that new. It had been poured exactly four months ago, on November fifth.

The morning of Bonfire Night.

The morning Daniel had disappeared.

He didn't expect Brian Pigeon to know that the way *he* knew it, but he still hated him for thinking of that day for any other reason.

Brian was yelling again. "When you put the rocker cover back on you must've pinched the gasket. Oil everywhere. All over Mr Knight's driveway too!"

James wouldn't have done something so careless. It was probably Mikey who'd pinched the gasket. He was rash and speedy, and if a car wasn't hooked up to the diagnostic computer, he was often lost. But James didn't say any of that. He just stood there, one hand at his side with a spanner dangling from it, the other over his head as he loosened the nut with his fingers, on autopilot now.

"What have you got to say about that then? Now the job has to be done again."

"Not by you!" Mr Knight shouted from near the office. "You'll pay for someone else to fix it or I'll sue the arse off you!"

Brian ignored that. "What have you got to say?" he demanded of James again.

"Sorry?" said James.

"Sorry, *bullshit!*" Brian shouted. "Mr Knight is our most valuable customer! Now we have to do the job again!"

"You're not touching my car," Mr Knight insisted.

"For free!" Brian kept on.

"Even for free," said Mr Knight. "I'm suing you!"

Brian ignored him again and shouted at James, "This is the last straw, James. Get out."

James let go of the Golf and wiped his brow with his elbow. "What?"

The spanner in his right hand suddenly felt very heavy.

"Get your stuff and get out." Brian jerked a thumb over his shoulder. "You're fired."

There was a brief silence — or what passed for it in the garage, with the radio still playing like static under their lives.

"Hold on," said Mr Knight, suddenly not so vehement. "I'm not . . . it's not —"

Brian held up a hand. "Don't you worry, Mr Knight. It's not your fault. Your custom is far too important for me to risk losing it over some *moron.*"

James felt the cold steel against the ball of his thumb. The spanner was beautifully machined and perfectly balanced. He tightened his grip.

"Seems a bit steep, *firing* the guy," said Mr Knight.

"Not a bit of it," said Brian. "Messed up your car. Messed up your driveway. Messed up my forecourt. Cost me a bloody fortune. But it's not about the money — we've got a reputation. We're professionals."

Mr Knight shrugged and nodded — slowly understanding that sometimes a man had to do what a man had to do.

Brian turned back to look at James. "Are you still here? What are you waiting for? The gasket fairy?"

James turned and, with all his strength, hurled the spanner across the workshop. It bounced off a bench, then skidded across the red-painted concrete floor of Pigeon's MoT & Diagnostics and slid into the old inspection pit with a loud metal clang. James stormed around his boss (*That's a Snap-On, you little shit!*) and past Mr Knight (*Made a helluva mess on my drive . . .*) and into the scummy little kitchen.

He sat on the only chair with a padded seat — the one Brian always took. He put a foot on another of the chairs and pushed it noisily around the lino floor for a bit, and then kicked it over with a deliberate crash.

There was a Formica table, a sink unit, the wooden bench where Ang slept, and five mis-matched chairs. The table was covered with old newspapers and junk-food wrappers and a mug without a handle that Pavel and Mikey used as an ashtray. The walls were pitted and smeared with dark finger-marks. Over the microwave was a calendar that was an excuse to hang photos of topless women on the wall. None of them ever looked at it, or changed the month; it was just there as a minor male defiance.

James tipped over another chair.

All the time, he heard indistinct voices under the usual echoing noises of pop music and of engines turning over. The voices became less and less heated. Brian talking to Mr Knight; Mr Knight walking away; the back and forth of departure.

Then the courtesy car started up. James would have known it anywhere; it was a Citroën diesel that sounded like a suit of armour falling downstairs.

Mr Knight was leaving his Audi for the work to be done. After all that bluster and bullshit. That's the way it usually went.

James listened to the Citroën bump off the garage forecourt and grind into second gear as it joined the traffic. Then he got up.

He walked to the back of the workshop, but Ang was already retrieving the spanner from the layer of assorted rubbish in the bottom of the disused pit. Ang was quick to volunteer for anything and Brian was not slow to take advantage of it. He put him to good use fetching sandwiches, parking cars and dialling phone numbers for him, because he was too busy to waste time on hold. Three years after arriving in England on the axle of a flatbed truck, Ang was still learning the language. So far he'd only really mastered the four-lettered words.

Brian Pigeon calling. Please hold. You have message? Ang practised his lines endlessly under his breath, but the task was a minefield.

10

Now Brian directed him from the edge of the pit, hands on hips, the poppers on his overalls starting to gape. James had noticed that lately, when Brian leaned into an engine bay, he had to find somewhere safe to rest his belly.

He glanced at James. "Spanner was a bit much."

"Sorry."

Brian shrugged, then said, "Did you like the gasket fairy though?" He laughed at himself, and then added a review: "Bloody hilarious."

James smiled faintly, and put out a hand to help Ang up between the old ramp and the pit wall. He was slim, so he braced himself, but Ang was as light as a feather and seemed almost to float out of the pit.

James followed Brian across the workshop to the office while Ang picked up his broom and turned the radio up, singing along, putting the wrong words to the wrong tune.

"Ang!" shouted Mikey. "You sound like a randy cat!"

"Thank you," said Ang, and went on singing. He loved that radio. It was on in the morning when they arrived for work, and still on when they left every night.

Brian looked up as James came into the office. "You don't mind, do you?"

"No," said James.

"So soon after . . ." Brian shrugged with his hands ". . . you know . . ."

"I don't mind," said James, and he meant it. He didn't mind about much any more. Nothing was important enough to mind about.

Brian took a crumple of notes from his pocket and tugged free a twenty. "Here," he said.

James tucked it into his top pocket without a word.

"Shit," said Ang from the doorway. "Money for old nuts."

"Rope," said James. "Money for old rope."

"So what is money for nuts?"

"I dunno. Peanuts, maybe? You get paid peanuts? Not much money, you know?"

"Oh," said Ang. "OK." He hovered at the door.

Brian was on the phone, sorting out another new lift. Four years ago when James had first started, they'd had three crappy old inspection pits; now two had already been filled in and replaced by hydraulic lifts. There was also a rubberized floor and a new cement forecourt — and they still had to put the coffee against the microwave door to keep it shut. Brian was rich but tight; James figured maybe he was rich *because* he was tight.

He shouted at someone about delivery slots and concrete-setting times, then banged the phone down and shouted, "Arseholes!"

Ang leaned into the office with his usual good timing. "I's fired for peanuts."

"What?" said Brian.

"I's fired. No James."

"James gets fired."

"But I's fired for peanuts."

"James gets fired," Brian repeated. "He's white and English so he gets fired. You're a Chinaman so I can't fire you because that would be racist, see?"

"Shit." Ang frowned. He toyed with the end of the broom handle, picking at the wood with his fingernail.

Brian sighed. "Are you going to clean the floor or am I going to have to call Immigration?"

Ang twitched upright and started sweeping. "I's Hmong person," he pointed out sulkily. "Not Chinaman."

"Well, now you're in England, and in England we work."

Across the garage, Pavel gave a hollow laugh into the wheel-arch of a Lexus.

James reached up and continued undoing the nut on the Golf's exhaust clamp. It was the thirteenth time he'd been fired. Two hundred and sixty quid's worth of humiliation. Brian Pigeon was some actor — he should have been in the West End, not running a grubby MoT garage in south London — and his anger was convincing, even when you knew it was fake. Sometimes Mrs Pigeon came to the garage, although she rarely got out of her sleek Mercedes — just issued orders to Brian through the window, as if she were at a McDonald's drive-thru. Brian never got angry with *her* though, and sometimes James wondered whether that was why he had a reserve of that emotion, all locked and loaded and ready to direct at *him* whenever a customer looked like getting litigious.

It always worked. Nothing appeased a rich bastard faster than seeing some grease-monkey fired on the spot for screwing up a job. Nothing made them feel more important.

It wasn't for real, but James still found it unpleasant. There was the embarrassment of publicly claiming a cock-up that was never his. There was the forced apology. There was the shouting and the submission and the spittle in the face.

It all made him feel like shit.

Even the twenty quid he got made him feel like shit. Brian always gave it to him as if he was doing him a big favour, singling him out for special treatment like a favourite son.

"Jesus," said Brian Pigeon quietly.

Ang stopped singing and stared sadly out of the double doors.

James followed their gaze and his heart sank even lower.

His wife was out there, sitting cross-legged on the edge of the forecourt, like Buddha in a blue anorak.

It only reminded him that feeling like shit was exactly what he deserved.

CHAPTER
THREE

Anna Buck was crazy. Anyone could see.

Every morning she sat in the street. Not against the wall like a homeless person, but right in the way, where commuters had to split around her with their phones and iPods plugged into their ears, and children circled her idly on their bikes like little Apaches.

Once a day, come rain or shine, Anna opened the grubby front door in the Victorian terrace and edged outside. No sooner had she opened the door than she slipped through and closed it again, fast, checking behind her as if she were trying to keep a cat in the house.

She always wore the same thing: a big blue waterproof, with sleeves that covered her right down to the fingertips. She kept her eyes down and the hood up, so that her face had an undersea pall. Head covered and bowed, Anna didn't need to look up to know exactly where she was going — diagonally across the wide pavement and on to the cement of the garage forecourt.

There she sank slowly to her knees and started to clean.

Every day, Anna Buck brushed the cement with a toothbrush, wiped it down with a cloth, and then polished it to a gemstone shine.

Nobody stopped. People were busy and had other places to be. If they looked they just glanced, and only if they glanced again might they have noticed what it was that she was cleaning.

Five footprints in the cement.

Five little footprints leading away from the sooty houses to who-knew-where . . .

Today was dry and the prints were dusty, and Anna used the toothbrush to clear the grit and dirt from the little rounded indentations where the toes had been. When the large pieces had been brushed away, she pressed her forefinger into the big toe-print, to lift away the dust. She thought of Daniel's toes — so small and pink and wiggly.

This little piggy went to market . . .

Pink and wiggly-giggly. She'd only had to start the rhyme to make him squirm with anticipation — his eyes made sparkling crescent slits by his chubby cheeks, and his small white teeth showing top and bottom with his squeals of laughter.

Her finger fitted cosily into the next toe-print.

This little piggy stayed at home.

She was still on the second toe — the tip of her forefinger fitted the second toe perfectly, all snug and cosy.

This little piggy stayed at home.

Daniel hadn't stayed at home. Daniel had gone and he hadn't come back.

No roast beef, no none, no *weee-weee-weee all the way home.*

Just.

Gone.

Anna pressed her pinkie into the third indentation, then the fourth.

The fifth — the little toe — was too small even for her pinkie, and she lowered herself like a supplicant to blow the dust from it, before wiping the rest of the footprint clean — careful along the inner arch because Daniel was so ticklish, and then around the heel, dabbing the last of the dust out with the cloth. As she did she could feel his heels in her hands again, cupping them in her palms during all those long-ago nappy changes, making his little legs pedal bicycles in the air, as he giggled to the scent of talcum powder.

He would laugh and she would laugh and James would laugh. It seemed impossible now — the very idea of laughter.

He'll be a sprinter — look at those thighs. He'll be a dancer, pointing his toes. He'll play for Spurs — what a kick!

Daniel had been easy to potty train. They said boys were harder than girls but Daniel had been out of nappies by his second birthday, and loved his big-boy jeans and his Batman pants. He called them his Bad Man pants and she and James had never corrected him because it was just so cute, and gave them a ridiculous level of pleasure every time he said it.

Anna sobbed. It happened sometimes without notice and she didn't try to stop it. She couldn't. Her tears were like breathing; there was no way of damming them. She'd tried in the early days, but it hadn't worked. Now she bent to her work and sobbed openly and didn't even care where she was or who saw her.

One tear plopped into the footprint and she cursed in her head and quickly soaked it up with the cloth. Salt and acid rain were death to cement and concrete.

After she'd got all the soot and dirt out of the prints, she opened the wax and started to polish them, to protect them.

Further up on the edge of the forecourt someone called Big Mike had written his name in the same wet cement. But nobody had ever cared for *Big Mike*, and already the shallow letters were starting to wear and fade, the edges softened by rain and passing feet.

That wasn't going to happen to Daniel's prints.

Never.

The fierceness of the thought stopped Anna's tears for a moment and she wiped her nose on a blue sleeve and drew a deep new breath, enlivened by her own determination to keep her son's last known steps as fresh and clean as on the morning they were made, exactly four months ago.

She couldn't stop people walking across them — not once she returned to the flat, at least. But she could make them shine, and she did every day that it wasn't raining. When it was raining, she just came out and sat leaning over them for a while, head down, like a dying squaw — saving the footprints from wear for a short while, before hurrying back indoors before the baby could wake up.

At other times she placed a tea-light there, and lit it with an old Bic lighter. Once a policeman blew it out and told her it was a fire hazard. Anna had screamed in his face — some crazed incoherence about Daniel and wasting time and catching real criminals — and the policeman had backed off and scurried away. After that he walked his beat on the other side of the street and let her light her candles.

Now Anna put out her finger and traced the outline of the last footprint. It was her favourite — the last point of contact Daniel had had with the ground. The print was twisted and a little misshapen, and more shallow than the others — as if he'd simply taken off and floated away, over the lime trees and into the sky.

Beyond it — where the sixth print should have been — the cement was smooth and undented.

"What are you doing?"

Anna looked up briefly and saw a girl. She was in school uniform — black trousers, black shoes and red sweatshirt, *St Catherine's Academy* embroidered around a cross on the left side of the chest.

Sometimes kids shouted at Anna as they went past in unruly groups, or called her names. Weirdo and Nutter and worse.

She bent and went back to her work.

"What are you doing?" the girl said again.

It was weeks since Anna had spoken to anybody but James. Maybe months.

"Cluh —" she started and then had to clear her throat of tears and disuse. "Cleaning."

"Oh," said the girl.

Anna polished the heel of the last footprint, making the cement as smooth and shiny as glass. While she rubbed, her anorak's nylon hood scraped synthetically back and forth against her ears, cutting out everything else.

Scri-scri-scri . . .

Anna went on rubbing long after she knew the footprint was done, just to maintain that noisy silence.

"Why?" said the girl.

"What?" said Anna.

"Why are you cleaning them?"

"Because —" She stopped and thought and then went on. "My son made them and I don't want to lose them."

"Why?"

Daniel had wanted to know *why* too. All the time. Why this, why that, why the other. It had driven her mad. Although — of course — at the time she'd had no idea what mad *was*; not the faintest idea. Now the lack of Daniel was showing her the true meaning of the word. Anna knew that. She knew she was going mad, but she didn't know how to stop it any more than she knew how to stop crying or breathing.

"Why?" The girl was still there. Still asking. "Why don't you want to lose them?"

Anna shrugged without looking up. "Because I lost *him*."

"Really?" said the girl, and her forehead wrinkled with mystery. "How?"

The *how* spun inside Anna's head so often that she knew it off by heart, the same way she'd once known every frame of Daniel's DVDs — *The Lion King* and *Toy Story*. She didn't want to replay the *how*, but once it had started, she could never stop it.

She'd been in the kitchen, making packed lunches for playschool and work. Peanut butter and carrots and a little chocolate bar shaped like a frog for Daniel, peanut butter and a Mars bar for James. From the garage next door the radio had gone on — the tinny sound of Duran Duran maybe, or Culture Club. Something from the Eighties. She'd glanced through the kitchen window at the street below, beating out its own rhythms: the number 32 bus waiting at the stop, the man walking two rocking Dachshunds, the woman jogging so slowly that the tall man with the *Daily Telegraph* under his arm overtook her with ease, the paving slabs cracking and tilting as the lime trees refused to be contained by concrete squares. There was a cement truck parked outside the garage, and the driver was laying thick, corrugated-plastic pipes across the forecourt.

In a minute, James would sneak up from behind and put his arms around her . . .

Oh!

She had turned her head and kissed him long and hard.

I'll bring home the fireworks tonight, he'd said.

She'd laughed and said, *I bet you will!*

He'd laughed too, and reached around her to pick up his lunch. Slowly. Their bodies touching all the way down.

Smiling.

See you tonight.

She'd see him a lot sooner than that.

And never the same way again.

Anna had heard him leave. Heard him go down the narrow, dark stairs, heard him open the door . . .

She hadn't heard the door shut. She hadn't even thought about it until afterwards — until it was far, far, *far* too late. James opened the door, James shut the door. That was what had happened every day for the three years they'd lived here. She knew it like *Toy Story* — so well that she could tune it out and have other thoughts while it droned on in the background.

Unheard.

Daniel!

She'd taken out the chocolate and put in another carrot.

Daniel! Come on!

She'd taken out the carrot and put back the chocolate.

She'd make cornflake cakes for tonight. Daniel's favourite. And she'd pick up some apples for bobbing, on her way to work.

She'd never go to work again.

Daniel!

She'd gone into his bedroom. She'd gone into the bathroom. She'd gone back to his room. She hadn't gone downstairs; there was no reason to. The only thing downstairs was the front door, and that was always shut because they were on a main road.

Instead she'd stood by the telly, wasting time, wasting *life*, wondering where he might be — and by the time she'd peered down the stairs, it was too late.

22

One hundred and twenty days ago, the door had been left open . . .

Everything after that was just a fast-forward blur of panic: of running and shouting and of the cement-truck driver looking up from the fat, jiggling hose to see what was wrong, of Pavel and Mr Pigeon scooting up and down the street, stopping strangers, holding their hands at hip height to show the top of Daniel's imaginary head. Of Ang clutching his broom, wide-eyed and tearful at the commotion. Of Mikey shouting *Danny! Danny!* from the alleyway behind the garage.

Of James finally appearing from the direction of the shops, with an armful of sparklers and rockets that he then forgot about so completely that they dropped from his grasp one by one as he ran frantically up and down the street.

All to the smell of fireworks in the dull air, and the sound of tinny hits floating from the garage.

The first police car had pulled right up on the kerb and one of the coppers had found this place. This place where five little footprints headed across the forecourt.

And stopped.

Nobody had seen him.

Nobody saw him again after that bitter November morning.

Anna didn't remember much more about that day, and didn't remember much about all the days since. The blur of police and cameras and newspaper stories growing smaller and smaller. DCI Lloyd calling now and then to pick her brains about things she might have remembered, just in case she had vital information that she hadn't bothered to share. The offers of medication and counselling — as if they could make her forget that Daniel was gone. As if that would be a good thing!

Anna couldn't honestly have said how she'd got all the way from that day to this; how she'd survived.

Why she'd survived.

The girl was still standing beside her.

Anna gathered up the cloth and the toothbrush and the wax polish and got to her feet. Now that she was standing, she looked at the child's face properly. It was round and ruddy and about eight years old. Black wire-rimmed glasses and dark-brown plaits with hairclips shaped like flowers.

"Where did he go?" the girl asked, and Anna realized that she must have thought all of those memories out loud.

"Nobody knows," said Anna, and that truth sounded as brutal to her ears now as it had when she'd first overheard a policeman saying it to a concerned passer-by on that fateful — careless — day.

"Did you look?" said the girl.

"I've looked," she said. "We've all looked. We'll never stop looking."

"Is he dead?" said the girl, with her eyes widening in horror.

"No," said Anna firmly. "He's alive. Somewhere."

The child nodded sombrely, relieved to hear the good news.

"If I see him I'll tell you," she said, and Anna was touched. She tried to say "thank you" but her mouth was too wobbly.

24

She'd forgotten how sweet children could be. A week after Daniel had disappeared, somebody had pushed a tatty drawing through the front door — two goldfish in a pond. She guessed it was from one of his nursery classmates at TiggerTime a few doors down. His teacher had knocked a few times too and offered comfort she had no real way to provide.

Anna and the little girl with the pigtails stared down together at the five footprints, now so glossy and dark that they were like works of art in a fancy gallery.

"They're all you've got left," the child said sadly.

Anna nodded. They were all she had left.

Then the girl said she had to go to school.

And she disappeared too.

CHAPTER
FOUR

The longer DCI John Marvel worked in homicide, the more he disliked people. He'd never met one he didn't hate — or despise, at the very least — and he could see the bad in anyone.

It was a useful quality in a detective.

Not so much in a human being.

Murder was DCI Marvel's favourite thing in the whole world — even above Sky Sports. There was no other crime that had the sheer black-and-white finality of murder, and it was one of the few things in life he took personally. He was good at it, too. He had hunches and insights; he had the dogged obsession to keep going when everyone else had given up — not because he wanted to solve the crime, but because he hated to lose. Solving murders was a competition, make no bones about it. The killer won, or the cops won.

How could you not love something that was so unambiguous?

So *biblical?*

Even when he used to go to the King's Arms of an evening, Marvel talked shop — as long as that shop sold murder. While his colleagues had tried to switch off and forget the underbelly, Marvel had mulled over the gory details; he mentally sifted evidence, he bullied colleagues into long, intricate discussions about blood spatter and rates of decay and dodgy evidence. And when they made excuses to leave early, he would sit alone and brood on the endless permutations of how and why and who and what and when.

He took case files on holiday. While other men read Lee Child or Wilbur Smith, Marvel pored over autopsy reports and crime-scene photos. And he got results — his solve rate since taking over South East's G Team was a staggering 84 per cent.

He looked at his watch.

It was exactly five minutes to opening time.

Old habits died hard.

He heaved himself out of his chair, went to the machine across the room and got a cup of tea. Or it could have been soup, it was hard to tell. Either way, he put two sugars in it.

He took the cup back to his desk and lit a cigarette.

The murder-squad room at Lewisham was a low-ceilinged, overcrowded place, with every sharp corner softened by towers of bulging brown files. Computers the size of wheelbarrows pumped out heat and hum on each desk, but the paperless office was still the stuff of science fiction. At an outpost of this information Jenga, Marvel had annexed a corner desk by pulling rank on DS Brady. As soon as he'd secured the desk, Marvel had turned it to face the corner, where he taped a *Reservoir Dogs* poster and a selection of case-file photos. Having his back to the room discouraged casual interaction. Marvel didn't give a shit what the rest of G Team did behind his back, as long as they were still there when he turned around.

He sipped his tea-slash-soup and grimaced, then sucked hard on the Rothman's, loving the acrid warmth that filled his throat, and squinted at the photos on the wall.

They weren't from the case he was working on now. That was about a thirty-four-year-old prostitute called Tanzi Anderson, who had been found in her wardrobe, with a lapful of her own skimpy clothing pulled from wire hangers, and a single bullet hole between her shocked eyes. Marvel had no doubt that very soon another whore would spill the beans and they would track down Tanzi's pimp, who had coincidentally disappeared on the night she died, along with Tanzi's money and heroin.

It was a no-brainer.

And if it didn't require a brain, it certainly didn't require photos on the wall to prick his memory.

No, the photos John Marvel chose to look at every day were from an unsolved case.

The case of Edie Evans, who had left home on her bike one dim January morning over a year ago, and had never arrived at school.

For one long, tortuous, timewasting day, Edie had been treated as a truant. She was almost a teenager; she was an adventurous child; she was on a bicycle; she knew how to catch a train to the city . . . The police did the maths, even though her parents insisted it didn't add up. Edie was young for her age, they said — by today's standards, at least. She didn't have a boyfriend;

she didn't wear make-up; she had a little brother she adored and a pet mouse called Peter. She was popular at school and good at her lessons, they said. Edie not going to school made no sense.

Not coming home made even less.

And they were right. Just before dark, a man walking his dog had found Edie's bicycle under a giant rhododendron on a stretch of green alongside the road, its back wheel buckled — folded almost in half — and its chain hanging in a sad loop.

That's when Edie Evans became a missing person.

And, early the next day, when a few drops of what proved to be Edie's blood were found on the pavement that ran between the green and the road, the case was turned over to the murder team. It was only logical — although they'd never found a body, and probably never would now.

Marvel tapped his cigarette against the edge of an ashtray shaped like a pair of lungs, then sighed at the photo through twin jets of smoke. He knew Edie's face better than he knew anyone's, apart from his own and the Queen's. Edie was a slightly goofy-looking child, with teeth she'd never grow into now, a sprinkling of summer freckles, and bobbed brown hair caught behind one sticky-out ear. In the photo, she was standing astride a BMX bicycle, in jeans and a Simpsons T-shirt, looking slightly upwards into the camera with a determined expression on her face.

"We call that her space face," her mother had told Marvel with a sad little laugh. "She wants to go into space."

He had wanted to go into space!

Marvel had forgotten it until the very moment Edie's mother had handed him the photo, but remembering it had brought a wash of memories that had left him glowing with long-lost happiness. Sneaking into the stone merchant's on Abigail Road with his best friend Terry Stubbs, to make an ascent of the giant grey-gravel mountain at the back of the yard. The favoured West face — to avoid being seen by the old man in the caravan-cum-office — and moving ponderously, to show they were on the Moon and lacked gravity. In the dirty, overstuffed city, the harsh gravel — made pale by the elements — was the closest landscape they could find to what they'd seen on grainy black-and-white TV. The winner was the one who could plant his flag closest to the summit without being seen. Although they didn't have flags: Terry's was a spatula and his own was a plastic sword with rubies on the hilt . . .

Sitting in the Evans's suburban front room, John Marvel had once more been able to feel the hot gravel under his belly, and the betrayal of sharp stones clicking down the slope behind him like unlucky dice. They'd been chased a few times, but never been caught. Not there, at least.

Not on the Moon.

They'd played in the stoneyard tirelessly, until they'd grown tired of it and never went back. Later he'd wanted to be a bus driver, then a scientist, then a fireman. He couldn't remember ever wanting to be a detective, but there you go and here he was.

Another day, another game.

It had been years — decades — since he'd thought of Terry Stubbs and the Moon, and it had given him a strange, syrupy feeling that anyone else would have quickly identified as sentiment.

After showing him the photo, Edie's mother and father had shown him Edie's bedroom.

As soon as he'd walked in, Marvel had known that she'd been taken, just as surely as *they* had known, from the very moment that they'd realized she was missing.

Edie Evans was going places, but not up to Oxford Street for a day out shoplifting mascara with a gang of girlfriends.

The walls of her room were completely covered with posters — not of pop singers and celebrities — but of *real* stars. There were planets and star maps and rockets and spaceships, Captain Kirk on one wall, Han Solo on another, Neil Armstrong on the back of the door; a space shuttle landing, and an Apollo mission taking off, robots and stormtroopers and willowy aliens with slanted black eyes. Between the big posters and pictures were cuttings and clippings and cartoons of constellations and close encounters, filling the gaps like grout. Even the ceiling was dotted with the pale-green stick-on stars that Marvel knew would suck up the sun and then glow in the dark over a child's head.

Marvel looked out of the window and into the mouse's cage. One looked over the neatly tended back garden to the trees beyond; the other was filled with curly wood shavings and old cardboard toilet-roll tubes, nibbled at either end. The mouse — Peter — pattered along in his wire wheel, going nowhere at a fair old lick.

Marvel had worked deep into every night in his efforts to find Edie. He had asked to have the case kept open long after it had started to chill; he had tried everything.

Even a psychic.

He hadn't consulted one, of course — that would have been the ultimate admission of failure — but when DS Short had suggested it, Marvel had only laughed derisively in her face, not forbidden it outright. And when the expense request came in, he had signed it — comforting himself with the thought that it said it was for "church-roof donations".

Nothing wrong with denial.

Marvel had only seen the psychic once, briefly and on TV, talking earnestly about his efforts to help.

Help schmelp. Marvel might as well have consulted the tea-leaves-slash-rehydrated noodles in the bottom of his cup of tea-slash-soup. All the psychic had done was bring the weirdos and well-wishers out of the woodwork. Sometimes it was hard to tell the difference; Marvel wasn't sure there *was* one. Mark and Carrie Evans had been inundated with letters and trinkets from around the world: visionaries, kindred spirits, children — all sending hope and Bible verses and talismans and charms.

There was even money. Twenty Australian dollars miraculously still stapled to a postcard from Perth, a hundred pounds in dirty notes stuffed into an ornately decorated envelope, and a crisp fifty with a long letter detailing another child missing in another place.

As if money would help.

There were the sickos too. There were always a few who trawled the papers for vulnerable targets, and reached out in their own repulsive way. Three Polaroids of a man's erect penis; a jewellery box containing a turd; and a newspaper photo of Edie with the eyes cut out and scrawled with the words *I kilt yuor girl*.

The world was full of wankers.

Including the so-called psychic, who'd had woolly visions for a few weeks before the trail had gone cold. Marvel had been so angry that he'd been to see Superintendent Jeffries about getting their money back. But Jeffries hadn't wanted to risk dragging their embarrassing experiment through the courts. A lesson learned, he'd said.

Marvel took another hard drag of his cigarette and felt the heat warm his thumb and finger.

The only tangible clue they'd had in the case was Edie Evans's bicycle.

It had been found half hidden under the rhododendrons on the broad strip of green that lay between the Evans's home and the school. Marvel had been there more than once.

More than fifty times.

It was a half-wooded, half-grassed area, where local people walked their dogs and children played hide and seek. In the summer, parents could sit outside the pub across the road and watch their kids kick a ball about.

Safe.

Not safe.

The line was so fine . . .

Marvel had never met Edie, but he had met her bicycle. The BMX was propped against a wall in the evidence room downstairs right now, still bent and drooping. It was an old, cheap bike and had been hand-painted in broad black and white hoops.

"Like a rocket," her father had said, looking at the photo in her room. "We painted it together."

"Did it have a bell?" Marvel had asked.

"Not that I remember. Why?"

"There are some scratches on the handlebars where a bell would go. But there's no bell in this picture."

Her father had shrugged. "It's an old bike. It had lots of scratches." He'd looked mildly puzzled. Not puzzled about the bell, but puzzled about why it even mattered when his daughter was gone and there was blood on the pavement.

It *didn't* matter, so Marvel hadn't pressed the point. He'd noticed it; that was all. It was his job to notice things, but sometimes the things he noticed weren't meaningful or logical, weren't things you could put in a report and call evidence. Sometimes they were just *things*.

But he noticed them all the same.

Not that it had helped. The case had gone cold; the mystery remained unsolved; Edie remained lost.

And the world moved on without her.

But still she watched him from the wall above his desk — as determined now as she had been on the day he'd caught the case. How could Marvel be anything but equally devoted to the mystery of her disappearance?

Somebody somewhere knew what had happened to her. All *he* had to do was find that person.

It seemed a very simple task when he looked at it like that. Not something he could just give up on. Not rocket science.

Along with fresh air and roughage, Marvel thought that children were overrated.

But he had a soft spot for Edie Evans.

CHAPTER
FIVE

The door was open.

Anna woke in a panic — already half out of bed.

"Is that the baby?"

"No."

"I think it's the baby."

"Don't get up."

"But —"

"Don't get up," said James. "Lie down."

She did, turning on her side away from him so he couldn't watch her creased brow, concentrating on listening for the smallest sound.

Behind her, she could feel James thinking. Feel him wanting to say something. Anything.

She waited and waited and waited and waited —

Then she got up to go to see to the baby — just as they'd both known she would. Once the thought was in her head, it must be completed. And, once completed, it would be repeated.

Endlessly?

Behind her, James got up and went to work.

Anna didn't go to work any more. She used to work for a company that made packaging for make-up. Not on the factory floor, but in the office — at a desk under her sixty-words-per-minute typing diploma, slender fingers flashing.

Now those same fingers were red and chapped from when she cleaned the flat.

And cleaned the flat.

And cleaned the flat.

Anna cleaned the flat on a loop, like the Forth Bridge. It wasn't a big flat, but it was in an old house, and it didn't stay clean for long — or not as clean as she needed it to be.

There were two bedrooms, a bathroom and toilet, a living room and a kitchen — and every single room was full of germs.

Full. Of. Germs.

Anna could hear germs breeding on counter tops and under sofa cushions. They filled her mouth when she yawned and gritted her lids when she blinked. She bleached the kitchen counters five times a day; she changed the baby even though he hadn't dirtied his nappy; and every item in the fridge was wrapped so tightly in plastic film that it took her four minutes to crack an egg.

Charlie was not allowed on the floor, and Anna kept antibacterial wipes in her jeans pocket. Twenty times a day, she got up from the table, out of her bed, out of the shower, just to swab his fingers and face. When Daniel came home, he would be *so safe*. Nothing would ever harm him again. Not a cough or a cold, not a stubbed toe or a paper cut. Not nits.

She often started cleaning before she got dressed, scrubbing the paintwork around the doors and bleaching the mugs. She swept James out of the front door every morning and then covered his tile tracks with cream cleaner followed by polish — running a cotton-wool bud against the bottom of the skirting to be sure she was getting right up to the edges.

She had James buy a foldaway three-step ladder, and scrubbed her way around the ceilings in concentric rings, coaxing daddy-long-legs into jars and releasing them through the kitchen window.

James did everything else that required leaving the flat — work, shopping, errands.

And he always returned.

The smell of him alone could make Anna panic. That dark, oily reek of the garage that kept her away from it like garlic does a vampire. Sometimes she could smell it seeping through the walls along with the tinny music, despite the pine and the lemon and the lavender that she lavished on every surface.

James always took off his steel-toed boots at the bottom of the stairs, but he refused to remove his overalls.

"I'm not taking off my clothes to come in my own bloody house," he'd say.

"Not your clothes. Just your overalls," Anna said anxiously.

But he wouldn't, even though it was all his fault — *all* of it!

So every night James led his smell up the stairs and across the kitchen to the sink, where Anna had already run a steaming bowl of soapy water and put out a pot of Swarfega and a nailbrush, for him to wash his filthy, black-grained hands and wrists. Right up to the elbows.

It was there, at the sink, that he would strip off his overalls so that she could bear them the three paces to the machine. She didn't start it immediately; first she had to wait for him to finish washing, so that she could swab down the sink and the counter and the floor where he'd been standing, and then she could wash that cloth too. Two biological tablets and a boil wash every night. Their electric and water bills matched those of a family of six, although it was only them.

And always would be, now that she wouldn't let him touch her any more. Not with those hands he scrubbed so hard but were never really clean.

Anna shuddered.

Then she looked up from washing the dishes and cocked her head.

She thought she'd heard Charlie crying. Not hard — more of a whimper. That was worse. Crying would show he had a healthy pair of lungs, while a whimper and then silence filled her with dread.

Some noises might be the children out behind the TiggerTime playschool a few doors down. But this sounded *inside*.

There it was again.

She removed her hands from the water and splashed Dettol liberally over them. A fresh towel was employed for drying, before she hurried into the nursery. Or the bedroom. It depended on who was talking.

By the time she got there, the baby had gone back to sleep. Anna breathed a sigh of relief.

"Hey, sweetheart," she whispered, as she pulled the soft lemon blanket over one adventurous leg. "Have you been kicking, you little monkey? Have you been dancing? Hmm?"

Charlie's golden lashes were laid on his peach cheeks; one wrinkled fist curled beside his ear. She laid a soft hand on his chest and his heart fluttered like a baby bird under his white towelling pyjamas.

Anna closed her eyes and — for a brief, precious moment — everything was all right.

Then the letter-box clattered and the circle started again.

The letter-box was in the door.

The door that was open . . .

Anna went slowly downstairs. Bills and junk all over the mat.

The bills she opened but didn't read; everything else she folded neatly three times. If she didn't, the kitchen bin would soon be full and her panic rose with its contents. She'd spoken to the postman about the junk mail but he'd explained that he got extra for delivering it.

"Why?" she'd asked. "So I can carry it from the door to the bin?"

He'd only shrugged, and at Christmas Anna hadn't tipped him — even though he'd knocked on the door on the pretext of handing her a small package that would certainly have fitted through the slot.

Two-for-one pizza with free garlic bread! *Fold*.

Release the CASH in your home! *Fold.*

£1,000 could be yours in TEN MINUTES! *Fold.*

THE DEAD ARE WAITING TO SPEAK TO YOU.

Anna stared at the leaflet. It was not glossy like the others — just cheap white paper and black ink. But somehow that, and the lack of an exclamation mark, made it seem more honest, made it seem that speaking to the dead was a more believable offer than free money and double pizza.

The dead were waiting to speak to her . . .

Anna swayed a little and touched the banister for support.

Daniel's not dead.

She'd been telling herself that for four months.

Daniel's not dead!

At first it had been a blind belief. Then a crazy hope. Then a desperate, marginal faith that made other people avoid her fevered gaze and nod at their own feet when she insisted it was a fact. As if she'd joined the Moonies.

Eventually the words had started to sound meaningless even inside her own head.

Daniel's not.

Dead.

Daniel . . .

Anna folded the leaflet once. Folded it twice . . .

Slowly, she unfolded it again.

THE DEAD ARE WAITING TO SPEAK TO YOU
Mediumship and open circle £2.
Private Consultations with the dead by

RICHARD LATHAM
(as seen on TV)
Why not come along and join us at
Bickley Spiritualist Church, Fridays 7 p.m.
Free tea and biscuits.
ALL WELCOME

Anna touched the words as if she could glean more meaning through her fingertips than through her eyes. She wasn't stupid; she guessed that "free tea and biscuits" was a sign of desperation on the part of the church, not generosity. And yet somehow they tempted her. She imagined dunking free biscuits into free tea, while someone who'd been seen on TV gave her all the answers to every question . . .

Daniel's not dead, she told herself fiercely. *I would feel it. I would know.*

Except that she *didn't* know.

Feeling and knowing were two different things, and not-knowing was the rat that gnawed at her heart in the dark early hours of the morning, before the buses started to rumble.

Was he cold? Was he hungry? Scared? Was somebody hurting him? Did he miss her? Did he wonder where she was and why she wasn't coming to get him?

Did he think she didn't love him any more?

That last thought was the worst, and had the power to make her twist in physical pain.

On Bickley Bridge she'd planned an end to the daily torture of not-knowing, and only the lies of a passing stranger had saved her.

But saved her for what?

For more pain? For more guilt? For more agony?

She stared at the flyer. If she'd been prepared to end her torture that irreversibly, wasn't this worth trying? Wouldn't it bring some kind of relief to know *something?* — even if that something was that Daniel really was dead?

For the first time since he had disappeared, the thought did not bring tears tingling into her eyes, only a deep, dull ache in her chest.

THE DEAD ARE WAITING TO SPEAK TO YOU.

Anna felt the words tugging at her in an insistent and seductive undertow.

Quickly she folded the leaflet again — once, twice, three times — and put it with the other junk mail. Then she pushed the whole bundle so far down into the kitchen bin that she had to scrub her arm with Dettol.

CHAPTER
SIX

After work on Fridays, the lads from Pigeon's MoT & Diagnostics all went for a drink at the King's Arms.

They were a motley crew. Tall, silent Pavel — always with an exotic black cigarette in his mouth that made him look like an angry poet; Mikey — as pale as a pint of milk, with ice-blue eyes, and hair of almost pure white on his head, brows, lashes and legs. His negative was Ang, with his tan skin, and jet-black hair and eyes.

Ang couldn't buy a proper drink; he swore he was twenty, but he had no ID to support his claim, and it would be years before he looked more than sixteen, so they'd long ago stopped trying to con the barman and just got drunk without him.

Every time they did, Mikey got louder and Pavel got darker, while Ang joined in by laughing at jokes he didn't understand — even if they were at his expense.

James got drunk too. With every beer he could do a better impression of a young man whose wife still loved him, and who hadn't lost his son. Sometimes, through the blur of the beer, he could barely see his own cracks.

But it took a lot of blurring.

Mikey had his leg propped on a chair and was showing his curly white shins to two giggling women.

"Is it white *everywhere?*" one of them said, predictably, and they both giggled like mad at their own daring.

"White as ice cream," leered Mikey. "If you're lucky I'll show you my 99."

They shrieked and clutched each other and swigged their vod-bombs.

"You girls are gorgeous," said Mikey. "Specially *you.*" He pointed at both of them and they roared with laughter.

He'd take them both home tonight; James would have put his next paypacket on it. Mikey was no oil painting — hell, he was barely a *finger* painting — but he had the swagger of a man twice his age, and girls were putty in his fluffy white hands. The kind of girls who drank vod-bombs, anyway.

James stared down into the dregs of his third pint and wondered whether it was worth going on, or if he should just stop and save the money. Take Anna to the movies, maybe.

He snorted into the glass. They hadn't been to the movies since before Daniel was born. So he finished his drink and got up to get another.

It had been a bad week, and he needed the blur.

The bar was three people deep, all waving their twenties at the sweaty staff. James stood and waited, letting the noise and the heat fill his head, pushing out any thinking he might do, any guilt.

Slowly he became aware of Mikey's voice above the hubbub — ". . . and him over there, so feck you too if you think you're hard enough!"

James turned slowly to look over his shoulder. Mikey could start a fight in an empty room, but on this occasion he was still in his chair, pointing him out to three clean-cut young men. They were in good shoes and neat-but-casual shirts, but James could see that the leader had a tattoo on his neck, low enough to be hidden by a collar and tie. He couldn't be sure, but he thought it was a swastika.

Although Mikey and Pavel hadn't got up, James noticed that Mikey had placed his pint on the window-sill, out of harm's way, and Pavel had rested his cigarette on the edge of the table, which for him was tantamount to loading an Uzi.

Ang was on the edge of his seat, his dark eyes drawing rapid triangles between Mikey, the men and the door. He twitched, as if to get up, and Pavel put a big hand on his forearm, forcing him to stay put.

James couldn't blame him for wanting to run; Ang had been beaten up a couple of times. Only a few months ago Brian had sent him off to Fryer Tuck's for lunch and he'd returned with a split lip, a swollen eye and the tattered remains of cod and chips five times, with extra gravel.

But sometimes you had to make a stand . . .

James straightened up, and the man with the tattoo looked him up and down. James could almost watch him think: now it was four against three, although Ang barely counted. James wasn't big, but he was an extra pair of fists, while Pavel was tall and unafraid, and Mikey looked like an enthusiast, even with the leg of his jeans rolled up.

46

James felt relief in his gut. Nothing was going to happen.

And nothing would have, if Ang had held his nerve.

But he made a sudden break for it — twisting off his chair and diving into the Friday-night crowd.

It stopped him like a wall and in a second they were on him, and James and Pavel and Mikey were on *them*, and a dozen lads who'd been preparing all night for a fight — *any* fight — joined in on any side that would have them.

It was the first fight James had been in for years, but by the time someone shouted that the police were coming, he had cleared a space around himself and a circle of people were regarding him warily. The three young men were nowhere to be seen.

Someone tugged at his sleeve and he knocked them away and turned to fight, whoever it was.

"Whoa there!" It was Mikey, ducking a bit. "Come on," he added urgently, "let's go out the back."

"Where's Ang?" said James, and Ang and Pavel appeared as if by magic. They were all a little dishevelled, and Ang's lip was split, but they were all in one piece.

"Thanks a bunch," Ang panted sincerely. "Thanks a fucking bunch."

They started laughing then. Partly Ang's words and partly the adrenaline high of having fought and survived.

James led them giggling around the bar, starting to jog. By the time they passed the toilets, they were running full pelt and laughing, and he hit the back door so hard he almost took it off its hinges.

It was raining outside but nothing could dampen their spirits — not even the kegs that Pavel knocked over, or the rusted nail that dug into Ang's hand. All of it was just hilarious, now they weren't dead.

Looking down the alleyway alongside the pub, they could see the flickering lights of a police car, so they turned round, following the high wall along the back of the yard. A train passed under the bridge and James pulled himself up the wall high enough to watch its curved, wet roof disappear into the darkness.

"Yahhhhh!" he shouted after it. "Yahhhhhhhh!"

"Nutter," laughed Mikey.

"Motherfucker," laughed Ang, and the other three looked at each other in surprise. Then James said, "More tea, vicar?" and they all laughed so hard that Mikey actually cried and they all had to shush each other constantly so the police wouldn't find them here behind the bins that smelled of chip fat and gangrene.

When they stepped out of the alleyway, it was into the crowd that had emptied from the front door of the King's Arms, illuminated in slow blue flickers by the lights of the police cars.

Mikey whistled for a taxi, and he and Pavel climbed into it. They lived in the other direction from the garage.

"You OK?" said Mikey.

"Yeah, mate," said James. "Bloody brilliant."

"You're a nutter," said Mikey, in a voice that sobered James up, because it didn't sound like Mikey was joking. He was looking at him hard, and James wiped his mouth on the back of his hand, in case he had blood there — or food, even though he hadn't eaten a thing.

"What?" he said.

"Nothing," said Mikey. "Maybe get some peas for your hands."

"Yeah, I will," said James, although he didn't know what the hell Mikey was talking about. *Mikey* was the nutter; everyone knew that.

They all said goodnight and fuck off and up yours, and then Mikey saw the two girls from earlier in the pub and called them over, and James and Ang watched as — somehow — he charmed them both into the cab and drove off across Bickley Bridge.

"Unbelievable," said James.

"Shit," said Ang.

They walked the short way to the garage together, both hunched against the rain.

Ang peeled off and started patting his pockets.

"Got the keys?" James hoped he did, because otherwise he would have to take him home with him, and Anna would be angry. They used to have Ang up for supper all the time, and on cold nights he would stay on the sofa. But now Anna wouldn't have anyone in the flat because of the germs. James suspected that even he wouldn't be welcome, if he wasn't the one paying the rent. Ang never said anything about it, and the only time James had tried to explain, he'd just nodded and smiled and said, *Is good* — as if he had never wanted a decent meal or a warm sofa in the first place.

Ang took the garage keys from his pocket and dangled them at James.

James opened his own front door just a few yards away, and they both raised a hand in goodbye.

James closed the door behind him —

never without thinking of Daniel

— and took off his boots.

He winced as his knuckles protested at being asked to perform intricate manoeuvres like pulling on a lace. Only then did he remember what Mikey had said about the peas. Frozen peas to take the swelling down.

He went up the stairs and opened the door of the freezer compartment. It was small, and made smaller by the overgrowth of ice around its entrance.

There were no frozen peas — just an empty ice tray and half a box of fish fingers.

James took them out and stared at the box. Fish fingers were Daniel's favourite. He put them back.

"Anna!" he said loudly. "We got any peas?"

She didn't answer. It didn't matter. Where would they be if they weren't in the freezer? And if they were anywhere but the freezer, they were no good to him.

He shook his head.

With the open fridge cooling his thighs, James spread his hands on the counter. They were red and swollen, and one knuckle had two short cuts on it right alongside each other — as if Bugs Bunny had nipped him.

He must have hit something very hard or very often to have got them into this state. He couldn't remember whether it was one or the other or both, but he felt a lot better for it.

He knelt slowly in front of the fridge and pushed both his hands into the freezer compartment. The overgrown ice pressed around him coldly.

"Anna!" he said again, but she was ignoring him.

He rested his head on the top of the fridge and only woke up when melting ice trickled slowly up his sleeve all the way into his armpit.

He got up and shut the door —

such a simple thing to do

— and went into the bedroom.

It was only then that James realized with a shock that — for the first time in four months — Anna wasn't home.

CHAPTER
SEVEN

The man who'd been seen on TV was a big disappointment.

Richard Latham was stocky and middle-aged, wearing thick glasses and beige slacks, and when he walked on to the small raised plinth that was supposed to be a stage, he bounced along on his tiptoes with the exaggerated gait of a puppet on strings. Anna thought there must be something wrong with his feet or his legs.

It was comical, but it was also a little bit disturbing.

He tapped the microphone and then bent backwards a little to look up at the ceiling.

"Can you hear me?" he said.

An amused ripple ran through the small audience. There were maybe fifteen people in total gathered together in the Bickley Spiritualist Church, which was a grubby little hall next to the King's Arms. There were bars at the high windows, plastic chairs instead of pews, and fake flowers in a vase: lilies and irises, gathering dust. On the wall behind the plinth was a clock that had stopped at a quarter past six, and a small, apologetic crucifix.

None of it calmed Anna's nerves.

She had taken nearly an hour just to get past the five footprints. She'd chickened out and gone back inside four times, hot and panicky despite the cold and damp, before finally making a run for it — hurtling down the uneven pavement with the baby jiggling and bouncing in his buggy.

Just being outdoors had been enough to make her nervous. Now that she'd seen the dusty flowers, being indoors was making her nervous too. The carpet was threadbare and crumbly, and nobody but her had left their shoes in the porch. She tried not to imagine the germs, but her eyes already felt gritty. She leaned forward and pulled the rabbit fleece almost up to Charlie's eyes so that the dust couldn't settle in his nose or mouth. She almost wished she hadn't brought him, but leaving him at home would have been worse. Better let him be exposed to the dirty air and filthy flowers than left with James.

James couldn't be trusted with children.

The woman sitting next to Anna leaned over and peered into the buggy.

"Awwww, isn't he lovely!"

Anna nodded, and smiled through stiff lips. She wished the woman would get her face away from the buggy. Her hair was too blonde and permed to within an inch of its sticky life, and she was wafting chemicals and germs all over him.

"What's his name?"

"D — Charlie." She'd almost said Daniel. It would have felt so good — to use his name in a normal way instead of a way that shredded her heart.

"Awwww," the woman said again. "Look at him blowing his little bubbles!"

A train rumbled under the bridge below them, and Anna thought of the eight twenty from Victoria. She felt that old desperation fluttering upwards in her like a bus ticket in a sudden gust, and had to slam a door on the feeling. She couldn't think of that. She couldn't think of the drop to the rails and the oblivion of the train. She had to stay strong if she was ever going to find Daniel.

Although the thought of finding him *here* made her want to cry.

She bit her lip and tried to focus on the man on the stage.

Knowing would be better than not knowing.

Perhaps.

"Good evening," the man said. "I'm Richard Latham. Some of you may have seen me on TV."

Two plump women in the front row nodded vigorously and Latham winked and said, "The camera adds ten pounds, you know. I used to be a large. Now I'm just a medium."

There were a couple of minor chuckles and the blonde woman leaned in to Anna and hissed, "He said that last week too. And he was only on TV a few times. Then they took him off."

This wasn't how Anna had thought it was going to be, and that was good. She'd thought it might be frightening, or stupidly mystical — or like the school-fair fortune-teller she'd been to once as a child: Mrs Smart the Geography teacher wrapped in a table-cloth and foretelling that she'd get an A if she worked very, very hard.

Richard Latham suddenly pointed at her and said, "I've someone here for you, sir."

Anna flinched — then she looked to her right, and realized that Latham must be cross-eyed to add to his other shortcomings. He meant the skinny young man sitting beside her in a bulky silver puffa jacket that was several sizes too large for him. His head protruded from its huge padded collar like a nodding dog's.

To add to the illusion, he nodded.

"Someone called Beryl. Can you take that for me, sir?"

"Yes," nodded the young man.

"Is it definitely Beryl?"

"Yes," he said. "Beryl."

"And is she your grandmother?"

"No, she was my grandmother's neighbour, but I knew her really well."

"OK," said Latham, and cocked his head at the ceiling. Anna followed his gaze nervously, but there was just a long cobweb there, and a damp patch in the shape of Australia.

"OK," he said again. "Beryl says to tell your gran it's all wine and roses up here. Wine and blooming roses, Mary. What's your gran's name?"

"Marie."

"Oh, Marie. Wine and blooming roses. That's *her* words, you see. Not mine. Nobody says blooming nowadays, do they?"

He looked at the ceiling again and this time Anna noticed she wasn't the only person observing Australia along with him.

"Anything else?" said Latham, and waited. Then he said, "No. That's all there is from Beryl."

"Thank you," said the young man. He didn't look a bit surprised to have had a message from a dead woman. Didn't rush off to phone his grandmother. Didn't whip out a notebook to write down the message while it was fresh in his memory.

He also didn't burst into flames for dabbling in the spirit world. Anna didn't believe in God any more, but she felt a little relieved by that anyway.

Richard Latham looked thoughtful again, and Anna felt herself tensing so hard that she began to shake. But he pointed to a very frail old man on the end of the front row, who sat with both hands clamped over the knob of a gnarled walking stick. He had huge ears — each containing a large pink plastic hearing aid.

"I've got someone here for you, sir, and she's very angry."

"Must be the wife," the old man quavered, and everybody laughed heartily.

"She says the doctor gave you a prescription, sir, is that right?"

The old man hesitated. Then he said, "Maybe."

"Don't you maybe me," said Latham sharply, then he softened his tone and added, "That's what *she's* saying, sir — I'm not being rude to you, honestly. She's saying, *Don't you maybe me, young man!*" Here Latham stopped and looked puzzled. "No offence, sir, but I wouldn't describe you as a *young* man. Are you sure this message is for you?"

The old man nodded. "I was younger than her, see?"

"Ahh," said Latham. "A toyboy."

The old man cackled and nodded and Latham cocked his head again, this time putting one hand momentarily alongside his ear — not quite cupping it, but close to it, as if the old man's dead wife was shouting from the back of the hall.

"Well," he continued, "I don't want to be rude, young man, but your wife — is her name Ellen? Ella?"

"Ella," said the old man.

"Well, Ella tells me you need to take that medicine because they're not ready for you yet, you see? She says you've still got a little way to go, and you might as well be healthy and happy while you're waiting. Will you do that for her, sir? Will you do that for Ella?"

The old man ruminated, and Anna could hear his dentures clicking from the back row.

"I'm not ordering you, sir," said Latham gently. "I'm only passing on a message."

"I'll think about it," said the old man.

"Good," said Latham. "But she's still a bit cross."

Everyone laughed again and the old man flapped a hand and said, "Oh all right then, just to shut her up."

This was *nothing* like Anna had expected it to be.

"Now," said Latham, "I'll let someone else have a go."

To Anna's surprise, the young man in the puffa jacket got up and walked to the front of the room and took the microphone from Latham.

"What's happening now?" Anna couldn't resist asking the blonde woman.

"It's open circle," she said. "We're all here to learn."

"Learn what?"

"Psychic powers."

"Oh!" said Anna. The idea that you could *learn* to be psychic was both stupid and intriguing.

The young man was frowning hard at the wall, waggling the microphone absent-mindedly.

"Right," he said finally. "I've got a Nnnnn . . . eville here. Neville or Nigel."

There was an undercurrent of non-interest and then a young woman just in front of Anna raised her hand. "I can take a Nigel."

"Good," said the man, and thought a bit more. "This Nigel, was he very fat?"

"No," said the woman. "Very thin."

Richard Latham got up and stood beside the young man, offering advice. "Now be a bit more confident. Don't be rushed. Wait until you're sure and then don't ask the person, *tell* them what you see. That way you'll get better results and not waste time with the wrong people."

The young man nodded like a plastic Pug on a parcel-shelf, and took some more time staring at the wall.

Before he could say anything else, a man with a port-wine birth-mark on his cheek put up his hand and said, "I can take a fat Neville. I only just remembered my father-in-law. He was a right porker."

And so it went on. Ghosts leaving messages on spiritual answering machines, as if they'd popped out to the shops, rather than died. One by one, random people stood under the damp patch and channelled the dead. It was all so *normal*. If Anna had expected anything, it would have been: *The will is under the bathroom carpet*, and *Margery did it and hid the knife in the shed!* Instead there was Carol remembering her blue felt slippers, John telling his brother to repair the chimney before winter, and Granny Mitchell confirming that Gramps had arrived safely and was as "happy as a sandboy".

As every would-be psychic got up, Anna's stomach fluttered with nerves, but the longer Daniel failed to put in an appearance, the less frightened and more relieved she got.

He wasn't dead! He couldn't be dead. If he was dead, he'd have come here and let her know, surely?

The tension drained from her and she felt exhausted. If it hadn't been a sort of church, she might have left to go home to bed. As it was, she felt obliged to sit and listen as the dead droned on. Her astonishment at their messages left her fast, and was replaced by a vague suspicion.

Finally she was just bored.

Dead people were every bit as dull as the living.

She felt her eyelids droop, and hid a yawn. She put a foot on a strut of the buggy and moved it gently back and forth — to keep herself awake as much as to keep the baby asleep.

By the time they got to the free tea and biscuits, Anna only stayed because she hadn't eaten all day and was determined to get her two quid's worth.

She helped herself to a cup of weak tea and two bourbon biscuits, because that was all there was.

The blonde woman who'd been beside her on the plastic chairs sat down next to her again. She had nice clothes and perfect make-up and a bag that matched her shoes. It stood out among the anoraks and jeans.

"I'm Sandra." She smiled and, before Anna could stop her, she had her head back under the hood of the buggy and was breathing all over the baby.

She sat up again and smiled. "He's very good, isn't he?"

"Yes," said Anna, "he's very good." But he wasn't Daniel and she didn't love him the same way she had loved Daniel. That didn't mean she wouldn't do all she could to keep him safe from harm.

And that included germs.

She leaned into the buggy herself so that Sandra could not, and rearranged the blankets. The baby's hand had fallen out and was cold, and she tucked it back in. Then she put her foot back on the axle and resumed the gentle back-and-forth rocking that kept babies on quiet.

"He your only one?" said Sandra.

"No," said Anna. "Daniel's four. Nearly five now."

"I don't have children. Couldn't. Blocked tubes, you know?"

"I'm sorry," said Anna, and she was.

"Oh well," said Sandra. "We all have our crosses to bear." She smiled, then said, "Is this your first time here?"

"Yes."

"What do you think?"

Anna looked around to give herself time. Australia caught her eye. "I'm not sure," she said.

"Don't be put off by the grotty hall and the carpet," said Sandra in a low voice. "Richard's a proper shut eye."

"What's a shut eye?" said Anna.

"A shut eye is for real. An open eye just pretends."

"Pretends what?"

"Pretends to have the gift. Talking to the dead and all that."

"Why would someone pretend?"

"To rip people off, of course!" said Sandra. "But Richard's not like that," she added quickly. "He's a proper shut eye. Especially with dogs."

"Dogs?"

"Mmm," said Sandra and rummaged in her bag. "He has a marvellous record, communicating with dogs. People swear by him." She took out a thick pile of photographs. "This is Mitzi," she said, handing one to Anna. "She won Top Puppy."

Anna said "Wow," although she had no idea whether that was something to be admired or not.

Sandra went on: "Richard likes to work from a photograph."

"A *photograph*?"

"Oh yes — he looks at the photo and he just *knows* things! Things only the dog would know. It's like magic."

Magic indeed. Anna had seen magicians on the telly. You couldn't see how they performed their illusions, but she knew that that was all they were — sleight of hand and smoke and mirrors. Not *real*.

Sandra seemed sad and a little bit crazy.

Anna looked doubtfully at the picture. It had been taken out-doors, somewhere on grass, and Sandra was wearing a beige belted safari jacket that made her look like a chubby Swedish commando. She was holding a small apricot poodle almost hidden by a big red rosette. Behind them, Anna could see a blue line that she assumed was the rope edge of some kind of show-ring, and a short row of blurred people in the act of clapping — which was a strange thing, caught in suspended animation.

Anna shivered, even though the hall was not cold.

Sandra leaned in conspiratorially. "Most people come here to get messages from their relatives, but dead people are so *dreary*."

Anna laughed, then quickly stopped. She hadn't laughed for a long, long time, and it felt sharp and guilty in her mouth.

"Have you ever had a message from your dog?"

"Oh yes," said Sandra. "Almost every time I come."

"What kind of things?"

"All sorts. Richard tells me things that only I would know. Like exactly how she used to give a little bark when she wanted a treat. And how she'd put her head on one side, like this, when I talked to her. And she *did* those things, you see? He's ever so good. And he gives me messages from her too. *I love you, I miss you.*" Sandra's eyes brimmed with sudden tears and she held her forefingers under her eyes to stop them spilling over and ruining her perfectly applied mascara.

Anna felt the burn of empathy behind her own eyes, even though she had lost her son and Sandra was only missing a dead dog.

Sandra found a well-used tissue in her bag and blew her nose discreetly.

"Do you have to pay him?"

"Who?"

"Richard."

"I don't *have* to. I make donations to the church-roof fund. That's only fair, isn't it? I have a private reading after the service. What Richard does takes time and saps his spiritual energy. But he's not in it for the money. No real shut eye is."

Anna nodded, but she glanced up at Australia. It had always been her experience that everybody was in everything for the money. Apart from James — which was why they never had any, of course.

She offered the photo to Sandra but she said, "You keep that. I have loads of them. My phone number's on the back."

While Sandra tucked the rest of the photos back into her bag and hooked it over her chair, Anna watched Richard Latham. He was sitting a few yards away with the two ladies who'd seen him on TV, while a half-dozen other people stood around him, listening intently, teacups in hand.

Anna tuned in to what he was saying:

". . . so I went to her house in LA," Latham told them, "and I said, '*Come on, Marilyn! You're dead!*' And I grabbed her by the hand, and I *pushed* her through the door to the other side."

There were murmurs of approval as Latham took a long slurp of tea. Anna noticed he had biscuit crumbs down the front of his jumper.

"Some people don't know they're dead, you see? So you have to tell them . . ."

Everyone nodded and there were murmurs of *true* and *that's right*, and Anna shied away from a new mental image of the soul lost between life and death, alone and afraid and never seeing a friendly face — in this world *or* the next. She couldn't think about it; it was worse than mere death. It made her hope that Richard Latham was a liar and a fake, and she comforted herself with the thought that if he really *was* psychic, he'd be in Hollywood by now, making millions off celebrities — dead or alive — not inventing outlandish stories about them in a grubby hall on Bickley Bridge.

She turned to Sandra. "What was he on TV for?"

Sandra dabbed tea from the corner of her mouth with the same tissue with which she'd blown her nose. It couldn't be hygienic; Anna moved the buggy away from her.

"He helped the police on a missing-persons case."

Anna's heart lurched.

"A girl called Edie Evans," Sandra went on. "They found her bike all mangled somewhere over in Bromley. It was a year or so ago. Do you remember?"

Anna shook her head slowly and her ears thrummed with blood. She felt drunk, yet more alert than she'd ever been in her life. So alert that she felt the tiny soft hairs on the edges of her ears tingle in anticipation.

"Did they . . . did they ever find her?"

"I'm not sure."

"But they didn't find her . . . *body?*"

"Oh no, I'd have remembered that."

Anna put her hand over her heart and felt it pulsing crazily under the skin.

"Sandra, is your dog dead?" The words spilled out of her so urgently that she wasn't even sure they were in the right order.

Is Sandra dog your dead?

"Oh no!" said Sandra. "Just lost! And Richard says she'll be home very, very soon!"

They didn't have to be dead for the psychic to find them.

Something expanded so fast in Anna's chest that it took her breath away. It was a magical bubble that left her dizzy and tearful with forgotten joy.

This was why she was here!

This was the reason she'd left the safety of the flat and brought the baby out into the filth of a London night. *This* was why she'd ventured past the footprints on the edge of the cement. Not to speak to the dead, but for *this!*

65

For something Anna thought had been lost to her for ever.

For hope.

CHAPTER
EIGHT

The body was small but it wasn't light.

He dragged it and lifted it and dragged it some more.

The dragging felt wrong. Not only because his hands were sweaty and kept slipping from around the narrow wrists, but because there was no dignity in it. Not for him, and not for the corpse.

He picked it up and carried it.

He tried to be kind to it.

That's all he'd ever tried to be. And if he had failed in life then it didn't mean he couldn't try to make amends in death. They were not separate things; he had lived with the dead for most of his life and understood that. Just because a body no longer contained a spirit, it didn't mean it should be treated with anything less than kindness and respect.

Even while he was trying to push it up and over the high railings.

He should have wrapped it in something. It was too late now. One loose fist swung gently as he struggled. He clenched his teeth. Rain ran into his eyes as he heaved.

His back cried out; his arms ached. He could feel the muscles stretching, trembling and starting to wobble.

The chiding fist bumped his cheek, reminding him, reminding him, reminding him.

He dropped the body.

It landed awkwardly in the damp grit, face down, and with the head twisted to the side under one hunched shoulder. The bare soles of the small feet glowing pale orange under the single streetlamp.

It was too hard. It was too horrible.

He started to cry.

He had failed the living and now he was failing the dead.

The rain on his face was swollen by sweat and then by tears and finally by snot as it ran over his lips and into his mouth in a salty flash-flood of shame.

Eventually, he sighed and wiped his eyes on the damp sleeve of his shirt.

Then he bent and embraced the body one more time.

CHAPTER
NINE

"Church?" James frowned up at the ceiling.

Neither of them had ever been to church. After Daniel had disappeared —

because you left the door open

— a priest had come round anyway, and asked if he could help.

Yes, Anna had said. *You can post these flyers through every letterbox on Northborough Road.*

She'd held them out angrily, and the priest had taken them and smiled and said *of course* — as if he was asked to deliver flyers all the time.

And he'd done it, too.

As far as James knew it was the only time either of them had ever spoken to a man of the cloth.

"What church?" he said.

"The one on the bridge."

"There's a church there?"

"It's like a hall. But it's a church."

"Oh."

"What?"

"Nothing," he said. "Are you going again?"

"Yes."

He lay in silence for a moment, then got out of bed and started to dress.

"What's wrong?" she said.

He sat on the edge of the bed to put on his socks. "You don't go out for months and the first place you decide to go is a church?"

"I went for Daniel," said Anna.

James got up and took his T-shirt off the floor and pulled it over his head.

"I went for *us*."

He snorted. "Leave me out of it."

"What do you mean?"

"Leave me out of it," he repeated. "I don't need you to go to church for me."

"But it's not —"

"I don't care what it's *not*," he said, suddenly angry, "I care what it *is*. And it's the last thing we need right now. Or any time."

Anna propped herself up on one elbow and watched him. James yanked open the wardrobe and started throwing random things at the bin bag in the corner that they used as a laundry hamper.

"What happened to your hands?" she said.

"Nothing."

"They're all swollen."

He didn't answer her. Kept throwing clothes she knew were clean across the room.

Anna picked at the edge of the duvet. "We all need hope," she said softly.

"*I don't*," he snapped, and looked at her properly for the first time that morning. "I don't need the kind of hope that's peddled by a church, Anna."

He balled up a pair of jeans and hurled it hard at the bag. "Shit!"

Then he turned on her angrily. "And I tell you what else I don't need. I don't need you sitting in the street like a crazy old monk. I don't need bloody refugees feeling sorry for me. I don't need the constant cleaning the house, and the stripping off and the taking off my boots in the hallway, and the guilt! And the no sex! And that *fucking baby!*"

Anna flinched. His face was in hers; the tendons stood out in his neck.

He might hit her.

He didn't.

He stood up straight. "And the *last* thing I need is for you to get all *religious* on me."

"It's not —"

"Where was that bastard when Daniel disappeared? Eh? Where is he now? *Nowhere.* That's where God is. Not in a church, not in this house, not with us, and not with Daniel! Just. Fucking. *Nowhere.*"

"It's not about God," she whispered.

"Good," he said. "Don't make it." He slammed the bedroom door so hard behind him that old paint flecked off the frame and spun silently to the floor.

Anna let out a trembling breath and lay back down. The bed had cooled.

It was a long time since it had been hot.

CHAPTER
TEN

"Have a seat, Chief Inspector."

Marvel knew something was wrong right there and then. Superintendent Robert Clyde was a taciturn man and Marvel could match him, monosyllable for monosyllable. Usually their interactions took place only in passing unless they were critical to a case. Even then, Marvel always stood and updated the super from somewhere near the doorway, a distance they both apparently found comfortable.

He had never before been offered a seat in his office.

He went in and saw it from a new perspective. It wasn't much of an office — just a cubbyhole with a door, a desk, two chairs and a grubby little window that looked down on the roof of the Happy Kebabby next door. It explained why the super's office often smelled of old lamb.

He scowled and sat down in a stained chair.

From here he had a close-up of a wooden plaque on Clyde's desk, which from the door he'd always assumed was a name plate.

Now he saw it was a Bible quote.

It is time for the Lord to act,

For your law has been broken.

"I'm taking you off the Tanzi Anderson case."

"What?" Marvel bristled. Being taken off a case he was almost sure to solve was a kick in the teeth. "What for, sir?"

"Scanlon can handle it. It's a no-brainer."

Both of those things were true, but they hadn't answered Marvel's question, so he didn't ask another one — just let the first one hang there.

Waiting.

"I need you on another case," Clyde said finally, but he glanced past Marvel's shoulder as he spoke.

Immediately Marvel knew two things. One: that it was not a murder case, and two: that Clyde was embarrassed to be asking.

The first thing was bad. But the second was good.

Really good.

Superintendent Clyde was a cold fish and Marvel could respect that quality, but ever since he had been transferred to Lewisham last Christmas to replace Superintendent Jeffries, it had been hard for Marvel to find a chink in the man's armour.

And DI Marvel loved a chink. It was his unshakeable view that everybody had a flaw in their make-up that allowed leverage to be exerted, and he liked to think he had a knack of identifying those weaknesses, those tiny human failings, that would give him the upper hand in any relationship. It was often race or affairs or homosexuality, but Marvel preferred the less obvious.

Less actionable . . .

Like Craig Reilly, one of G Team's DCs. He had a disabled son and was always begging for time off for doctors' appointments, which meant that when he *was* at work, Marvel could give him the shittiest jobs with the longest hours, without fear of complaint. And Detective Sergeant Brady's chink was Argentinians. Colin Brady's father had been in the Falklands War and had taken Port Stanley — pretty much single-handedly, if his son were to be believed. Now, thirty-five years on, Brady still fumed about Maradona's Hand of God goal every time *Match of the Day* came on, and his wife was banned from playing the soundtrack album to *Evita*, even through headphones. Argentinians — or anyone he suspected might *be* Argentinian — made DS Brady lose all reason, and he had to be steered away from them.

Or towards them, if Marvel thought it might be useful . . .

Oh, what a circus.

Everybody had *something* that Marvel could exploit to his own end.

Superintendent Clyde, on the other hand, had so far appeared to be chink-free. But now that he was looking unsure about this other case, Marvel's antennae twitched.

"Is it a murder case, sir?"

"Um," said Clyde, and Marvel sat up straighter. "No," the super continued carefully, "a disappearance." He handed Marvel a photograph of a buxom blonde woman with too much lipstick, sitting on a sofa.

"What's her name?" Marvel asked.

"Mitzi."

"Mitzi what?"

"Just Mitzi," said Clyde. "It's the dog that's missing."

"The *dog?*"

Marvel looked again at the photo. The blonde woman had a poodle on her lap. It was small and pale ginger and had a pink bow on the top of its head.

"My wife's dog," added Clyde, as if it made all the difference.

Which it did, of course, thought Marvel, with a little bud of anger unfurling in his chest.

Clyde was pulling him off a murder case to look for a lost dog.

Shit, he thought. *You shit.*

He was a murder detective, not a cub scout. What next? Would Superintendent Clyde have him shinning up trees to rescue cats? Opening a hedgehog hospital? Marvel didn't even *like* animals — *any* animals — and dogs, especially small fluffy ones with bows on their heads, were his most un-favourite animals of all.

He cleared his throat. "And this is your wife, sir?"

"Yes," said Clyde, looking uncomfortable at having to admit to something as human as a wife. "Sandra."

Marvel nodded while his mind worked overtime to find the leverage.

"The dog disappeared in the park," said Clyde. "While my wife was talking to a friend."

"I see," said Marvel. "So is there a lead attached to it?"

"No."

Marvel nodded at the photo. "Collar?"

"No."

"*Microchip?*"

"No." Clyde cleared his throat and made a stab at being in charge. "Listen, John," he said, and Marvel cringed inwardly at the use of his first name. It made him think of Debbie and his mother in the same mental breath, which was just *wrong*.

"Listen, John, I know it's a bit out of the ordinary, but there's more to it than meets the eye. So I thought I'd put my best man on it, get it sorted and get it over with."

My best man. That stung like a salted slug. You didn't put your best man on the trail of a lost poodle.

Marvel had to resist a sudden childish urge to tear the photograph into small pieces and toss them over his shoulder.

Next . . .

Instead he stared at the photo of the wife and the dog, hoping for divine inspiration that might absolve him from the task at hand. He could call down the rule book, he could call down his value to the South East's G Team, he could call down the murder of Tanzi Anderson, or any one of his unsolved cases. He could even call down Edie Evans on her Apollo 11 BMX. He should. He should call them *all* down and nip this bollocks in the bud right here, right now.

The dingy little office reverberated with tense silence. If Superintendent Clyde had had an ounce of pride he would have told Marvel it was all a joke, and he'd almost had him. But what he actually said was, "Listen, John, she's driving me mad about the dog. Day and bloody night. She's even been to see a bloody psychic."

Marvel almost laughed. A wife. A poodle. And now a *psychic*! Out of nowhere, there was so much leverage in this that it would almost be criminal *not* to exploit it.

Marvel wondered just how much he could get out of it.

As much as a promotion?

He'd only been a Chief Inspector for a couple of years, so it would be unusual to climb another rung of the ladder so soon. But not unheard of. And not unwelcome, now he thought about it. His knees were starting to play up. And the thought of controlling a whole room of murder detectives — of having his finger in every pie — appealed to him. Not to mention getting more money and a fatter pension to sit on his arse behind a desk all day.

Promotion was like committing a crime. You needed means, motive and opportunity, and although Marvel reckoned he'd always have the means and the motivation, opportunity didn't always knock exactly when you needed it to. But it was knocking now, and he'd probably never get a simpler crack at promotion.

Marvel had no illusions about his chances of promotion to superintendent — or his suitability. He wasn't a political animal, and knew he'd never be the first-choice candidate. DCI Lloyd would be the arse-creeper at the head of that queue, all things being equal.

But in life all things were rarely equal, and the Metropolitan police force was no exception. Very often, what was more important was a nod and a wink, and friends in high places.

The superintendent was in a high place.

And the psychic was the bow on the gift-wrapped, lever-shaped parcel he'd just been handed by his new friend, who was suddenly looking chinkier than chain mail.

"I see your problem, sir," he nodded sympathetically.

In the face of such sympathy, Clyde's superintendent-of-police façade momentarily slipped and his real, haggard, haunted face was briefly revealed. "I'll not get any peace until that dog's found, John. Until it is, my life is going to be an utter bloody misery."

Then, with a reverberating sigh, he looked Marvel straight in the eyes and added, "I'd be very grateful."

And — only because he was *absolutely sure* that that was true — Marvel nodded eagerly and said, "Don't worry, sir, I'll find it."

CHAPTER
ELEVEN

Anna Buck was on a mission.

Often, after James left for work, she would slide back into sleep. That oblivion was such a temptation to her that sometimes the sound of a child crying was the only thing that could rouse her. Occasionally — in that netherworld between dreams and misery — the crying sounded so like Daniel that she would wake up, run into his room and stand there, naked and shaking beside his empty bed, as brutal reality slowly reclaimed her. It was a car horn, an ice-cream van, the garage radio, or a dog wailing mournfully for its owner gone to work.

But today Anna swung her legs from under the duvet before sleep could reclaim her, quickly pulled on yesterday's clothes and changed and fed Charlie with an unaccustomed air of urgency.

The gas meter was in the cupboard under the stairs. On top of it was a short stack of 50p coins. The meter was secured with a padlock but they never locked it because it was just them in the house. The landlord, Brian Pigeon, kept spares in the ground-floor rooms — boxes and boxes and boxes. He had a spare front-door key but rarely came in.

Anna twisted the padlock out of the metal loops on the meter and pulled open the little drawer, counting out the money in the sickly yellow glow of a low-wattage bulb.

Thirty-two pounds. Not as much as she'd hoped.

She couldn't take it all, either. But she could turn off the heating, wear more jumpers, put another blanket on the baby. It would be warmer soon. Soon*ish*. Maybe by the time the meter was read and the bill came in, she could have reduced their consumption so much that the shortfall would be negligible.

Or maybe by the time the meter was read and the bill came in, Daniel would be home and they wouldn't give a shit about being able to pay the gas bill — or about anything else that might ever go wrong in their lives again.

She wondered how much Richard Latham charged for a consultation. She couldn't begin to imagine what something like that would cost. A token? Or a fortune? She should have asked Sandra.

She took twenty-five pounds. Fifty big coins bulging in her pockets and fists. It felt like a lot.

In the kitchen she put the coins in an old carrier bag and left it on the counter top. It gave her a thrill to look at it, sitting there, waiting to change their lives like a pouch of gold coins in a fairy tale. She thought about a beanstalk stretching from this world to the next — connecting the two, allowing passage between them.

She decided to have a cup of tea and think about what Richard Latham might tell her. She didn't often entertain fantasies about Daniel's return because it was too painful when they ended. But this felt different, exciting, and she decided to indulge herself just for five minutes, before cleaning the flat.

As she filled the kettle at the kitchen sink, she peered out on to the footprints — five dark smudges across the yellow-grey forecourt. Her lips tightened as a boy in baggy jeans rode his bike over them. There was nothing she could do about things like that. Nothing. Not without a bazooka.

She wished she could build a barrier around the prints, or stay out there all day guarding them, but she had the house to clean. And a new baby to look after, of course.

Charlie grizzled in his cot and she called through to him in a soft, sing-song voice. *Hey Charlie . . . Hey Charlie Barley . . . Mummy's here, baby . . . Mummy's right here . . .*

But today it felt automatic, and she had no desire to go through and pick him up and feel the weight of him, safe in her arms. Going nowhere.

Instead she sipped her tea quickly at the kitchen window. As she did, she reached into the pouch of her hoodie to get the elastic that she used to keep her hair off her face while she worked. She took it out, along with a piece of white card with a phone number on it.

It was only when she turned it over that Anna realized it was the photo of Sandra and her dog, Mitzi.

She studied the photo. Sandra's dark roots were showing a bit in the picture, but her make-up was perfect. A long time ago, perfect make-up was something Anna cared about. She used to get free samples at work and try out different "looks". Hours in front of the mirror applying Cleopatra eyeliner, dabbing at kohl with a makeup sponge, lining her lips so they seemed fuller than they really were.

Often while Daniel played on the floor behind her with bricks or books.

Entertaining himself while she stared at her own stupid face.

It made her clammy with shame.

She put the photo down on the counter and stared out of the kitchen window on to a beautiful garden with curved beds, filled with wrong flowers and not-right shrubs against a backdrop of fuzzy trees.

She blinked, and it was gone.

Before she could even think about how odd that had been, Anna was overtaken by a desperate need for water. Tea was not enough. She leaned over and turned on the tap so hard that water ricocheted off the sink and sprayed across her T-shirt. Anna didn't care; she was so *dry!* No time for a glass or a mug or even a cupped hand. She twisted her head under the flow and gulped at the water that hammered out of the spout, greedily sucking it down, as it overflowed and ran into her hair and her ear.

Once, when Anna was four or five, her mother had bought her a paper lily that was packed tight into a tiny plastic bubble only an inch across. They had run a sinkful of water and dropped the little pink knot into it and watched it magically uncurl and blossom into a wonderful flower nearly a foot wide. Anna thought of it now for the first time in years, as she felt the water race through her body like an electrical current, making her alive again, when she had been dry and dead and tightly packed.

After a few moments she straightened up a little unsteadily. Her hair dripped on to her shoulders and she felt lightheaded and foolish.

She should eat something. She had to think hard about what she had eaten — or when — before the two biscuits at the church last night. She got all the way back to a boiled egg for lunch on Thursday. Had she *drunk* anything since then? She must have. But she couldn't think when.

No wonder she was hallucinating!

Anna took a slice of bread from the loaf in the fridge, and made toast and another cup of tea.

She needed to take care of herself. She needed to be here when Daniel came home.

And, for the first time in months, she felt she was actually *doing* something to make that happen.

CHAPTER
TWELVE

"Would you like a cup of tea, Chief Inspector? And a piece of cake?"

Marvel looked up from the pink velour sofa and confirmed the order, and Sandra Clyde bustled off to the kitchen.

So, this was where the super lived.

Marvel looked around and mentally snorted. Even though Clyde was probably in his mid fifties — only ten years older than him — he lived in the house of an old fart.

There were lace cloths on the side tables and antimacassars on the backs of the chairs, and a plastic runner in the hallway to protect the carpet. There were photos of babies that Marvel assumed were grandchildren, and of adults he assumed were children, doing expensive things like skiing and climbing that place in Peru with all the bloody steps. There were crap trinkets from foreign holidays — a bon-bon dish shaped like a sombrero, and a bull's pizzle twisted into something disgusting you could hang on the wall.

The sofa was pink, the carpet was pink, the wallpaper was maroon — which was just dark pink really. Marvel suddenly wondered why it was that men allowed women to control the way their homes looked. Now that he thought about it, when Debbie had moved in, *his* stuff had started to move *out*. His sofa had been the very first thing to go. Marvel had spent many a long, happy night on that sagging dark-blue corduroy, sipping whisky at one end, his feet wearing a hole in the arm at the other, all the while berating the England cricket team as they lost to the Aussies on Sky Sports. But within days of Debbie moving in, it had been replaced by a blocky cream-leather Habitat couch. Debbie said it was retro, which meant you couldn't put your feet on it.

Then he'd found his lung ashtray in a box she was taking to charity. She'd said it was a mistake, but he'd taken it to work for safekeeping. And then, on the night he'd stopped on Bickley Bridge, he'd come home to find his Jameson bar towel collection had disappeared from the coffee table, in favour of two red candles and a pale chunk of pink rock on an ornate wooden stand.

"Rose quartz opens the heart chakra," she had told him, embarrassingly.

"Interesting," he'd said. "Where are my bar towels?"

"Under the sink. I hope that's OK."

Marvel had stayed quiet while she'd bent and lit the candles, even though she was right in the way of San Marino versus Belgium.

And then he'd said, "What's that smell?"

"What smell?"

"Like a hippy's armpit."

"Patchouli," she'd said, looking crushed.

"Why?" he'd asked. "Are we smoking pot now?"

Debbie's heart chakra must have snapped shut at that point, because they hadn't had sex that night or for several nights afterwards.

A while later he'd realized it had been Valentine's Day.

He'd have to make it up to her next year.

Sandra Clyde brought tea in a pot on a tray, delicate china cups and a slab of Victoria sponge that would have choked a carthorse.

Marvel felt more cultured just holding a cup and saucer. More sensible. Older.

Closer to death.

Sandra sat down in the wing chair opposite and looked expectant. It reminded Marvel that there was no such thing as free cake.

"Any news?" she said — as if he would have kept it from her if he had found Muttley already.

No, not Muttley. Mindy.

Not Mindy.

Something *like* Mindy.

Morky.

No.

Marty, Mandy, Monkey, Mopsy. Shit, he'd forgotten the name of the bloody thing now.

He shook his head. "Not yet, I'm afraid. But it's early days."

"Mitzi's been gone for five weeks," said Sandra a little reproachfully.

"Early days for the official investigation," soothed Marvel. He took out his notebook and wrote MITZI in big letters on the first blank page so that he wouldn't forget it again. Then Sandra told him everything she'd done to try to find the dog since it had disappeared in the park. She'd printed photos and flyers and bumper stickers; she'd got her grandson to upload Mitzi's picture to the internet; she'd put cards in newsagents' windows, and offered a reward.

"Reward?"

"A thousand pounds," she nodded. "No questions asked."

Marvel tutted. "We don't encourage that," he said. "In fact, we don't approve of it at all. I'm surprised the super allowed it."

"You don't approve of offering a reward?"

"Saying 'no questions asked'," said Marvel. "It confuses the investigation and could be seen as an obstruction of justice."

"What do you mean?"

"How many calls have you had about Mitzi since putting up the cards?"

"Oh, lots. Everyone wants to help."

"A thousand quid buys a lot of so-called help," said Marvel. "Especially when there are no questions asked. If the dog was nicked, then the criminals feel safer about bringing it back for the reward because they reckon you won't be calling the police, you see?"

Sandra got all flustered at that and Marvel put up a hand to wave the issue away. "What's done is done. We'll let it go."

"Thank you *very* much, Chief Inspector," she said.

"No problem," said Marvel magnanimously. He filed it away though, for future reference. It was minor, but minor things could become major things — especially for people in positions of responsibility. Like police superintendents. What kind of police officer wouldn't ask questions? It would be a dereliction of duty *not* to!

"Now," he said seriously, "I understand you've consulted a psychic?"

"Oh yes," said Sandra. "He's been very helpful too."

"Has he found Mitzi?"

"Well, no. Not yet."

"Then he hasn't been that helpful, has he?" said Marvel.

"Well, he *has*," said Sandra, a little defensively. "He's told me not to give up hope and that Mitzi will be home soon."

"And how has that been helpful?"

"Well," she said again, "it's given me hope, you see?"

"I'm sure it has," agreed Marvel. "But what if it's false hope?"

Sandra Clyde's face crumpled. "You mean Mitzi might be dead?"

"No, no, no!" Shit, he didn't want her crying! He didn't want to make the super's wife *cry*. How in hell was *that* going to help his chance of promotion?

"No, that's not what I meant," said Marvel. "Not at all. I only mean that if somebody is desperate, like you are, to find . . ." he glanced at his notebook ". . . Mitzi. Sometimes that hope — that *completely valid* hope — can be abused by an unscrupulous person."

"Oh, he's not unscrupulous, Chief Inspector! I was very careful. He's not some fly-by-night. He's even helped the police on a case! That's how I knew his name. Richard's been on TV and everything."

"Richard Latham?" said Marvel with a heavy heart.

"Yes," nodded Sandra Clyde eagerly. "Do you know him?"

"Not personally," said Marvel. "But I worked on the Edie Evans case and I have to tell you, Mrs Clyde, that he was really no help at all to us. None whatsoever. A year on, and Edie's still missing. All Mr Latham did was waste police time and possibly distract us from what might have been more fruitful lines of inquiry."

Sandra looked crestfallen all over again.

"Have you paid him any money?" Marvel asked.

"Oh no!" she said instantly. "Only some little donations for the church roof."

Marvel grunted and reddened and pretended to write something in his notebook while he gathered his thoughts.

The church roof! It sounded so . . . so *stupid*! It *was* so stupid, and it made him furious to think that he and Sandra Clyde had that stupidity in common. The coincidence knocked the *Schadenfreude* right out of Marvel, so, instead of being scathing, he just said wealdy, "Well, don't give him any more, OK?"

Sandra bit her lip and nodded and became slightly less red in the face and the danger of tears seemed to have passed. Marvel was relieved. He was no good at riding the rollercoaster of female emotions.

"Listen," he went on. "We'll find Mitzi without the help of a conman like Latham. If he or anyone at the church contacts you, claiming to have a message or a vision or a dream or *anything* about Mitzi, I want you to tell them you're not interested, OK? Tell them the police are now involved in the investigation and you don't need their help. If they don't take no for an answer, let me deal with it."

Sandra nodded, but looked far from convinced. "But if we can't believe Richard's visions, we're back to square one!"

Marvel wasn't crazy about her use of the word "we". It made it sound as if they had *both* believed Latham's so-called psychic visions at some point, which he absolutely never had.

"Square one is a very good place to start," he said brusquely. It was a great line, he thought: like something out of a Quentin Tarantino movie. He'd have to remember it if he ever needed to deliver a motivational speech to G Team that went beyond "Do your fucking job."

Sandra Clyde gave a tremulous smile. "Like Julie Andrews in *The Sound of Music*. Do-Re-Mi!"

"Of course," he said, although he had no idea what she was talking about, and wished she hadn't introduced Julie effing Andrews just as he was thinking about blood and guns and Tarantino.

But he let it go. He was so exhausted by having to be nice to the super's wife that he just wanted to get the hell out. He closed his notebook with a flourish and got off the low sofa with surprising difficulty; Christ, the Clydes must have hydraulic knees.

Sandra Clyde showed him out.

On the doorstep she said, "So what happens now, Chief Inspector?"

"We'll take it from here," Marvel said, planting the seed in her head that there would be some kind of *team* dedicated to finding Mitzi, not just him, so that if something went wrong in the future, there was someone else to blame. Someone imaginary.

"Thank you so much," she said, and, without warning, the super's wife leaned forward and gave him a big hug.

"OK," he said when it was over. "We've got things in hand now."

"Thank you, Chief Inspector!"

He walked to his car. Normally he'd have a pool car but there had been a spate of bumps and write-offs and he'd been driving his own for a few weeks now. It was a black BMW M3, with tinted windows and Wolfrace wheels, which had once belonged to a drug-dealer called Jimmy the Fix. After Jimmy had been sent down for fourteen years, Marvel had bought it cheap from the police pound before it could go to public auction, and it was his pride and joy. He paid ten grand a year for a garage to keep it nice — and to keep it his.

Just as he pulled open the car door, Mrs Clyde called from the doorstep, "Ooh, wait a minute, Chief Inspector, I have something for you."

Marvel waited, imagining cake in a tin-foil wedge.

Instead Sandra Clyde bustled out and handed him a bumper sticker that read FIND MITZI. It was pink and at either end there was a heart-shaped photo of the poodle, with a bow on its head.

The bow was pink too.

"For your car," Mrs Clyde said.

In a Tarantino movie, Marvel would have pulled out a .357 Magnum and blown Mrs Clyde's head clean off her shoulders, in an ironic pink spray.

In the movie of his own life, he took it and said, "Interesting."

"Robert has one on his car," smiled Mrs Clyde encouragingly. "And he's given them to everyone at work."

If Superintendent Clyde had told his wife that, it was a boldfaced lie.

"So you should really have one," she added, "as you're in charge of the case."

There was no denying that annoying truth.

And, because she was standing there watching, Marvel had to peel off the backing and place the bright-pink poodle sticker on the rear bumper of Jimmy the Fix's shiny black BMW.

That night over dinner, Debbie said brightly, "You should put up Wanted posters. Like in the cowboy films."

Marvel snorted. "Dead or Alive?"

She nodded. "It would catch people's imagination. Make them remember what she looks like. Maybe put a little cowboy hat on her," she mused, then quickly said, "No, that would be silly."

As if Wanted posters weren't.

92

Usually Debbie didn't like to discuss his cases. Usually she got all touchy if he read a file over dinner — especially when he shifted her candles aside so he could lay out autopsy reports.

"Not at the dinner table, John," she'd say. "It's sick."

"This is my *job*!" he'd snap back. "I don't expect you to take an interest, but the least you could do is let me work!"

"Well, *I'm* trying to eat!"

"Eat then! Who's stopping you?"

Trust her to enter into the spirit of things on a case that wasn't even a murder, thought Marvel.

"You should go to Battersea Dogs Home," she suggested as she helped herself to more green beans. "If someone found Mitzi that's probably the first place they'd think to take her. We had a dog from Battersea when I was little. A funny old scruffy thing like a dust-bunny on legs."

She smiled softly and added, "He used to drag our shoes into the garden. We'd be getting ready for school and we'd have to go hopping around in the bushes looking for our other shoe!"

Marvel thought that if a dog did that to his shoes, it would be back in the pound before it could say "euthanasia". Still, he smiled because Debbie looked so happy at the memory. He hadn't seen that look on her face for ages, and he wondered briefly whether something or somebody had been upsetting her.

He reached out and took her hand, and she looked up in surprise and gave a small smile. Then she sighed deeply and pushed her beans around with a fork. "I was heartbroken when Pip died. But losing him and not knowing where he was would have been even worse."

Marvel thought of Edie Evans and grunted his agreement around a mouthful of spaghetti Bolognese.

"Maybe you could look on the internet," said Debbie.

"For what?"

"They have those sites where people put pictures of dogs they've lost or found. Doglost or Lostdog. One of them, anyway."

"I'm already doing that," said Marvel, although he wasn't. But it sounded like a good idea. It was just as well, because when it came to finding lost dogs, Marvel realized he didn't have many ideas of his own.

"Good," she said. "And if you get some more copies of the photo I can give them to the girls at work."

"OK," said Marvel. Women and other do-gooders all loved animals and children. He started to wonder whether he could hand the whole operation over to Debbie and just reap the spoils of the promotion to superintendent.

"Anything else?" he encouraged her.

She hummed a little while she thought, and Marvel wondered when they'd stopped being like this all the time — with Debbie interested and backing him up, and being happy to do it. Certainly, it was before she'd started making the faces that told him his feet were on the Habitat couch, or that there were photos of corpses on the kitchen table.

"You could offer a reward," she mused.

"Good idea," he said — even though it was redundant — because he wanted to extend the moment of mutual goodwill.

Debbie smiled again, all pleased with herself. "And you should put on it, *no questions asked.*"

CHAPTER
THIRTEEN

The next Friday night, Anna left the flat much more easily. She only went back inside twice, her tummy fluttering, before hurrying past the five footprints with the hood of the blue anorak blinkering her view.

She had the money.

The drizzle was slow but meant business, and by the time she reached the hall her jeans were soaked up to the shins by the spray from the wheels of the buggy.

There was a shiny new red plastic bucket under the damp patch. Queensland now bulged slightly sideways into the dirty white Pacific ceiling. There was also a new, smaller patch on the lower right, which Anna thought might be the start of Tasmania.

Sandra wasn't there, but otherwise the congregation was mostly the same as last week's and the dust certainly was. Anna could feel it in her throat.

The format was the same too. Latham bouncing slowly about the stage like a Thunderbirds puppet, poking his glasses up his sweaty nose and giving living people pointless snippets of non-information from dead people.

Dad says he saw you break your heel.

Toby's here and he wants to say everything's going to be fine.

Caroline's showing me you have pain in your hip.

Ugh. Anna thought Richard Latham *must* be communicating with the dead, because if he were making this stuff up, surely it would be more interesting?

It didn't get better when he threw the floor open to the amateurs. The nodding-dog boy was still confused by which spirit was which, and a small woman with the ruddy nose of a cider drinker stood for a full minute, swaying back and forth without speaking into the microphone, before they realized she'd gone to sleep.

Last time it had been novel and bizarre enough to hold her attention. This week — with her new-found hope making Anna itch with impatience — it was like a slow-mo action replay of something that hadn't been worth watching the first time around.

There was no message from Daniel, and with every dead dullard her spirits rose. He wasn't dead; he wasn't dead; *he wasn't dead.*

The low buzz of anticipation in her gut grew and grew until she could barely sit still. She jiggled the buggy compulsively with her foot, careless of whether Charlie was sleeping or not.

The session ended and the two ladies at the front got up to make the tea and put the biscuits on a plate.

Anna couldn't wait any longer. She edged through the little knot of people around Richard Latham, who was telling a story about how he'd come to the aid of a Rolling Stone. A dead one, presumably.

"Hi," she interrupted. "Can I have a consultation?"

"A chat, you mean?" He smiled.

"Well, yes. But a proper one. One you pay for."

Latham looked a little embarrassed and so did the people around him. He put down his cup of tea and pointed at the chair opposite his. "Why don't you sit down and have a cup of tea and a biscuit and we'll have a chat afterwards?"

"OK," she said. She sat down, feeling the panic of having passed the point of no return. She'd done it; she'd asked. She'd even told him she'd pay, so she would be able to ask him anything she wanted to about Daniel.

She gripped the handle of the buggy so hard that her hands hurt.

She hadn't asked how much it was going to be. Shit. What if it was hundreds of pounds? The bag filled with the gas-meter money had felt very substantial when she'd left home. But here, now, it didn't seem like a lot at all — not for someone who'd been on TV.

Anna felt sick with worry. She'd asked now, and she needed answers. What if Latham laughed at her heavy, light money and refused to tell her what had happened to Daniel? What would she do then? What *could* she do?

She bit her lip and felt her eyes grow hot with threatening tears.

She would *make* him help her. She would beg or threaten, or cry and get angry. Something would work; something would *have* to, because Anna Buck was crazy and anyone could see —

"Now," said Richard Latham, "what would you like to talk about?"

Anna looked around to see that while she had been panicking, everyone had left, and it was just her and Latham in the dingy little hall. Her eyes lit on the crucifix over the doorway, and she felt guilty that she wasn't praying, instead of paying for help.

But James was right. Where was God when Daniel disappeared?

Nowhere.

This was the moment of truth. A minute from now she might know where her son was. The hope in her heart felt as swollen and fragile as a soap bubble.

For a second she couldn't speak at all, and thought she might cry instead. Then she pulled herself together. She had to stay strong for Daniel. She couldn't fall here at the very first step.

Anna drew a deep breath and her words came out in a rush. "I need to know where my son is. He's been missing for over four months. He's nearly five now and his name is Daniel and here's a photo of him, it was taken last summer so his hair will be longer now but you can see it's him, and Sandra told me you can just look at photos and you *know* things, so can you look at his photo? Please? I can pay you. I have money. I only have twenty-five pounds at the moment but I can get more if it's more. I just have to know where he is, or whether he's —"

Daniel's not dead.

She took a deep breath and rushed on. "He's not dead. I know he's not dead because I'd *feel* it, I think. I know I would, so I know he's not dead, but can you please just look at it? Please? And tell me?"

She held out the photo to Latham, but he didn't take it from her trembling hand.

"Please?" she said, and her voice cracked.

Latham reached out, but instead of taking the photo, he took both Anna's hands in his.

"I can't," he said.

"Yes, you can. Sandra said so. She said you're a shut eye and you talk to her dog and you can just look at a photo and —"

"I can't," he repeated. "I'm very sorry."

"She said you can. Can you just *look* at it? I mean, that's all I want you to do! It's not much to ask! My son's *gone*! He's four years old and he got out of the door because James left it open when he went to buy fireworks and now he's *gone*! Please just look at it."

Latham hesitated, then took the photo from her and Anna's stomach churned frantically. She could feel the blood heating her cheeks, and she shook in anticipation. Felt faint with it.

But he didn't look at the photo. He looked at her through thick lenses with moony, uneven brown eyes.

"I'm sorry," he said again. "I don't do this any more."

The blood in Anna's ears was so loud that she cocked her head and asked, "You what?"

"I don't do missing people any more. I'm sorry."

"You don't *do* them any more? What do you *mean*? Won't you even *look* at it? Look at the photo! Please!"

"I'm sorry."

"But this is what you do! You helped the police look for another child; why won't you help me find *mine?* I need your help! Nobody else can help me. Please! Please! *Please just look at the picture!*"

He blinked slowly behind the thick lenses. "I'm sorry."

Anna looked down. He was offering the photo back to her, but she didn't take it. She stared at it. Daniel smiled up at her from next to Richard Latham's big thumb. There was a black mark on Latham's nail where he'd dropped something on it, or hit it with a hammer. It was her best photo of Daniel. He was in his red dungarees, like a jolly little hillbilly. She'd got them from Oxfam and they were his favourite things. Loose and cool and with lots of pockets for lots of things: crayon stubs and pennies, and discarded toys from other children's Happy Meals. She thought of the way he was so fascinated by the dungarees' bib fastenings that she always had a job to do them up, because his head was always in the way. His little blond head, with the short curls, craning to see how the metal button slid into the buckle. She never minded how long it took to do up the bib, as long as she could kneel there and breathe in the heady aroma of Daniel: innocence and joy.

Innocence and joy.

"I'm sorry." Latham said it again. He wasn't going to change his mind.

Slowly Anna reached out and took the photo.

She had been ready to beg him, to threaten, to shout and scream. She would have slapped him; she would have slept with him.

But when the moment came, she had nothing.

She was empty.

So empty, she couldn't even ask *why*.

"OK," she whispered.

"I'm sorry I couldn't help you."

Couldn't? Or wouldn't? No difference.

"OK," she said again. She got up and put the photo back in her pocket.

"Please come back next week," he said. "Maybe somebody else will bring you a message from Daniel."

She didn't answer. She couldn't think about other possibilities. The pain of losing this one was too great.

"Goodnight," he said.

Anna pushed the buggy up the old green carpet and put her wet shoes on at the door.

"Don't give up hope," he said.

It was too late for that.

Outside the rain was coming down hard and the baby bawled loudly all the way home.

CHAPTER
FOURTEEN

The smell of dogs filled John Marvel's nose, and their echoing barks made him wince.

"This is it," he said and showed the photo of Mitzi to the perky girl in the peaky polo shirt. She had her name, *Rachel*, embroidered under the Battersea Dogs Home logo on the slope of her bra-less breast.

"I don't recognize her," she said. "But owners usually like to look at the dogs themselves anyway, to be absolutely sure."

"Surely you'd know if you had a ginger poodle in?"

"I think it's called apricot, not ginger."

"*Apricot* poodle."

"Well, dogs that come often don't look like their pictures," said Rachel. "Specially if they've been gone for weeks or months or even years. Sometimes they've been stolen and when they're found they're unrecognizable."

"Why would nicking a dog make it unrecognizable?"

Rachel's pretty brown eyes widened. "They might be fatter or thinner, or injured, or clipped to disguise them and be sold on, or mutilated."

"*Mutilated?*"

She nodded sombrely. "Some dogs are stolen for fighting."

"We're talking about a ten-pound poodle."

"Or baiting," said Rachel. "To train bigger dogs to fight. Give them a taste for blood."

"You're joking," said Marvel.

Rachel shrugged. "It happens," she said, then added hurriedly, "Not to *your* dog, I'm sure. All I'm saying is, when a dog's been missing for more than a week or so, you have no idea how bad they can look and smell when they come in here. She may not even look like a poodle any more. So it's best you check them all, really."

Marvel finally conceded the point. "OK," he said. "How many do you have here?"

"About five hundred."

"Five hundred *dogs?*"

"Give or take."

Marvel frowned. This case was turning into a huge pain in the arse. Plus, somebody had talked. Nobody had *said* anything, but somehow word must have got around the squad room about his new case.

First a toy dog had appeared on his desk. A blue puppy with a bone in its mouth.

Hilarious.

He'd made a free shot with it into the rubbish bin.

Then people had started barking at him. Not to his face, but behind his back. Small growls and whimpers — now and then a yap. It got so that even when nobody growled at him, he imagined it anyway. He snapped "Fuck off and die" at the vending machine gurgling as he walked past, he turned furiously and glared at a small child making car noises in reception, and rounded on DI Averiss in the lift when he mentioned that he had no new leads in his case.

What the hell does that mean? No new leads? Are you trying to be funny?

If he wasn't fast-tracked to superintendent after all this hassle, he'd put in an official complaint.

Rachel was unlocking a door with a little window in it.

Marvel sighed. "Just show me the small ones."

Rachel laughed and swung open the door. The echoing noise and the smell increased tenfold and Marvel nearly gagged. The corridor between the rows of steel kennels stretched off into the middle distance like something from a spaceship in a sci-fi film.

"Jesus," he said. "How do you stand it?"

He meant the noise and the smell, but Rachel was made of kinder stuff. "I know," she said, making a sad face, "it's heartbreaking, isn't it? A third of them will have to be put to sleep. I only wish I could take them all home with me."

Marvel wished she could take them all home with her too, and save him the bother of trudging up and down the stinking passageways.

With a heavy sigh he set off down the first corridor, cursing Debbie and her good ideas.

Marvel looked at thousands of dogs. He was sure of it. Thousands of yipping, yapping, yowling dogs — every one of them on a tireless spring, and all stinking of shit and old sofas.

He reckoned he'd spend ten minutes in the corridors and then go back to the office and tell Rachel some cock-and-bull story about being called out on a triple homicide. Dazzle her with murder.

But by the time he was halfway down the first corridor, he found he couldn't stop. The next cage might contain Mitzi, and the next cage was only a few feet away. How could he not take those three more paces that could ensure him his promotion? It would be stupid not to. And at the end of the first corridor, how could he resist the second? And the third? And so on. Hundreds of kennels; thousands of dogs; three paces at a time, his hopes raised and shattered and raised again, every few seconds.

Every dog was so *hopeful*, so bright of eye and waggy of tail, and the noise and the smell were extreme. The whole thing was emotionally and physically exhausting. By the end he was walking with his hands cupped over his ears to take the edge off the high notes, and after a while he went dog-blind, and started to think that almost any small dog might be Mitzi. None of them were, but it was lucky he had her photo with him to refer to, or he might have left the place with a red spaniel, a panting ginger Pom, or a tan mutt with a dick that almost touched the floor.

Instead he left with a scruffy terrier that looked like a dust-bunny with legs, and with an expression on its face that said that this was a shock to both of them.

He paid Rachel two hundred pounds for the dog — which was worth at least twenty — and bought a cage for another eighty in which to take it home. Fifteen more on two bowls, twenty-five on a collar and lead, and a tenner on a sack of food.

By the time he put his debit card into the machine he was so hysterical with altruism that he rounded the payment up to £350.

"Oh, thank you!" gushed Rachel. "Please let me know if there's any other way we can help you, Chief Inspector."

Marvel gave her a photo of Mitzi, which she promised to copy and give to all the dog wardens.

"Great," he said. "What else do you suggest?"

"You might want to offer a reward," she said. "No questions asked."

Marvel drove the suspicious dog to the flat and left it in its cage with food and water in the kitchen, where Debbie would see it as soon as she got home.

He hoped she would understand that this meant they were quits for Valentine's night.

As he shut the cage, the little dog licked his hand with a surprisingly strong pink tongue — as if to say thank you.

Marvel was almost fooled.

But when he got back into the BMW he found the dog had also left him the gift of a small turd on the back seat. He had nothing to pick it up with, and had to drive through drizzle with the windows open all the way to Lewisham.

So he was already in a bad mood when he pulled into the parking garage back at the station.

As he got out of his car, DS Kominski glanced down at his bumper sticker and said, "Lost your dog, sir?" in a tone that was so bland, so neutral, so *completely inoffensive*, that Marvel just *knew* he was taking the piss.

He told DC Kominski to fuck off, but instead of following orders, Kominski stopped and said, "There's no need for that, sir."

"What?" said Marvel angrily.

"I said, there's no need for that language, sir."

"Come here and say that!"

Looking a bit bewildered, Kominski did.

Marvel threw a punch and missed, then Kominski threw one back and missed too. There was a split second of relief on both sides that they hadn't connected — and then they just grabbed each other by the sleeves and fell on the ground and rolled around in the dirt for a bit until Marvel got lucky when Kominski caught his funny bone on the wall. It allowed Marvel to roll to his knees and scramble to his feet while Kominski was still shaking his arm and going "*Shit!*" — thus affording Marvel the victory.

He helped Kominski up and told him to let everyone know that he would do the same thing to any bastard who gave him shit.

"Shit about what?" panted Kominski.

Marvel didn't dignify that with an answer, just strode away.

"*Shit about what?*"

CHAPTER
FIFTEEN

Anna hadn't cleaned the flat, and it was shocking how fast the germs took over. They started in the kitchen sink, where the dishes piled up and where food dried and hardened in the pans until cleaning them would have meant cleaning the last of the nonstick right off them too.

The germs overflowed from there and ran along the counters, down the cabinet doors and across the floors — out of the kitchen and into the lounge and from there to the bathroom.

And every time the germs met a wall, they bounced off and colonized a different angle, another corner, a new space.

Even James noticed how fast things got dirty when you didn't keep them clean.

Eventually — after three days of eating cereal from a mug — he did the washing up. Afterwards he went into the bedroom where Anna was still in bed and said, "What about the baby?"

"What about him?" she said dully.

"Aren't you afraid he'll get sick?"

"No," she said. "I'm not afraid of anything any more. What could happen to us that's worse than losing Daniel?"

James stood at the door for a while, wondering whether there was anything he could say that would cheer her up. Or get her out of bed, at least. But there was nothing. Anna was right: nothing could be worse.

"Are you going to church again?" he asked tentatively.

"No."

He nodded slowly. "What happened?"

"Nothing. I thought it would help, but it didn't."

"Oh," he said. "I'm sorry." He *was* sorry. Even though he was relieved she wasn't going to church again, he was sorry that she had found no comfort there, or anywhere.

He slowly drummed his fingers on the bedroom door and said, "When I get home I'll clean the house."

When James got to work, Ang's sleeping bag was still unrolled on the bench. There was water on the floor where he had used the tiny handbasin to wash himself, and on the table were little bits of wire, a pair of pliers, and a bottle of aftershave with the face of a famous footballer on it.

James felt awkward — as if he'd walked into Ang's home without knocking.

"Sorry," he said, as Ang edged past him to roll up the sleeping bag.

"Is good," said Ang.

He used to have a mattress, but Brian had bitched about it taking up all the space in the kitchen, until Ang had dumped it in the old inspection pit, where it leaned uselessly against a wall, while he slept on the bench.

"You want some tea?" said James.

"Yes, please."

James put the kettle on and picked an intricate piece of wire-work off the table. "What's this?"

"Car," said Ang. "See?" He picked up a second piece and showed James how they would fit together to make bodywork and a chassis.

James grinned. "Clever," he said. "Daniel would love that."

There was a loud silence, until the kettle switched itself off with a click.

"You should make more of this stuff," said James. "Sell it, you know? Get some extra money."

Ang shrugged at the car in his hands. "Is not for money," he said. "All Hmong make this." He put the car down and opened the old broom cupboard next to the sink, and stuffed the sleeping bag on the high shelf.

"Did you make that too?" James pointed at a broad strip of colourful material that was pinned to the inside of the door.

"No," said Ang. "My mother."

"What is it?" said James.

"*Paj ntaub*," said Ang. "Umm, iiiiiis . . . Story, umm . . . cloth."

"Story cloth?" James opened the door wide so that the light fell more fully on the material. It was beautiful. A foot wide and two foot long, it had a dark-red background, with intricate curlicues and spirals and zig-zags sewn on to it in repeating patterns of wildly clashing pinks, oranges, magentas and greens.

"That's great," said James.

Ang grinned proudly and his slender brown finger pointed out various symbols, as he struggled to tell James their meanings. "This iiiiiis . . . snail. This iiiiiis . . . I don't know English. This iiiiiis . . . flower . . ."

"Very beautiful," said James.

"You want?" said Ang, and started to peel off the sticky tape at one corner.

"No!"

"I give," Ang insisted. "For Anna is happy."

James's nose tingled with sudden emotion. It would take more than a strip of needlework to make Anna happy.

He felt a sudden prick of anger at Ang. His guilt wasn't Ang's to fix. Let the little bastard find a guilt of his own and fix that!

"No!" he said, more roughly than he'd meant to. Ang flinched and stopped picking at the tape.

Immediately James felt bad. Ang wasn't being mean: he had seen Anna's pain and offered up the only thing of value he appeared to own.

Unselfishly.

"Thanks, mate," James said. "But your mother made it. You keep it."

"Two sugars in mine," demanded Mikey from the doorway, and Ang swung the cupboard door shut.

"Feck, it's freezing." Mikey was only five-eight, but he filled any room with his big voice and his restless nature. He sat noisily in one of the chairs and picked up the aftershave. "Goal." He read the name, then punched the air with both fists. "GOOOOOAAAAAALLLLL!"

They all laughed. Mikey had the knack of making everything feel OK again. James was glad he'd walked in when he had.

Ang held out his hand for the bottle, but Mikey sniffed it and winced. "Jesus! That's one nostril won't need picking for a week! Who's the lucky lady, Ang?"

Ang looked at him blankly and Mikey tapped the bottle in salutation. "You got a girlfriend?"

"Girlfend?"

"Girl. Woman. You know," said Mikey and traced a universal hourglass with his hands.

Ang shook his head. "Shit, no."

"You should get one," said Mikey. "Shouldn't he, boys?"

"Get what one?" said Pavel, hanging up his coat. "He should get a girl," Mikey went on. "Young fella like him. Good looking, sense of humour, own teeth."

"Own broom," snorted Pavel, as he lit a black cigarette.

"Ahh, girls *love* a man with a broom," said Mikey. "A broom's a big turn-on to the ladies."

He winked at Ang, who grinned and held out his hand again. This time Mikey gave him the aftershave and Ang put it under the sink.

James put a mug of tea in front of each of them.

"How long have you been here, Ang?" said Mikey.

Ang held up three fingers.

"Three years. And how old are you?"

"Twenty-one," said Ang.

"Bollocks" said Mikey, and he and James laughed while Pavel merely raised an eyebrow. "But you should get a nice girl," Mikey went on. "Even better, get a nasty one, hey, Pavel?"

He winked at Pavel, who only shrugged and blew three perfect smoke rings.

Ang shrugged and gestured at the kitchen. "Where?"

Mikey looked around and then waved away his concerns. "Easy. Get this place done up. Brian won't mind. Bit of carpet on the floor. No windows, so you don't need curtains. Get a lamp —"

"A double bench," said James.

"That's right!" laughed Mikey. "You'd have a girl in no time. I mean, you're almost as gorgeous as me!"

"Of course," said Pavel, "but he never as *white* as you."

"*Nobody's* as white as me," said Mikey proudly, twisting the hairs that curled like vermicelli around the strap of his wristwatch.

"He had a girlfriend," said James. "Zij or Zoe or something. He was going to meet her parents and everything, remember?"

"Ah! That's right!" said Mikey. "What happened there, mate?"

Ang shrugged sadly. "She break my hat."

"She what?" said James.

"She break my hat."

They all stared at him quizzically until James had a lightbulb moment. "She broke your *heart*."

Mikey spat tea across the room he laughed so hard, and even Pavel chuckled without smiling, making his cigarette wobble between his lips.

114

Ang looked mournful enough to make the whole thing even funnier, and they didn't stop laughing until Brian Pigeon came in and told them to stop enjoying themselves and get to work, or they could all go back to whatever third-world shithole they came from and stop stealing his money for doing *bugger all*.

James could have reminded him that he paid shite wages and *bugger all* national insurance by employing illegal immigrants. But he didn't, of course.

He worked in Brian's garage and he lived right next door in Brian's flat, so he wasn't saying a *thing*.

He had enough troubles of his own.

CHAPTER
SIXTEEN

It only took ten minutes of feeding Charlie at the cluttered kitchen table for Anna to realize that she could never not care about germs. James was naturally untidy, and after only three days without her input the table was already covered with junk. Torn envelopes, bills, pizza boxes and dirty plates.

She didn't rush the feeding though; she enjoyed it too much. The weight of the baby in her arms, the ritual of the spoon in the jar and the choo-choo train to the rosebud lips.

If she closed her eyes, she could easily imagine it was Daniel, safe and warm and at home with his family.

So she took her time.

But as soon as she had dabbed the last of the Mixed Vegetable Medley off the baby's chin, Anna put him down to sleep in the bedroom and got to work.

She flapped open a bin bag and used her forearm to sweep a great swathe of rubbish off the table. There was no room for sentiment when it came to cleaning the flat, and Anna was brutal with rubbish. James knew that if he put something down in the wrong place for too long, he was liable to lose it.

As the junk slid off the table, Anna caught a fleeting glimpse of Sandra and Mitzi. The photo had been under the pizza box. She stopped and reached into the bag to retrieve it, and stared at the blonde woman and the curly dog.

She nearly dropped it back into the bin then. What was the point of keeping it? Mitzi was only a dog, after all.

But she didn't throw it away. She wouldn't want someone throwing away a photo she'd given them of Daniel, even if the odds of recognizing him from it were a million to one. She wouldn't throw it away. She couldn't.

She propped it on the window-sill behind the sink.

And suddenly she was looking at the garden again.

My God! It felt so familiar!

The angle was odd and the flowers were *wrong* and the smell was wrong, too — it was grease and dry dust, not grass and blossoms — but Anna was *right there*, even though the flowers were far away. Or were they? The perspective wasn't right and she couldn't tell what kind of flowers they were, even though her father had loved to garden and had taught her some names. She squinted but she didn't see anything she recognized — not even common flowers like roses and daisies. They were big and coarse and the edges were . . . black? And there was something on the window-sill . . .

She reached out a hand to pick it up —

There was nothing there. Her hand hovered between the sink and the kitchen window, with nothing in its grasp but air. No flowers, no grass, no misty trees. Just the stale air of a messy kitchen.

Anna shivered so hard she had to put out a hand to steady herself against the table to keep from stumbling sideways. She felt as if she'd been stretched out like a piece of elastic and now she'd pinged back, made limp by the effort.

Barely breathing, Anna waited for something else, but there was nothing, and already she couldn't recapture the feeling of *something*.

She needed water. Again. She was desperate for water.

She hurried to the sink and turned on the tap and gulped greedily at the stream that flowed from it.

More.

More.

And more.

She drank more than she needed. More than she wanted. She drank as if her life depended on it. And even after she'd retched a couple of mouthfuls back up into the sink, she continued to let the stream pour down her lips and cheeks as the water spread fast inside her stomach, her legs, her fingertips, her *brain*.

Anna started to laugh and splutter at the glory of water filling her whole being. She was exhilarated. She put the "high" in "hydration"! *Oh my God! Oh my God!* She felt so alive!

Finally she turned the tap off and stood over the sink, panting with relief.

She looked out of the window, giggling a little as she felt her pumping heart-rate slowly return to normal, and then — just as suddenly — she was overwhelmed with sorrow.

She stood in a puddle of water and cried and cried and cried until she'd emptied herself of what felt like every drop she'd just drunk.

What was wrong with her?

What if this sudden raging thirst was a symptom that there was something physically amiss? This was twice it had happened in a week. It was extreme, and bizarre. So bizarre that Anna wondered whether she should see a doctor.

She had refused to see anyone after Daniel had disappeared — not doctors and not counsellors. What could they have done? How could they have helped? Given her sedatives to make her sleep, make her forget? When she woke up, Daniel would still be gone. What mother wanted to forget her missing child? What doctor would try to make her?

But this . . . this felt *wrong*.

Wrong enough to see someone now?

As she stood, shivery-wet and sniffing, Anna imagined the scene.

Doctor, I get very thirsty.

Do you have a tap?

Yes.

Then turn it on.

The thought brought a wry smile to her lips. It was a simple solution to a simple problem. She *should* drink more water. She'd read somewhere that *everyone* should drink more water. Maybe this extreme thirst was just nature's way of telling her that she was falling behind on her quota.

But even if that were true, then what was the vision of the garden telling her?

Something.

She just didn't know what. And now that it was gone, it seemed to be no more than a momentary flash of wild imagination.

But in her heart Anna knew it had been more than that: she had been *there*. And it had been almost close enough to touch . . . She closed her eyes and reached out her hand and tried to re-conjure that vision, but it was just a memory now, and no more or less vivid than any other.

And what would the doctor say about *that* craziness? Probably plenty.

If Anna was going mad, she didn't want anyone else to know. Even *she* didn't want to know.

She opened the cupboard under the sink to find tea-towels to clean up the water on the floor.

He looks at the photo and he just knows things . . .

Anna straightened up as Sandra's words popped into her head, unbidden.

She stared intently through the kitchen window at the grey street and the red buses, but her mind saw only the sorry crucifix on the wall and the crumbs on Richard Latham's jumper.

He just knows things.

Anna just knew things too!

120

She knew the garden as if she were there. She knew that the flowers were somehow *wrong*. She'd seen it all twice, and both times she'd had that raging thirst.

And both times she had been looking at the photo of Sandra and Mitzi.

What did it mean? Was she getting visions? Like Richard Latham? Like . . . what had Sandra called him . . .

Like a shut eye?

How else to explain it all? Was Mitzi in a garden somewhere? Or in a house where she could see the garden from the window? Was the dog trapped somewhere without water? Anna hoped not; the thought of that thirst without the relief of the kitchen tap was horrific, and she shuddered.

Was she in psychic communication with a lost dog?

It was ridiculous. Ludicrous.

Embarrassing.

Down below, through the kitchen window, the garage came into focus, and she wondered whether she should tell James what had happened, what she'd seen. With his good sense and logic, she was sure James could explain it.

Explain it *away?*

It would not be hard to do. Anna could be easily persuaded out of it. Because — as Sandra had also said — it was like magic, and everybody knew that magic was just a clever distraction, a misdirection. Sleight of hand and smoke and mirrors, and a willingness in the observer to be deceived, baffled and bamboozled.

But what if it wasn't?

What if there was even the tiniest sliver of real magic to be found in the layers of lies and self-deception? Wasn't that why crowds still flocked to watch the girl sawn in half or the confetti turned into doves? Wasn't it because people *wanted* to believe that somewhere, somehow, there really *was* such a thing as magic? That their lives might one day also be transformed into something wonderful?

Or, at least, bearable.

That was why magic flourished down the centuries, just as religion did — because they both brought hope.

Anna had lost *everything* the day Daniel disappeared. The meagre possibility of his return was all that kept her alive — and then only just. She had felt the joy of hope in her heart that first night at the church, and the desolation of losing it on her second visit. But here it was again, a resilient little shoot poking upwards from the black earth.

The last thing she needed was James stepping on it, pointing out that there would soon be a frost.

Anna picked Sandra's photo off the window-sill. She looked at it with new eyes. The pride and happiness in Sandra's face — the content expression of the apricot poodle. Mitzi had the look of a dog who was used to being tucked under an arm and doted upon.

Anna took her phone from her pocket, then hesitated. Was false hope better than none? Or far, far worse?

Then she thought of how Richard Latham's refusal to even *try* to help had emptied her, hollowed her out and replaced her heart with a cold stone of misery.

122

Anna Buck wasn't stupid; she knew that magic wasn't real.

But sometimes it *felt* real.

And sometimes that was enough.

CHAPTER
SEVENTEEN

The phone rang and rang and rang before Sandra finally picked up.

"Hello? Sandra?"

"Yes?"

"Hi. This is Anna. I met you at the church a couple of weeks ago?"

There was a long confused hesitation.

"I had the baby in the buggy?"

"Oh yes!"

Anna was glad she had called. Sandra seemed like a nice person and she hoped she could help her. She took a deep breath and decided to cut straight to the chase before she lost her nerve. "Sandra, twice now when I've looked at that photo you gave me, I've had this weird sort of vision, and I wondered whether, if I described it to you, maybe it would make sense, and maybe it would help you to find your dog."

There was a short silence and then whispering at the other end — Sandra turning away to tell somebody something. A friend? A husband?

Anna hurried on: "I mean, these pictures in my head don't mean anything to me, but maybe they would to you. I mean, I'm not a psychic or anything like that, and I know it does sound pretty stupid, but I thought, if there's even a small hope of it being any help to you, you know?"

Anna stopped talking, partly because the more she talked about a vision, the nuttier it sounded. And partly because she was getting nothing back from Sandra. There were no encouraging murmurs or excited interjections.

Just silence.

"This is Detective Chief Inspector John Marvel. Who's this?"

Anna blinked. "Anna," she said.

"Anna who?"

She hung up.

Breathing shallowly, she stood very still, as if she were hiding. As if Detective Chief Inspector John Marvel might see her if she moved or made a sound. She didn't know why; she hadn't done anything wrong. She'd *never* done anything wrong! It was just so unexpected . . .

Why would a policeman be interested in her phoning Sandra about her lost dog? Why would he want to know who she was? Did he have her confused with somebody else? What was going on?

She flinched as the phone rang. She stared at it until it stopped, and then continued to stare at it until it beeped to let her know there was a message waiting for her.

She picked the phone up and listened warily, as if she might hang up — even on the message.

This is DCI Marvel of Lewisham police. We're investigating a possible theft and if you call this number again, you may be charged with obstruction of justice.

Anna immediately deleted the message. She'd never been in trouble with the police — not even as a teenager — and it felt somehow shameful to be suspected of something, even when she'd done nothing wrong.

She sat down slowly and tried to think logically about what was happening. Logic was possible; it had to be — even when it came to visions. Maybe she'd hallucinated because she hadn't eaten enough, and she'd got thirsty because she wasn't drinking enough. That was all there was to it. She wasn't psychic.

Was *anybody*?

If Richard Latham were psychic then surely he would have helped her find Daniel. Why wouldn't he? How *couldn't* he? If you really had such a gift and you could help someone in desperate need, surely you had to do it.

You *had* to help.

She had to help!

She had to help. That was all there was to it. The feeling wasn't rational but, like the thirst, it was not a want, it was a *need*.

It was raining outside and the baby was asleep, but Anna didn't care about either. She picked him up, wrapped him up warmly, put him in his buggy and put up the hood, then pulled on the big blue anorak, took a deep breath and left the house.

This time she didn't turn back — not even once.

CHAPTER
EIGHTEEN

The reception area of Lewisham police station was lined with wooden benches that had been polished to a high sheen over three decades by the arses of the guilty and the innocent alike.

PC Emily Aguda liked to guess which was which, as they came through the glass front door on a conveyor belt of crime and punishment.

It was her privilege and her burden to man the front desk on an almost permanent basis. At a time when the Metropolitan Police was making efforts to counter claims of racism and sexism, Emily Aguda ticked two boxes for the price of one and so was thrust under the noses of the local populace whenever possible, as a shining example of a black woman police officer. *Look!* The Met crowed over her like a toddler with a frog. *Look what we caught!*

And then they kept it in a box until it died.

Emily Aguda had been on the front desk for nearly two years now and it was really pissing her off. She had graduated from Reading with a first in law. She could have done anything! At twenty-six she could have been a detective sergeant by now. But instead she'd been put behind a glass window like a ticket seller or a zoo exhibit, and the loudly unspoken understanding was that her job was to be nice to people and smile — what with her being black and a woman and a symbol and all.

Despite that, Emily took her job seriously. She was firm with drunks, cynical with liars, helpful to the vulnerable, efficient with casualties, accommodating to lawyers and sympathetic to victims.

But she wasn't sure how to categorize the young woman who had just walked through the door.

White, skinny, drowning in a huge blue anorak that hid her face and reached almost to her knees, and pushing a baby in a cheap buggy.

The only description that came easily to Emily's mind was *crazy*.

Even when she reached the window, the skinny woman didn't meet her eyes: she looked beyond Emily to the rest of the small front office, where officers wandered about holding papers or paper cups.

Looking for someone else.

Someone better.

Although Emily was used to it, it never failed to sting. But she smiled because she was a symbol and being a symbol was her job. For now, at least.

"How can I help, ma'am?"

The woman focused on her for the first time and said, "Hi."

"Hi," said Emily, thawing a little at the greeting; the woman didn't seem impolite, only distracted.

"I'm looking for a Detective Marvel."

"Sure," said Emily. "Do you have an appointment?"

"No. I just need to see him."

"OK," said Emily. She had worked out that saying words like *sure* and *OK* reassured people that you were on their side, even if you were actually nowhere *near* their side. "Can I take your name, please?"

The woman hesitated and Emily thought for the first time that she might be trouble. She didn't *look* like a troublemaker, but Emily couldn't help her instincts; they were generally great.

"Why do you need my name?"

"So I can let DCI Marvel know who wants to see him."

The woman chewed on her lip.

Emily gave her time. She was good at switching off and thinking about other things. Like now, she thought about what she'd do after work. She'd go to the pool and do fifty laps. Then she'd stop for a pizza at the place on the high street. Goats' cheese and jalapeño peppers. Then she'd go home to her flat and feed Piggy, her cat, and wait for Marion to come home from her job in the City. Maybe finish the bottle of red they'd opened on Saturday night. Cuddle up on the sofa and watch *Friends*.

"Anna Buck," said Anna Buck.

There you go. Emily wrote her name down in the log. "And what's it about, Mrs Buck?"

"A dog."

"DCI Marvel's a homicide detective, ma'am. He doesn't deal with dogs."

"He's dealing with this one."

"O-kay," said Emily slowly. "I'll see if he's available. Would you like to take a seat?"

The woman glanced over her shoulder at the benches that lined the foyer. There was a motley population already there. By Emily's taxonomy, four victims, three liars, and a casualty holding a blood-spotted tissue to the side of his head. The casualty was also one of the liars, which made a total of seven people. Her system was a little confusing, but Emily understood it. Anna Buck would be the only crazy on the benches so far today.

"OK," Anna said doubtfully.

Now that the woman had become compliant, Emily softened and leaned forward to peer down at the baby. She didn't necessarily want one of her own, but she liked babies and this one was very sweet, with long pale-gold eyelashes and a tiny little bubble on his rosebud lips.

"Gorgeous," said Emily.

The woman nodded. "Thank you," she said, but she seemed too distracted to be flattered. She pushed the buggy to the far end of one of the benches and sat down.

Emily called G Team. DS Brady picked up, and flirted with her briefly. Emily flirted back. She kept her girlfriend a closely guarded secret at work. Not because she was ashamed, but because if the powers that be found out she was a lesbian as well as a black woman, she'd be the Holy Grail of Equal Opportunities and she'd *never* get off the bloody reception desk. So if flirting with Colin Brady helped her cause, she was happy to do it.

He put her through to DCI Marvel.

Not Emily's favourite person. She'd never actually *heard* him say anything racist or sexist, but he always looked as if he might be *about* to.

She told him that there was an Anna Buck in reception about a dog, and he told her he'd said all he needed to say to the woman.

"So what would you like me to tell her, sir?"

"Just that," said Marvel, and hung up.

Rude git.

Emily tapped on the glass to get the skinny woman's attention. She came over to the window.

"DCI Marvel is busy on a case at the moment, Mrs Buck."

The woman stared at Emily for a moment with a frown splitting her brow. "So is he coming down?"

"No."

"But I need to see him."

"He can't come down at the moment," said Emily. She always had to suppress her natural inclination to preface any such statement with the words "I'm sorry but . . ." Drunks, fools, and almost all men seemed to think it implied that *she* was somehow to blame. Life was much simpler when she was a bit ruder, even if it didn't come naturally to her.

"I have to see him," Anna Buck said firmly. "I might have important information for him."

"About a dog?"

"Yes, but . . ." She looked uncertain for a moment, then visibly stiffened her resolve. "Yes."

"He told me he'd said all he needed to on the case."

Anna nodded slowly. Then said, "I'm not leaving till I see him."

If Emily had had a penny for every time somebody told her that, she'd be sunning herself on a beach somewhere right this moment. People who said it usually stomped back to the benches and crossed their arms angrily, then waited for her to go off shift, or leave the window to fetch a form, before taking the opportunity to slink away without her seeing them go.

But Anna Buck didn't go and sit down and cross her arms. Anna Buck pulled a photograph from the pocket of her big blue anorak and pressed it against the glass to show Emily.

"Do you see this photo?"

Emily looked at the photo of a tubby blonde and a small poodle against a grassy backdrop.

"Yes."

"There's something in this photo. There's something in this photo that's getting inside my head and telling me things. Showing me things."

Crazy! I knew she was crazy!

"I know it sounds crazy," said the woman, making Emily blink with exposure. "I *know* that. But I lost my son and this woman lost her dog and all I want to do is to help her find it again, do you understand? Because of my son. He went missing in November and if I can help *her*, then maybe somebody somewhere will help *me*. Find Daniel. Do you understand what I'm saying?"

132

Emily nodded. She couldn't help herself, because the tears starting to gather on the woman's lower lids and lashes spoke the truth about her son.

"So please can you tell him that? Please can you let him know that I'm only here to try to help? I'm not asking for money or anything. I only want to help her get her dog back, because of Daniel."

Emily hesitated. "I'm just not sure you have the right officer —"

"I do!" said Mrs Buck. "He left a message on my phone. About the dog. Her name is Mitzi. You ask him. Please just *ask him!*"

Emily hesitated. The woman *seemed* crazy, but there was something about her story that *wasn't*. She wondered what it was and realized it was the name of the dog.

Mitzi.

Who the hell had a delusion so intricate and so ridiculous that they named a dog Mitzi? That just didn't seem likely to Emily Aguda, and if it didn't seem likely to her, then it was probably not true.

She stared up one last time at the photograph of the woman and the dog, and then decided. "Hold on just a moment, Mrs Buck."

She picked up the phone and dialled G Team again. She flirted with Colin Brady again; she got Marvel on the line again.

"Sir, I'm sorry to trouble you again, but Mrs Buck seems very insistent that she can help you find . . ." here Emily lowered her voice so as not to embarrass DCI Marvel". . . a lost dog?"

In the face of Marvel's silence, Emily lowered her voice even further. "Called Mitzi?"

"Oh, for *Christ's sake!*" Marvel shouted in her ear.

Emily tightened her lips and her backbone. "Sir, the lady's becoming quite —" She had been going to say "agitated". But as she spoke, Emily glanced through the window at Mrs Buck and her eyes widened in alarm. "Sir," she said firmly, "I think you should come down here *right now*."

Then *she* hung up on *him*.

It's all circles.

The voice spoke quite clearly and Anna flinched and turned to see who was behind her at the window.

There was nobody. She looked back at the desk officer on the phone and could no longer hear her speaking, although she could see her mouth moving, very, very slowly.

She looked at the photo in her hand. Sandra's dark roots, the contented little dog, the blue rope and the blurred spectators.

It's all circles.

The voice was in her head. It wasn't her voice, or even her thought. For some reason, that didn't bother her.

She tried to tap the window to ask the officer whether she could hear it too. But she never raised her arm, never made a fist, never knocked on the glass, never opened her mouth — because it was full of circles, and so was her head.

Circles and circles and circles.

134

The young woman behind the counter was staring at her now, and hanging up the phone, and Anna tried to reassure her that it was all circles and everything was OK, because everything was endless and it would all begin again.

The officer's eyes widened as, very slowly and deliberately, Anna backed a couple of steps away from the window and drew a big, slow loop in the air, using her whole arm to do it. A little part of her felt foolish, but she *had* to do it, because everything *was* circles and that was *important*.

She turned slightly and drew another full round and felt better again.

So she turned and drew another one, this time facing the benches and the buggy and the baby.

Circles and circles and wonderful circles.

With each circle she drew in the air, Anna felt better.

Everything *was* better because of circles. How had she not seen this before? How had she missed it? It was right there in front of her eyes! The very act of making the circles was liberating; she wished everybody could share it, and she smiled to encourage the other people on the benches, but she couldn't speak to them because she was in a joyous bubble of turning and circles and turning and circles.

She finally stopped, facing the little window again — breathless and euphoric. And for a moment she and the young woman stared at each other in perfect understanding of the universe and their place within it, which was *everywhere* —

Then Anna doubled over in sudden agony and dropped to her knees.

"Water," she croaked. "Water!"

Emily Aguda leaped up from her chair and shouted for help and barrelled through the security door as fast as she could to help the crazy woman.

But by the time she reached her side, Anna Buck was dying.

CHAPTER
NINETEEN

Anna Buck was dying.

She was curled on her side like an old corpse in a lifeboat, eyes sinking, lips cracking, a yellow pallor spreading across her skin.

"Water," she whispered.

"Get her some water!" Emily yelled it straight at the liar with the cut on his head. The man looked blank, so she pointed at the door marked *Gentlemen*. "In there! Quick!"

He bounced off his bench in startled obedience and hurried through the door.

"All of you!" she shouted at the rest. "Help him!" and the whole lot of them — guilty and innocent alike — leaped to their feet like soldiers and trooped into the loo after the first man.

Two more officers banged through the security doors and knelt beside Anna with a defibrillator and a first-aid kit.

"What happened?" said one.

"I don't know. She was in a kind of trance, and then she fell over and started asking for water. She looks terrible. She didn't look this terrible before. Thirty seconds ago she looked OK! This is mad!"

Anna Buck stared past her at the ceiling, but her lips were moving and Emily bent close so she could hear her.

"Eighty-eight," she whispered.

Emily looked up but there was nothing there. "Eighty-eight what?" she said.

"Water," the woman croaked, and closed her eyes.

"What the bloody hell is going on here?"

Marvel was already in a bad mood because of Mitzi Clyde, and had come all the way downstairs to give a public bollocking to that bitch on the front desk.

Aguda.

How dare she hang up on him? How *dare* she? And who else had she told about Mitzi? Was she down there now, laughing about it? Sharing it with the bloody peanut gallery? The cheeky little cow. Well, now she was going to get what was coming to her; he'd report her to the super for insubordination and put a nice dent in her future.

He'd run down the stairs, too angry to stand still in the lift, and by the time he'd hit the ground floor he had worked up a real head of steam. It was ages since he'd been this angry with anyone, and he was looking forward to venting his rage on a target that couldn't hit back.

But all hell had broken loose in the foyer.

Two officers were kneeling next to a thin woman who was sitting awkwardly on the linoleum floor in a widening pool of water. There was a defibrillator unit off to one side, not being used, and a steady line of

138

people hurrying to and from the toilets with little paper cups. Not police officers, but civilians — four men in jeans and hoodies, a woman with tattoo sleeves and a ring in her nose, an elderly man in a homburg hat, even a local burglar called Dickie Dixon, who had a cut on his head.

Aguda was directing operations — whipping the line into speedier action like the drummer on a slave ship. As each person handed their cup to her, she passed it to the woman on the floor, who gulped it so fast it splashed over her shoulders and down her T-shirt, then held out her hand for the next, while the first cup was returned to the water porter, who hurried back to the toilets for a refill, slipping and sliding on the spillage, but never daring to stop while the drummer urged them on.

Marvel was stunned. It was like a bizarre game show that everyone knew how to play but him.

"What's going on?" he demanded of Aguda.

"This is the lady who wanted to see you, sir. She had a funny turn. She needed some water."

Marvel looked around the foyer. *Some water?* This wasn't *some water.* This was madness!

But he said nothing. He just stood back and watched in amazement as the thin woman continued to suck down water, soaking herself and those near her in her desperation.

Slowly the gulping got more measured, the spillage reduced, the line slowed and finally stopped. The line of random helpers backed up. They maintained formation though, hovering anxiously in case their services were needed again, each carefully holding a paper cup, like choirboys with candles, while Aguda controlled them with a hand, a look, a presence.

The woman on the floor handed the last half-full cup to one of the officers and said, "Thank you," and then burst into tears.

It was only then that DCI Marvel recognized her.

The girl on the bridge, looking down between her shoes at the glistening rails. Crying.

Small world, he thought irritably.

The water line broke up slowly, and its constituent parts went back to the benches, talking quietly among themselves. A couple remained standing, watching Anna Buck with concern. All had oddly bonded. "Well done, everyone," said PC Aguda quietly. "Thank you all for your help."

She had done a good job, Marvel noted grudgingly. He'd save the bollocking for another time.

The two officers helped Anna Buck to her unsteady feet, holding her elbows. She stared around her with dazed eyes, not recognizing him even though he'd once saved her life.

Marvel bent and picked up a photograph a few feet away. It was swimming in water, and he shook it at arm's length so that droplets flicked off the corners.

"Don't touch him!"

Marvel froze, but the girl wasn't talking to him. She was shouting at the big woman with the tattoos and the nose ring, who was reaching into the buggy.

"Don't touch my baby!" she yelled. She tried to shrug off the two police officers holding her arms, but

140

their instinct was to tighten their grip, and they held her fast.

Aguda spoke soothingly. "It's OK. She's not going to hurt him, Mrs Buck, calm down."

Mrs Buck didn't calm down. She started to thrash against the two men holding her, shouting and trying to break free. The woman with the tattoos looked frightened; the child was in her arms, but she didn't know what to do next.

"It's OK! Look, it's OK!" Aguda quickly crossed to the big woman and carefully took the baby from her so that the mother could see him. "Look! Mrs Buck, look! He's fine. I'll bring him to —"

She stopped halfway between the buggy and the hysterical mother, staring down at the baby in her arms.

"Don't hurt him! Give him to me! I have to keep him safe!" The woman lunged and writhed, but Emily Aguda didn't move. Instead she looked straight across the room at Marvel.

"Sir?" she said, and the hackles on the back of his neck went up like a dog's.

Then she dropped the baby.

Anna Buck shrieked and Marvel moved so fast to catch the falling child that he skidded across the wet floor and fell to one knee with a furious crunch.

"Shit!" he yelled at Aguda. "What are you *doing?*"

The blue blanket slid to the wet floor but the baby was suspended in mid-air, dangling by one arm from Aguda's hand.

Anna Buck thrashed and shouted and Marvel thought, *This'll cost us a fortune in damages.*

Aguda looked down at Marvel, wide-eyed. Then she made a fist.

Marvel held up his hands to stop her. "No! No!"

But too late.

She rapped her knuckles on the baby's head and Anna Buck screamed.

The baby didn't flinch.

The baby didn't cry.

The baby didn't even wake up.

"It's not real," said Aguda.

"*What?*"

"It's not real, sir."

Marvel realized he was down on one knee in front of Aguda as if he was going to propose, and got wincingly to his feet. He hadn't moved that fast since he was sixteen. He'd pulled a groin muscle and his knee was a ball of pain.

"What the hell?" he said.

Aguda held the baby out to him and he took it from her gingerly.

It was remarkable.

Even through his anger and pain, and Anna Buck's hysteria, Marvel was amazed. Every eyelash, every vein, every fingernail. The weight of it; the way the head lolled. It was all absolutely perfect. There was even a little bubble of saliva on the wet lips. He touched it with a finger, and it was solid, like glass.

"But . . . but the heart's beating," he said; he could feel it under the heel of his hand.

Aguda leaned in curiously and opened the top buttons of the little blue romper suit.

"Don't hurt him!" cried Anna Buck. "Don't hurt him!"

They both ignored her.

Stitched to the cotton body of the baby there was a soft, heart-shaped pad, with two wires running from it, that beat a baby rhythm.

"Jesus Christ," said Marvel in awe. "That's the creepiest thing I've seen in my whole fucking life."

All around him, the thieves and the victims and the liars got slowly off their benches and moved closer to wonder at the fake baby, like fake wise men and shepherds.

Marvel let them. They'd earned the right and it could do no harm.

Mrs Buck had screamed herself out and was sobbing quietly between the two officers now.

"Let her go," he told them. "She's nuts."

They did, and she rushed across the room and reclaimed the wondrous, hideous doll, picking up the wet blanket and wrapping it up, then placing it carefully back in the buggy, weeping all the time.

They all stood and watched her, stunned by the depth of her madness.

The burglar held the door open for her and she left, still crying.

When the glass door closed behind her, there was a subdued silence. Then, very slowly, things started to return to normal. Aguda began to soak up the water from the floor with paper towels; the two officers picked up the defibrillator and went back to work; the sergeant who'd taken over behind the window called out a name and the old man in the hat shuffled over to him to report whatever he'd come in to report a hundred years ago.

Marvel bent to pick up the photo he'd dropped in his skid across the floor.

"Is this hers?" he asked Aguda, and she looked at it and nodded sadly.

"She said it was telling her things," she said. "Poor woman."

He snorted. "Telling her how to pull a scam. The fake baby was probably a part of it."

Sandra Clyde's roots were showing in this photo, and he wondered idly whether Debbie dyed her hair. He wouldn't hold it against her — not after the mind-blowing thank-you sex they'd had when she'd come home to find the dog.

Then Marvel's heart pitched like a rollercoaster ride. It got stuck in his throat and swelled there like a sponge.

"Get her back," he choked.

"Are you OK, sir?"

He shook his head. It felt like a heart attack but that wasn't important. He hobbled to the benches and sat down heavily next to the woman with the tattooed arms, still staring at the photo.

"Get her back! *Get her back!*"

Aguda dropped a ball of wet paper towels and yanked open the door. Through the glass he could see her running, hear her calling.

Marvel looked again at the photograph.

Not at Sandra; not at Mitzi. But beyond them to the line of blurred people caught in mid-clap.

So far, so faint, so fuzzy.

So familiar.

One of them was Edie Evans.

CHAPTER
TWENTY

For a long while after she was abducted, Edie Evans hoped it was by aliens.

She woke from a deep sleep — still wearing her space helmet — and stared up at a dark ceiling with gleaming pipes and flared ports running along it.

She recognized it immediately; it was the ventilation system of a spaceship.

A little flower of mist blossomed and died on her visor every time she breathed out and breathed in. The close sound of her lungs filling and emptying only added to her certainty.

She was in space!

Edie was excited by it. The mist on her visor bloomed a little bigger at the thought.

She started to turn her head to look at the walls, but it hurt to do that and she winced and stayed still for a couple of minutes, blinking at the pipes.

But now her head was hurting.

She tried to ignore it, and to think about how she might have got here.

She had been riding her bike to school . . . and then she'd woken up. And between those two moments things were fuzzy. Edie frowned and tried to remember if there had been a bright white beam, or any sense of floating. But because she couldn't remember either, they both remained possible in her mind, like that cat in the box. Dad had told her the story about some guy who had a cat in a box that was both dead *and* alive until you opened the lid and found out which it was. So, until she remembered something different, she definitely could have been abducted by aliens.

Edie could remember earlier things though. She could remember saying goodbye to her mother as she pedalled away in the half-light of the early January morning. A brief glimpse over her shoulder, and the feeling of the bike wobbling slightly as she raised a quick hand in farewell. She could remember doing a good swerve to miss a dog poo on the pavement. She could remember stopping to zip up her anorak because it was even colder than it looked.

She could remember cutting across the corner of the wide green patch they all called the woods. There wasn't a proper path there, but local people had made one just by taking the shortest route through the grass. In the winter the path was mud; in the summer it was flat and hard. Today it had been cold and dry — the grass alongside it encrusted with dark diamonds of frost.

She could remember swinging out of the woods and on to the pavement next to the road . . .

After that she couldn't remember anything until now.

Edie tried turning her head again and this time when it hurt she thought about being at home in bed, with

Mum stroking her forehead and Dad calling the doctor.

Maybe she'd ask the aliens to take her home. She was pretty sure they would at some point; there wasn't much Edie Evans didn't know about aliens, and she knew that nobody got abducted for ever.

She was sure they'd take her home right away, if she asked.

For some reason, thinking about going home made her throat ache and she nearly cried and her visor misted right up.

It wasn't really a space helmet; it was a skateboard helmet that Dad had fixed with a tinted visor so she could be an astronaut as she rode her rocket bicycle to school every day.

One small BMX for mankind, he always said.

Without turning her head again, Edie carefully reached out her hand and felt around the floor for her bike. It wasn't there. They must have left it on Earth. She got a pang, and hoped Frankie wasn't riding it already. Much of Edie's life was devoted to keeping her bicycle out of her little brother's clutches. He never took care of anything. He'd left his own bike outside so often that his trainer wheels had rusted right through. The thought of him mistreating her bike the whole time she was in space was infuriating and, at the same time, made her miss him.

Her visor misted up again, obscuring the gleaming pipes overhead.

After a while Edie fell asleep with her arm still outstretched, her delicate fingers curled and weightless.

148

When she woke for the second time she was in a bed, but it wasn't her own. Even though it was so dark that she couldn't see a thing, Edie felt sure that was true because this bed smelled like a road.

She sat up carefully. Her head had stopped aching and she was sorry she'd cried. Cross with herself for being a baby. Being in space was the most exciting thing that had ever happened to her, or to anyone she knew, and she should make the most of it. Then when she got home she could tell people all about it, especially Dad. He'd be gutted he'd missed it.

Slowly she stuck her left hand straight out into the darkness and moved it about. There was nothing in front of her, but to her left she felt a smooth, cold wall. She kept her hand there, feeling safer for touching something solid.

"Hello!" she shouted.

Her voice sounded short and dull and like it wasn't going anywhere. She didn't like it, so she didn't shout again.

From somewhere a long way off there was the rhythmic hiss and underwater thudding of a great engine.

The spaceship was on the move.

Where were they going? Were they leaving their orbit of Earth and heading for the stars? She got a little thrill of terror.

With her left hand flat against the cold wall, Edie felt the bed with her right. It wasn't a proper bed; it was like a camping one. The canvas sides were stitched over

149

a tubular steel frame. She crawled slowly to the end and bumped her head on a wall. She felt around and found her space helmet and put it on. Then she turned and crawled even more slowly to the other end until the helmet hit another wall. Wherever she was, it was only as long as the bed.

Edie leaned as far as she could to the right without leaving the anchor of her left hand on the wall, but couldn't feel the floor or another wall.

Maybe she was in a pod hundreds of feet up a wall in a hive of other captives. She imagined the beings around her — of every intergalactic species, each one thinking it was alone in the dark.

It was exciting when you thought about it.

"Hello?" she said carefully. "I'm Edie."

Nobody else said anything. Maybe they didn't understand English. Maybe to them English was just like an oink or a purr would be to her. She wouldn't talk back to a pig or a cat.

There was a blanket folded at one end of the bed. It wasn't a nice soft one like the one they put over Nanny's knees when they took her out in the wheelchair. It was cold and itchy.

In the black nothingness, and with one hand flat against the wall, Edie fingered the thin, rough wool.

In all this weirdness, the blanket was the only thing that made Edie really uneasy.

Since she'd been a little girl, Edie had read hundreds of books and watched dozens of films and TV shows about space. She knew that the first spacemen were fruit-flies and monkeys and a dog called Laika; she knew that Neil Armstrong was the first man to walk on the Moon, and that Buzz Aldrin was the second and that Michael Collins had stayed in the getaway car. That's what Dad always said. *They got dropped off on the Moon and he stayed in the car for a quick getaway.* She knew about Sally Ride and Helen Sharman and satellites and Hubble and the rings of Saturn. She knew that the sun was really a star and that all the other stars were so far away that it would take her years and years to get there, even if she went in a beam of light, like a speck.

Alongside all the real stuff, Edie knew all about Vulcans and Jedis and Close Encounters. She knew about their light sabres and mind melds and the metal chips they put in your head so they always knew how to find you again. And even though that stuff wasn't real, maybe one day it *would* be — or already was, on another planet.

So there wasn't much Edie Evans didn't know about aliens.

And she was pretty sure that they didn't have itchy blankets.

Edie started to worry then, started to be afraid that she had been taken by a human being, and for another reason entirely.

She knew about those things too.

But before that fear could properly dig its claws into Edie's fertile imagination, a light went on — and an alien walked into the room.

CHAPTER
TWENTY-ONE

Marvel got Anna Buck a cup of tea from the machine. This time he made sure it was tea, because that's what she had asked for.

"Thank you," she said softly when he put it on the desk in front of her.

"Do you want something to eat?" he asked.

She shook her head.

Marvel had brought Aguda into the room with them. Partly because she was a woman, which might be useful, and partly because he was grudgingly impressed by the way she'd handled things so far. Handled herself and handled other people.

Even hanging up on him made sense now, with the benefit of hindsight.

Aguda spoke carefully to Anna. "Do you want me to call someone to come and fetch the . . . baby?"

Anna hesitated, then shook her head and looked at the table top. "I don't trust James," she said. "Not with children."

Aguda shot a quizzical glance at Marvel, who sat down opposite Anna, wincing at the pain in his knee and his groin.

Like everything else on this case, he wasn't sure where to start. He wasn't even sure which case he was working on.

Did Anna Buck know that Edie Evans was in the photo of Sandra and Mitzi? Was she a dumb stooge in the opening gambit of a cruel negotiation? Or an unlikely mastermind? Each option had a million implications and permutations — all built on the bizarre quicksand of a five-by-seven snapshot carried into his world by a mad woman and her phoney baby.

Whatever the answer, Marvel needed to know what the hell was going on. And if that meant being all touchy-feely with a nutcase while he found out what she had to tell him, then he was prepared to do it.

For Edie Evans.

The photograph lay on the table between them, starting to curl at the edges now that it was drying out.

"This photo . . ." Marvel started, then looked at the picture and stopped.

Every time he saw it, it hit him again.

Edie was the third person along, behind the blue rope. Her face was turned away from the camera, and even if it hadn't been, it would have been too blurred to be identified as anything more than a girl by almost anybody else.

But Marvel *knew* it was her. He'd spent a year learning Edie Evans. A year learning her shape. The way she stood. How her hair hung, pushed behind that one sticky-out ear. He knew her like a parent, with his *gut*. And when he'd studied the photo more closely, the strange, abstract, angular *thing* glimpsed between the hazy legs of the people had suddenly become Edie's bicycle — lying in the grass behind her.

It had almost brought tears to his eyes to see it there.

He thought he had exhausted the evidence in the Edie Evans case. He'd been over it so often he knew it by heart. It had become meaningless with repetition.

But this was *new*.

Out of nowhere — a tiny spark that might illuminate everything.

And it had come in a photo of Sandra Clyde and her lost poodle, Mitzi.

John Marvel didn't believe in coincidence any more than he believed in global warming, and the convergence of the two cases made him deeply suspicious.

But it also made him feel like the very start of being drunk: foolish and disorientated.

"Tell me about this photo."

"It's of this woman, Sandra, and her dog."

"Do you recognize anyone else in the picture?"

She frowned. "There isn't anyone else in the picture."

"Do you know where it was taken?"

"No."

"Or when?"

"No."

"And where did you get it?"

"From Sandra. A few weeks ago. At the church."

"Did you speak to anybody about it?"

"No."

"Nobody from the church?"

"About the photo? No."

Aguda interrupted. "May I see it, sir?"

Marvel nodded and she slid the photo across the table and bent closely over it.

He turned his attention back to Anna Buck. "You called Sandra earlier today. Why?"

She shrugged. "I told you already. On the phone. It sounds stupid now."

"Tell me again."

There was a long, reluctant silence before Anna said haltingly, "I saw . . . things. Because of the photo. I think I did, anyway. I wanted to see if they meant anything to her, in case it would help her to find her dog, because my son —"

She stopped and swallowed, then went on, "My son, Daniel, he's missing too."

"Daniel Buck."

She nodded.

Marvel knew of the case. He and DCI Lloyd over in Serious Crime had compared notes briefly a few months before, but the two cases hadn't had anything in common apart from vague geography. One boy, one girl; one toddler, one twelve-year-old; one who'd run out of a door left open, the other the victim of what looked like a planned abduction and possible foul play. A few miles wasn't all that separated the cases.

Anna nodded and went on, "I suppose I thought — I *hoped* — that helping her . . . I mean, if I helped her, maybe . . . somehow, someone would help me find Daniel too. Do you see?"

She looked at him with such hope and sincerity that Marvel found himself nodding in ridiculous agreement. "What goes around comes around," he said.

"Exactly!" She smiled, and when she did, Anna Buck's face lit up, as if from within. "Exactly that. What goes around. Like karma, you know? I wasn't trying to interfere or . . . or . . . *obstruct* anyone. I was only trying to help find the dog, in case someone could help me . . ."

She tailed off into silence and wiped her nose on the back of her hand.

Marvel sighed. "The dog's back home," he said without pleasure. "It was returned this morning."

Marvel had been driving to work when Sandra Clyde called to say Mitzi was home.

"I just opened the door and there she was! And she *jumped* into my arms and gave me a million kisses and then went running, running, running round the house and the garden and her bowl and her little green monkey! So happy, weren't you, baby girl? Who's mummy's Mitzi Mitzi Moo-moo? Hmmm? Who's mummy's —"

"Who found her?" Marvel interrupted.

"A boy!" said Sandra. "A dear, sweet little boy! He had her on a lead made from his school tie! It was like something out of *Just William!* I just opened the door and he said, *Is this your dog?* and I said, *Yes, it is! I've been looking everywhere for her!* and I kissed him and I kissed Mitzi. I think he was quite embarrassed, poor child!"

156

"How did he know where you lived?"

"He said he just knocked on doors and someone recognized Mitzi from one of the photos I'd given out. I put them through hundreds of doors, you know."

Marvel knew that. He also knew it meant the dog wasn't home because of anything *he'd* done. That was bad news. How could Superintendent Clyde be very grateful to *him* now that some random brat had returned the bloody dog because of the efforts of his *wife?*

If that was what had happened.

Marvel's natural suspicion stirred in his belly. How could he find out? He needed to regain his lost leverage. His mind darted about, feeling for a chink.

"Don't pay the reward yet, Mrs Clyde."

There was a stuttering break in her stream of doggy consciousness and Marvel knew before she even said so that the reward money had already been paid. A thousand pounds. The idiot.

". . . He didn't want to take it, of course," Sandra Clyde was babbling. "He was such a sweet boy. I had to make him, and then you should have seen his little face —"

"Cheque or cash?" he interrupted bluntly.

"Cheque."

"So you have his name?"

"Well, no. I mean he's just a little boy, you see, so he doesn't have a bank account and so I made it out to cash."

Marvel swore under his breath and did a U-turn under a No U-turns sign, to a chorus of disapproving horns.

"I'll be there in ten minutes," he told her roughly. "In the meantime, call your bank and put a stop on the cheque."

"Put a *stop* on it?"

"Yes. Stop the cheque. Right now."

He hung up on her before she could irritate him further.

The cheque would be stopped. The reward money would not be paid.

Even a guilty person would come back to find out what had happened . . .

And Marvel would be there when he did.

Anna Buck had paled.

Now she looked Marvel steadily in the eye for the first time since they'd sat down.

"What time this morning?"

"Around seven thirty."

"Oh," Anna said softly, and looked away again. "That's before . . ."

She trailed off, but her face was an open book. If there had been guilt and deception, Marvel believed he would have read it. There was neither. If anything, Anna looked embarrassed. With good reason, thought Marvel: Mitzi was safely back home before she'd had her so-called visions. Before she'd phoned Sandra Clyde. And long before she'd had a funny turn at the police station.

It all made her look pretty stupid.

"I'm happy for Sandra," she said dully, then looked at him earnestly. "I really am."

John Marvel nodded. He could see the bad in anyone, but he was having trouble with Anna Buck — and that uncertainty confused him. Mentally and physically, she looked smaller now, weaker and less *connected*. It might have been because her plan to extort money from Sandra Clyde had been thwarted. Or because her karmic leverage on the universe had disappeared the minute Mitzi had been found.

Just like his own.

His instinct was to pin her to the wall like a butterfly, pour scorn on her visions and force her to confess that she was just a scammer looking for an easy mark, foiled by a schoolboy sleuth.

But something stopped him and for a moment he was at a loss.

Then Aguda cleared her throat and made eye-contact. "Sir?" She lowered her voice and he leaned in to look at what she was pointing out in the photo — the gold lettering printed on the ribbons of the rosette.

Marvel squinted and leaned back. He kept a magnifying glass in his desk drawer for small print, but he didn't have it here.

"What does it say?" he asked testily.

"Beckenham Show, 1999."

"Beckenham?" Marvel frowned. Beckenham wasn't far from Edie's home. That made sense. "When was last year's show held?"

"I don't know, sir."

Marvel nodded and was about to let it go. It was minor; it was meaningless; it didn't matter.

But it would get Aguda out of the room, which suddenly seemed like a good idea.

"Go and find out, will you?"

"Yes, sir," she said, and left.

The door clicked shut and there was a deep silence — as if they'd both been waiting for her to go.

"I remember you," said Anna softly.

Marvel nodded a brief acknowledgement. He didn't expect a *thank you* and he didn't get one.

Without the inhibition of a witness, he tapped the picture. "Mrs Buck, can you tell me what it was that you saw when you looked at this photo?"

"What does it matter now? The dog is home."

"That's true," he acknowledged. "But indulge me. Tell me what you told Sandra. And anything else you can remember."

She looked at him warily.

"Please," he said with sincerity that sounded genuine, even to his own ears. "I want to know what you saw."

He held the photo out to her again. This time she took it, but immediately put it face-down on the table between them.

For a long moment he thought Anna Buck was going to refuse to say anything else.

But then she sat a little more upright in her chair and said softly, "I saw a garden . . ."

Marvel went cold.

His fingers pressed so hard on the Edie Evans file that the tips went white. Under his splayed hands were the interviews with the psychic, Richard Latham. Marvel didn't believe a single word the man said, but he knew every one of them off by heart. Latham's visions were random and unverifiable. A broken glass jug, a white disc with a red centre, rolling across a floor . . .

A fake garden.

Marvel's voice was tight. "What kind of garden?"

"Just a garden," said Anna. "But it wasn't . . . *right*."

"What do you mean, not right?"

"I don't know." She shrugged. "There was just something a bit wrong with it. Like it wasn't *real*."

CHAPTER
TWENTY-TWO

Edie Evans drew a garden on the wall of the tiny concrete room.

She'd said she was bored, and two days later the alien had brought her hundreds and hundreds of wax crayons, all broken stubs, in two plastic carrier bags.

She was lucky they had crayons aboard the spaceship, but all the good colours were gone. There was no bright red or orange and those were her two favourites, but she started drawing flowers on the wall beside the little camp bed whenever the light was on, which usually it was.

Sometimes the alien switched it off as he left, and on those days (or nights) Edie had to be very, very patient because the gaps between stars were huge, and you couldn't expect to see the next one soon — maybe not even in your lifetime.

But whenever the light was on, she drew flowers. Mostly blue and purple and a few yellow ones, but there weren't that many yellow crayons either, so she had to make do. She made all the middles yellow, so that the blue and purple flowers weren't so dark. There were a few maroon crayons and she used them sparingly too, and a blue that was too dark for anything

— even the sky. There were lots of whites and blacks and browns, so she made a white window frame so that it was like looking out of her bedroom across her garden to the woods beyond. She coloured the trees, enjoying the bobbly-rough sensation of the wax passing from each crayon to the cement trunks. It wasn't like using a pen; the crayons shrank in her determined fist as they escaped to the wall, layer by layer. She could watch it happening and wondered at the change from coloured stick to coloured wall. Often she would have to stop and peel back paper from the wax crayons so she could keep colouring.

After Edie finished the window and the garden, it wasn't enough, so she re-created the rest of her bedroom around the walls — all from memory. Her wallpaper, her posters, the door with Neil Armstrong on it, the old fireplace, the shelf with the clock and Pink Ted and Pengie the penguin, and her books. She wrote the title on each spine, trying to remember all of them: *Island of Adventure, Chocky, The Silver Sword, Matilda*. There were more, and so she drew blank books so she could write on the spines as she remembered. She drew Peter in his cage and hoped Frankie was feeding him and playing with him. She drew his cage much bigger than it really was, just in case, and put in extra toys. Then she made sure there was plenty of water, and lots of brown-and-black food in the little purple bowl.

It was hard to fit everything on to the walls because the room was so small — only as long as the camp bed and three times its width — but Edie did her best. Her

163

fingers quickly smelled of wax, and were tipped with little crescent rainbows under each nail.

The alien came every day. He was tall and skinny and his face was a mask above a flowing black shroud that hung to his hips. The slanted black eyes did not blink, and in the wan glow of the small fluorescent strip, the teeth glimmered sharply within the rictus of the lips.

At first she was scared of the mask. She had been scared a lot at the beginning, despite her mind's best efforts to construct a story she could live by.

Remain sane by.

But after a while she became more scared of what might be behind the mask, and hoped she never found out.

On that first day, the alien had brought a dead chicken with him, and Edie had crouched in mute terror as he'd sung a strange song and swung the chicken over her head in circles. There hadn't been any blood, but white feathers had fallen from the bird on to the bed, and after the alien had left, Edie had gathered them together and cried for the poor chicken. There were seventeen feathers ranging from the little tufty fluffy ones right up to the single long quill, like something you could write with. It had slender spines that separated with an actual tiny sound, and then knitted back together so perfectly you couldn't see the join.

Every day after that, he brought her water in a tall glass jug, and proper food. Bread and butter, old bananas, and dented pots of custard or rice pudding. A

164

mug for drinking and a plastic spoon. A bowl, and a bar of yellow soap that smelled like lemons but tasted like soap.

"What do you want?" she asked him once, early on, and when he didn't answer, she got cross and shouted, "What do you *want?*"

"Ssh," he said. "Ssh, ssh." And then he left.

Every time he went, Edie shuddered with relief — and then fretted in case he didn't come back. But he always did, with more water and a bruised apple or a box of Ritz crackers. They were soft, but she didn't care. She was in a space station where you couldn't go out, and supplies had to come from Earth once a year. Right now they were having to eat up all the stuff from the back of the cupboards, but soon the supply ship would dock and then they'd have Brazil nuts and shampoo, and Marmite sandwiches.

Edie wondered whether the other astronauts —
prisoners
— were humans too. Maybe if they were beings from all over the galaxy, like on *Star Trek*, then the cupboards were full of all kinds of foods from all kinds of planets. She wondered if there was an alien whose job it was to feed the right thing to the right species — just like she gave Peter mouse food, not dog food — or if they all had to eat Ritz crackers.

When she wasn't drawing on the walls, she liked to wear her space helmet and imagine that she was piloting the ship and that the other astronauts were right next door and she only had to call out or knock on the wall and they would call or knock back. She

165

didn't do it, of course, in case they were busy with scientific experiments, or in hypersleep. And because that first shouted *Hello!* had scared her so badly that she didn't want to put another to the test.

Getting nothing back would be confirmation that she was really alone.

Once, the alien reached out slowly and touched her hair. Edie pressed herself into the corner at the far end of the bed.

She started to cry; she couldn't help it.

"Please don't," she whispered. "Please don't touch me."

The alien withdrew.

For now.

CHAPTER
TWENTY-THREE

"Take a tray," said DS Brady, handing him one.

"What for?"

"Cover."

Marvel dropped the tray back on to the pile with a clatter.

Brady held on to his, and put an iced bun on it defiantly.

They were a dozen people behind Richard Latham in the queue at the Marks & Spencer café. They'd gone to his little terraced house and knocked on his front door until his neighbour had come out and told them where he'd probably gone.

"He goes there all the time," she'd added.

"Yeah?" Brady had said. "Why?"

"The company, I think."

Now Marvel looked around at the coldly corporate café and wondered how that could be true. The low ceiling, pale floor and dark chairs made the place feel cold and unwelcoming. There was a long line of mostly elderly people shuffling slowly towards the till, sliding their trays along a system of rails so they didn't have to carry them and walk at the same time. Inappropriate pop muzak encouraged them to pick up the pace a bit, but they weren't having any of it.

The King's Arms it wasn't.

"Anything to eat, my love?"

A middle-aged woman smiled cheerfully at Marvel. She wore the round-collared tunic of a performing monkey, complete with a matching hat that was not unlike a fez. Before Marvel could even hesitate, she took the glass covers off two huge cakes and held them up like cymbals. "Lovely bit of carrot cake?" she said. "Ever so moist."

"OK then," he heard himself saying without thinking, and she laughed as if he'd made her the happiest woman in Bromley, and chose the biggest slice there was for him.

"Put it on your tray," Marvel ordered Brady.

Latham was already at the till. His tray had a teacake on it.

Marvel watched the be-fezzed woman behind the till beam at him. Over the music, he heard her say, "Morning, Richard!"

Marvel couldn't hear the response, but there was a friendly exchange. The woman giggled and chatted while Latham handed over his money and got his loyalty card stamped. Marvel watched him shuffle along a bit and pick up a cup and a pot of tea, then stand there for a moment, looking around — apparently for his company.

Was it friends?

A woman?

The accomplice who knocked on the church ceiling?

Latham walked across the café and Marvel saw for the first time that there was something wrong with his feet, or legs. He had a strange, lilting walk, a slow bounce to his gait. He kept his elbows high to avoid spillage, and people turned their heads absently to watch him pass, even as they talked and ate, alert to the abnormal.

He put his tray down on a table for two, alone.

The queue edged forward.

"Lucas! Hold on to the *handle* or you won't get any *cake!*"

Marvel turned to see a woman behind him with a pushchair. A boy of about three was beside her. Lucas.

The boy sidled back over and fixed his chubby fist around the metal bar of the pushchair, and when his mother set off to catch up with the queue, his arm jerked and he had to jog a few paces to keep from falling.

Marvel stared at the child. When *he* was that age, his mother had kept him on reins. Like a pet pony. Years after they had grown out of them, Marvel and his brother had taken turns using them around the house — riding each other from room to room, flapping the reins to go faster and pulling them back and going *whoa!* to stop, then pawing the air with their hands to show they were rearing up. Reins were much safer — much more fun — than having to hold on to the handle.

"Can I help you?" Lucas's mother was looking at him in a challenging way.

"No," said Marvel. "I was just wondering, whatever happened to reins for children?"

The woman narrowed her eyes at him and tutted, then put a hand around Lucas's wrist in a belt-and-braces gesture that almost made Marvel laugh. Parents saw danger in all the wrong places. Children were stupid and easily distracted, and predators were alert to the slightest opportunity. There wasn't much anyone could do about that fatal combination; it was the luck of the draw.

He picked up the file marked *Evans, Edith 23778/SE-G* off Colin Brady's tray and — under the suspicious eye of Lucas's mother — peeled out of the queue and walked over to the table where Richard Latham was shaking a sachet of sugar.

"Mr Latham? DCI John Marvel."

Latham squinted up with big brown eyes, and Marvel sat down. He never bothered to ask if he could, because nobody ever said yes.

"Can I help you?" said Latham.

"Yes," said Marvel, and laid down the photo Anna Buck had brought in. "What can you tell me about this?"

Latham blinked so hard it was close to flinching. "I don't . . ." he started. "I . . . What do you mean, what can I tell you?"

He was rattled. Marvel liked that.

Colin Brady put his tray on the photo. There were two slices of carrot cake on it, a cup of coffee and a glass of water. Brady was on a diet and had decided that drinking water before eating anything — however calorific — was the way to do it.

"I got you an Americano, sir."

"Take the tray off the bloody photo, will you!"

Brady raised the tray so that Marvel could slip the photo out from underneath. But, annoyingly, it had given Latham a chance to regain his composure. Now he was looking away from Marvel and up at Brady instead.

"Hello, Sergeant."

"Mr Latham."

"This photo," insisted Marvel. "Nothing mystical. Just, what can you tell me?"

"Nothing mystical, eh?" Latham tipped the sugar into his tea. His movements were deliberate, and Marvel knew he was playing for time.

He took a bite of teacake, then leaned forward and peered at the photo. "Well now, let's see."

He stared at the photo for so long that Marvel could almost hear his brain formulating an adequate answer.

Finally Latham said, "Yes. I believe this lady comes to our church."

"You know her name?"

"Errrr . . . Sandra."

"And?"

"And I can't tell you much, I'm afraid. She lost her dog and thought I might be able to help her find it."

"And did you?"

"I still hope I can. I believe the dog is alive, so that's a good thing, isn't it?"

"Depends," said Marvel, "on how much you like dogs."

"I suppose so," said Latham. "I'm a cat person myself. How about you?"

Marvel said, "Did Sandra give you a photo too?"

"As I recall she gave out a lot of photos of the dog. I probably had one."

"This one?"

"I really can't remember." Latham looked around the room as if for an exit, and pushed his glasses up his nose.

Sweating.

"Do you recognize anyone else in this photo?"

Latham studied it again. "No," he said.

"OK," said Marvel. He slid the photo away from Richard Latham, and saw the relief in his eyes as it went. He loved it when a suspect thought the hard part was over.

"Mr Latham, how do you know Anna Buck?"

"Who's Anna Buck?"

"Young woman," said Marvel. "Came to your church a few weeks back for the first time."

Latham looked blank.

"Had a baby in a buggy. Never cried."

"Oh, yes," said Latham. "I remember."

"So that's how you know her then."

"Well, I didn't know her name."

"Did you talk to her?"

"No."

"She says you spoke."

"I don't think so."

"She says —"

"Bit of cake, Richard?"

They all looked up at a woman in a fez. She was clearing tables and held a damp rag in one hand and a teapot in the other.

"No thanks, Denise. The teacake will be fine for now."

"You sure now, darlin'? Don't want you wasting away!" Denise laughed and looked at Marvel and Brady and said, "Richard used to be much larger, you know, but now he's only a medium!"

She cackled and patted Latham's shoulder with the damp rag before bustling away, leaving an awkward silence in her wake.

"She says she spoke to you about her son," Marvel started again.

"Oh yes," said Latham. "She did."

"Then why tell me she didn't?"

"You weren't specific. She didn't speak to me the first time, but a week later she came back. She wanted a private consultation."

"In return for a donation to the church-roof fund, I presume?"

Latham's composure wavered again. Only a flicker, but it was there — and Marvel noted it.

"No," said Latham. "I couldn't help her."

"Why not? Isn't it your job to help her?"

Latham sighed and shook his head. "That's not how it works, Mr Marvel. Spirits choose what to show, and whom they show it to. I can only be open to them — a conduit for communication. But I'm not the one in control."

"If you're not in control, who is?"

"The dead," said Latham. He gave a grim smile. "The dead are in control."

"Great," said Marvel. "Maybe I'll take this up with them."

"Maybe you should."

Marvel resisted the temptation to continue the childish exchange. Latham had started out shakily when he'd seen the photo, but was getting more comfortable now, and Marvel needed him off balance again, where he might trip over his own ego, if not his own lies. "You know what else Anna Buck saw in this photo, Mr Latham?"

"No."

"Edie Evans."

Latham frowned. "Where?"

Marvel put a finger above the blurred image and Latham bent down until he was just inches from the picture. "How can you tell?"

"I can tell," said Marvel. "Trust me."

"Really?" said Latham. "I wouldn't have recognized her."

"What did you tell Mrs Buck about Edie?"

"Nothing."

"You didn't discuss the case at all?"

"No. Why would I?"

"Interesting," said Marvel. "Because when Anna Buck looked at this photo she had a vision."

"Did she?" said Latham. "Well. Good for her."

"Of a garden."

Blink.

"Just like you did."

Blink.

"And do you know what she said about the garden?" Marvel waited for Latham to respond, but when he didn't, he flipped open his notebook and read from the interview with Anna Buck. "She said, *There was just something a bit wrong with it. Like it wasn't real.*"

He closed the notebook. "Sounds familiar, doesn't it?"

Richard Latham looked down at the spoon stirring his tea. *Click, click, click.* "A garden is a common spiritual motif, Mr Marvel."

"You remember what you said when you were shown Edie's picture a year ago?"

"Not really."

"I do," said Marvel. He didn't bother opening the file. "You said, *She's looking at a garden through a window, but there's something strange about it. As if it's not real.*"

He looked steadily at Latham, who raised his eyebrows and shrugged and said, "Well."

"That's some coincidence," said Marvel.

"If you believe in coincidence," said Latham.

"I don't," said Marvel,

"Nor me."

"Well then, Mr Latham, it can't be a coincidence that Anna Buck comes to your church. It can't be a coincidence that she has a private consultation with you about her missing son, when you were involved in the hunt for another missing child. And it can't be a coincidence that a few weeks later she has the same so-called vision as you claim to have had a year earlier."

"I grant you, that *is* strange," said Latham.

"I don't think it's strange at all," said Marvel. "I think it's a logical progression with one important step left out. You told her about the Edie Evans case."

"Why would I do that?"

"Simple. You tell her, she tells us, we tell the family. And, somewhere along the line, somebody pays you for more of your useless information."

"Except I didn't tell her."

Marvel gave a grim smile. "This is all in a day's work to you, Latham. You squeeze suckers over lost dogs and dead relatives every week at your so-called church. But missing kids pay better than dogs, don't they? You know *that*, if anybody does."

"I don't know what you're talking about, Mr Marvel. I'm not in this for the money."

"Yeah, but it never hurts, does it?" sneered Marvel. "Puts a few slates on the church roof, right?"

Latham shrugged. "It's a big roof. And a small church. All donations are gratefully received."

Marvel lowered his voice menacingly. "You took two grand off us in donations and gave us *nothing*."

Latham looked at him with amphibian eyes. "I did all anyone could for Edie Evans."

"Maybe," said Marvel. "Maybe not. Or maybe Anna Buck is just better at this than you are. I mean, if you *didn't* tell her about Edie Evans . . . if she really *did* see something in this photo that even you can't . . . Maybe

176

she's the real shut eye, Latham. Maybe you just weren't up to the job."

Latham's lips tightened and Marvel knew he'd scored a direct hit on the man's fat ego.

"You forget something, Mr Marvel," said Latham. "It wasn't my job to find Edie Evans — it was yours. *Your* job. And you couldn't do it."

Marvel's fist twitched. "*Excuse* me?"

Latham shrugged and went on. "I'm not *blaming* you. I'm sure you did your best, but I suppose you can't win 'em all."

"You can't win 'em all?" said Marvel angrily. "That's your answer?"

Latham shrugged, picked up his napkin and carefully wiped his buttery fingers. "Either way," he sighed, "it makes no difference in the end."

Marvel wanted to smash his face in. "It made a big difference to Edie Evans!" he shouted. People were looking at them now; Marvel didn't care. "Your stupid fantasies about white wheels and broken glass. Wasting our time. Wasting *her* time."

"You're wrong about wasting time," said Latham, who had somehow regained an infuriating air of calm. "To people like you, life's a long line that starts *here* and ends *there*. But existence is a continuum of life and death, a grand circle, and a circle never ends. Life and death are one and the same, and time is irrelevant."

Marvel snorted and Latham smiled. "You snort at Einstein, Mr Marvel. Did you know that his theory of general relativity postulates that the past and the future may exist simultaneously? So is it so unscientific to think that some of us can see that nexus, right here and now? And I *do* see it. Not *all* of it, and, believe me, I don't always *want* to see it. But —"

He leaned across the table and stared intently at Marvel through his thick lenses. "*Your* future," he whispered, "is *my* memory."

Marvel felt an illogical chill. For one gut-wrenching moment he was on a precipice, with his own destiny gaping blackly before him and the past at his back, pressing him gently but firmly towards the edge. Somewhere in his soul he could hear the overhang crumbling under his frightened feet; pieces of stone clicking away like unlucky dice —

"Can you remember next week's Lottery numbers?" said Brady.

They both ignored him, but it broke the spell, and Marvel leaned across the table so that his nose almost touched Latham's.

"Mumbo. Fucking. Jumbo. You can't see Edie Evans and you never could. You see nothing but money. I see *your* future, Latham, and it's in handcuffs."

Latham dabbed carefully at his mouth with the napkin. "Is that some kind of threat, Mr Marvel?"

"You bet your arse it is," said Marvel. "And DS Brady is my witness."

Latham screwed up the napkin and dropped it into his teacup, where it browned and swelled. "Then next time you're feeling guilty about Edie Evans, Mr Marvel, don't come crying to me."

178

"Fuck off!" said Marvel. He stood up furiously. Brady looked up at him in surprise, then he stood too, with a forkful of carrot cake in his hand.

Marvel jabbed an angry finger across the table, making Latham flinch. "I'll find out what happened to Edie without your so-called help." He turned, then remembered: "And you can stop tapping Sandra Clyde for cash, too, because her dog was returned to her this morning, no thanks to *you*!"

Latham gave Marvel a sanctimonious smile. "Isn't the important thing that she has her dog back?"

"To her, maybe. Not to me."

"I'm sure she'll be unsurprised to hear it."

"And *I'm* sure you'll be giving her a refund on her donations to the church bloody roof."

Latham raised his brows mysteriously. "Who knows?" he said. "Maybe, in the future, I already have."

"You piece of —"

"Are these gentlemen bothering you, Richard?" Two middle-aged ladies were suddenly at the table. One was thin, the other was dumpy, but both had faux fezzes over their wispy grey hair, little round glasses, and the redoubtable self-confidence bestowed upon them by an M&S uniform and a reserve army of beige back-ups.

"Yes," said Latham. "Actually they are."

"Time to go, I think, sir," said the dumpy one, holding out her arms to usher Marvel out.

"I'm a police officer," he protested.

"Well then, sir, you should know better."

If she'd been a man Marvel could have hit her, but what could he do with an old woman who barely reached his armpit?

Nothing but obey.

"Come on, Brady," he said.

They'd only taken a couple of paces away from the table when Latham called out, "Sergeant Brady?"

They stopped and turned around. Latham was looking at Colin Brady with an earnest expression on his face.

"There'll be complications when your wife gives birth. You'll be worried the baby's going to die, but it won't; it will be just fine."

Brady gave a hollow laugh. "I've had the snip, mate. Shows how much *you* know!"

"Oh," said Latham. He frowned — and then gave the smallest of smiles. "In that case, maybe you could give my message to your milkman."

Brady swore and started towards him, but the dumpy woman said, "Now, now, sticks and stones and all that," and — somehow — herded them both out of the café and into Menswear.

"Bastard," said Brady.

"*Fucking* bastard," said Marvel.

They strode past the fey white mannequins with their gilets and their man-bags, and out to the car park.

Marvel fumed, "Did you see his face when he saw that photo?"

"Yeah," said Brady.

"White as a sheet. Then he tries to say he doesn't recognize her."

"Yeah," said Brady.

"Bloody fake. Preying on the weak and vulnerable."

"Funny about that garden thing, though."

"Not if Latham told Mrs Buck about it."

"Yeah," said Brady. "But if he didn't."

Marvel gave a dismissive snort and stormed through the car park while Brady hurried to keep up. But the question did nag at him. What if Latham *hadn't* told Anna Buck about the garden? Where did that leave them?

Nowhere he felt comfortable being . . .

"Maybe he hypnotized her or some crap," he thought out loud. "He was on TV. You know what those pricks are like."

"Yeah," said Brady thoughtfully. "You think he meant that about the milkman?"

"Course not," said Marvel. "He's just winding you up."

The pink bumper sticker made Marvel's car easy to spot. "Bloody thing," he said, and slapped the Edie Evans file against Brady's chest. He squatted behind the BMW and picked at one corner of the sticker. "He's a fake, no question," he went on. "But he's hiding something else."

"What?" said Brady.

"I don't know," said Marvel. "But I'm going to find out."

He yanked off the sticker with a single Elastoplastic rip.

The paint came off with it.

When Marvel got back to the station, Emily Aguda deepened his bad mood by telling him that last year's Beckenham dog show had been held on 14 September.

"Impossible," said Marvel. "Edie was abducted on January twelfth."

"I checked with Mrs Clyde —"

Marvel waved that away dismissively. "Mrs Clyde doesn't know whether she's Arthur or bloody Martha."

"Mmm." Aguda pursed her lips diplomatically and read from her notebook. "So then I spoke to the show secretary. There was a show in April last year and another in September, but the April one was indoors."

"I don't care if it was indoors or outdoors," said Marvel. "She couldn't have been at either. It must have been held earlier than that."

Aguda looked puzzled.

"Check again," he told her. "Get it right."

CHAPTER
TWENTY-FOUR

When Anna got home, James was in the nursery with Daniel's red dungarees in his hand.

"What are you doing?" she said.

"Nothing," he said. "Putting these away. Where have you been?"

Anna took the dungarees from him and went to the chest of drawers. "They were already away."

"No they weren't; they were on the bed."

He was lying. She never left them out. Before she laid them in the bottom drawer with the rest of his clothes, Anna pressed them to her face — to her nose. They still smelled faintly of Daniel. That was why she never washed them. The only thing in the flat she hadn't washed and scrubbed and washed again. She'd have to wash the baby's clothes now, after what that woman did to him, and the blanket that had fallen on the floor. And his bedding; and *their* bedding and everything —

"Where have you been?"

"The police station."

"What for?"

"I thought I could help someone who'd lost their dog."

"A lost dog? How?"

Anna hesitated, but she was not a liar; she'd never seen the point, when the truth was so much simpler to remember.

"I had a vision," she said. "I looked at a photograph of the dog and I had a vision."

"Since when do you have visions?"

She said nothing. She opened another drawer and smoothed the clothes in it — just for something to do. They'd all have to be washed, but not today. She would have to do everything in the correct order. Efficiently, so that one thing did not contaminate the next.

"Is this about that bloody church?"

When she didn't answer him, James said, "A vision of what?"

"Of a garden. And of circles and ... and ... eighty-eight." She shrugged.

"Eighty-eight what?"

"I don't know."

James sighed. "You know all this makes you sound mental, right?"

"I know. I just thought they might be something to do with the dog."

"Of course. Why wouldn't they?" Sarcasm didn't become him. James never used to be sarcastic with her. Before.

"Nobody believes shit like that," he went on.

"The police took it seriously," she said without inflection.

"Were they wearing white coats?"

184

She knew he was trying to be mean, but she ignored it. "They asked me all about it and to draw pictures of all the things I saw. They had me there for two hours."

"Yeah?" said James. That obviously surprised him and he lost that knowing expression.

"It was nothing to do with the dog though. The dog had already been found."

James laughed — relieved to be back on solid ground.

"They thought it might have something to do with a girl who went missing."

"What girl?"

"Her name's Edie Evans. She was in the photo."

"What photo?"

"Of the dog."

"Where is it then?"

"The police kept it." Anna opened another drawer — this one full of bits and bobs. The tie James had worn to his mother's funeral, spare batteries, a small sheaf of Daniel's drawings that had been transferred from the playschool to the fridge and then were too precious to make their logical way to the bin. Wax crayon on butcher paper; random three-legged animals and wonky houses with curly smoke.

"Why are we even together?" Anna said suddenly.

James looked at her in surprise, but Anna felt calm inside — as if she were on a slow summer ocean. She couldn't believe that just a few hours earlier she had been curling up to die on a police station floor . . .

"I mean, we only got married because I was pregnant with Daniel."

"*What?*" He looked at her in disbelief. "You know that's not true."

Anna avoided his eyes. "And now he's gone —"

She stopped. She had said that without crying. She said it again.

"Now he's gone . . ."

The second time was a charm, and she felt the lump growing in her throat that meant that soon she wouldn't be able to speak at all. She stared into the drawer filled with her son's baby clothes and whispered, "You can go too. If you want."

James went.

On his way out he slammed the door, and opened the floodgates.

James only got as far as the King's Arms, where he drank until he ran out of money. Then he drank until he ran out of goodwill, and then he got into a scuffle with someone who wouldn't buy him another pint.

Then he got thrown out.

In revenge he pissed into the drooping pansies planted in barrels along the front wall. They were already fighting a losing battle against the waterlogging and the traffic and the cigarette stubs, so it was a mercy killing really.

He headed for home. Anna had told him to leave, but he was going back. She might claim to have married him because of Daniel, but that wasn't the only reason *he'd* married *her*.

186

So he was going home. Or, at least, to the place where he paid the rent — and if she told him to leave again, he'd ignore her again.

He'd drunk so much that he couldn't make it home before he also needed to relieve himself again, so he stumbled down the alleyway next to the mini-mart and pissed with his forearm against the wall and his face cradled in the crook. Hot and cold in shivery waves, dimly feeling the rain seeping under his collar and the splatter on his trainers.

He thought of the red dungarees, and the way they smelled of Daniel, and his eyes overflowed too.

"James?"

"What?"

"OK?"

"Piss off," he snuffled into his elbow.

There was silence bar the sound of rain gurgling down the supermarket gutters.

"You want to eat?"

James turned his head to see Ang standing a few feet away, his thick black hair plastered close to his small head.

"What?"

"You want to eat?" repeated Ang, and gestured that James should follow him behind the building.

James pushed off the wall gently, but still too hard, and stumbled backwards as he zipped up. Then he followed Ang round the back of the supermarket.

He had disappeared.

"Hello," said Ang. He was in a skip, holding a sandwich in a cardboard wrapper.

"What are you doing?" said James.

"Eating."

James peered over the lip of the skip and Ang switched on a torch. James noticed it was the one Brian Pigeon kept in the office. Ang directed the beam at the rubbish. Cardboard, plastic, a couple of black bags, and scattered food in broken packaging. Ang had collected a little pile of booty at his feet: bread rolls in plastic wrap, fish fingers and yoghurt; two boxes of eggs, only half crushed.

James wiped his face on his arm and said, "No. Going home."

Ang nodded doubtfully. "OK," he said. "Me too."

He put his food in a plastic bag and clambered out of the skip and they walked together, James stumbling and Ang hovering around him like a worried bee, touching him now and then to keep him steady and headed in the right direction.

Halfway home, James threw up.

"Shit," said Ang.

James swayed and wiped his mouth and wondered how much the puddle of vomit had cost him. Whatever it was, they couldn't afford it. Maybe Anna would start working again, now she'd started going outside. Maybe going to the church hadn't been such a terrible thing, if it had reminded her that going out was what *normal* people did. Not going out to polish your dead child's footprints, but going out to the shops and the post office and a job, and coming home to a husband who wanted you back.

Outside the garage, the footprints were filled with rain, and dancing with more.

James stared down at them, and then squatted awkwardly. He put out an unsteady hand to touch the nearest of them, and only Ang's quick grip on his shoulder stopped him from falling on his face.

He didn't try again.

"So sorry, James," said Ang tenderly.

"Me too," said James.

The five footprints didn't remind him of Daniel; they reminded him only of doing something so wrong that he could never make it right. Anna would never forgive him. He couldn't blame her.

When James got in the lights were out, so he didn't turn them on. Anna was a restless sleeper. The kitchen floor was wet and the washing machine was on. Anna had obviously begun a major sweep of the house. He knew that the next few weeks would be chaotic as she took the clean flat apart and put it back together even cleaner.

It was mad, but it could be worse. Better a clean flat than a filthy one. And things would improve with time. James lived in the hope that they would, that they *must*.

Although he was drunk, James knew he wouldn't be welcome in their bed tonight — even hanging off his own edge of the mattress. So, with a sigh, he opened the door to Daniel's bedroom and switched on the light.

"*Jesus!*" he breathed, and sobered like ice.

It was all covered with paint. Blue paint. James recognized the can on the chest of drawers as one of several that had been in the cupboard under the stairs for a few years. He'd used it to paint Daniel's toy chest, which had been pink when they'd got it from the charity shop.

Anna had painted four huge circles on the walls, each the radius of her own arm, wonky and sloppy, with drips all over the floor and furniture. Three circles filled one wall, and the fourth ran on to the next. She had moved the chest of drawers to accommodate the last one, and there were blue handprints all over that too.

It made him realize that she hadn't even used a brush. He looked at the circles and saw the unmistakeable trails of fingers and palms. His wife had interrupted her obsessive cleaning operation to vandalize her own home.

Unless someone else had done this.

It suddenly seemed more likely — more horribly possible — that some crazed smack-head had broken into the flat while he was out getting pissed, assaulted his wife, vandalized the room, taken what little they had —

Had he left the door open?

James rushed into their bedroom and banged on the light with a frightened fist.

Anna woke with a start. "What?" she said. "What's wrong?"

She shielded her eyes with a single blue hand.

CHAPTER
TWENTY-FIVE

"My wife tells me you told her to stop the cheque for the reward money."

Superintendent Clyde had sneaked up on Marvel like a bad smell.

"That's right, sir. A thousand pounds is a lot of money. I thought you'd like to make sure this boy deserves it."

"He brought the dog back," said Clyde flatly. "He deserves the money."

Marvel was rendered almost speechless by the naivety of the man. What was it that plaque on the super's desk said? Something about the Lord taking over when the law was broken. Marvel suddenly wondered just how appropriate it was for a senior police officer — or *any* police officer — to have that motto on his desk. As if day-to-day police operations had been contracted out to the Almighty like catering or cleaning. It smacked of the same sort of abdication of responsibility as *no questions asked* — as if Clyde's heart really wasn't in this crime-fighting lark.

He spoke carefully. "What if he pinched the dog in the first place, sir? People will do a lot for a thousand quid."

"You should have a bit more faith in human nature, John."

Marvel almost laughed in his face. *What an idiot!*

Out loud he took a more conciliatory tone. "Sir, I just want to make sure you and Mrs Clyde aren't being ripped off, that's all."

"Thank you for your concern, but *I'm* sure and I think that should be enough, don't you?"

Marvel didn't reply, but the super seemed to assume the affirmative.

"You'll be reassigned to another case shortly, and I'll deal with the matter from now on, thank you."

Marvel remained mutinously mute.

"Understood?" said Clyde.

Marvel understood. Clyde wanted the Mitzi business over and he didn't want anything happening that might prolong it — even if that meant ignoring an infringement of the law.

Marvel understood that. And he wanted the super to *know* that he understood.

So he looked steadily up at Clyde and said, "No questions asked, sir?"

"That's right," snapped Clyde. "No questions asked."

"No questions asked?" said Debbie. "But that's what *everybody* puts on posters."

"Well, everybody's *wrong.*"

The dog, now named Buster, lay between them, its round pink belly stretched by food. Buster was allowed

192

to have all four feet on the Habitat couch, while Marvel still wasn't allowed even one.

"People aren't wrong just because they don't agree with you, John."

Marvel pursed his lips and glared at the TV. It was about koala bears so he knew he wouldn't be allowed to change channels. Debbie was crazy for koalas. They were her second-favourite TV animal behind meerkats. She'd sit for hours with her knees tucked to one side, a glass of rosé in her hand, watching the anthropomorphism of anything small and furry.

She was watching them now, and stroking Buster's belly, while she was talking. "And now you've fallen out with your boss," she said, "over something so silly."

"It's not *silly*. Jesus Christ! It's obstruction of *justice*. By a senior police officer!"

Debbie sipped her wine. "But it's a very *small* obstruction."

"Oh, for God's sake!"

Marvel picked up the remote and started changing channels. "It's not the *size* of the obstruction that matters. What matters is that there has *been* an obstruction at all. And that he *knew* that and allowed it to remain there! A copper's job is to solve crimes, and to solve crimes you have to ask questions. If you don't ask questions, criminals get away with crimes. *Now* do you understand?"

Debbie made a face and emptied her glass. "You're just grumpy because we had hummus for tea."

"No, I'm grumpy because you're so *fucking stupid*."

There was a horrible silence and Marvel felt guilt crawling up his neck and behind his ears. But he couldn't say sorry because he was *right*. She must be stupid not to see that.

Debbie said nothing. She watched the flickering television while her fingers moved gently back and forth over the coarse fur on the dog's chest.

Marvel ran through the channels again, but there wasn't even anything on that was better than the koalas. Infuriatingly, he'd finally made a stand over the control of the television in the only five minutes of the decade when nobody was showing *Top Gear*.

Debbie watched in cool silence until he finally switched the TV off completely and tossed the remote across the coffee table with a clatter.

Buster twitched, and farted in surprise, and gave Marvel the excuse he needed to get up and go to bed without apologizing.

CHAPTER
TWENTY-SIX

Evans, Edith.

For the millionth time, Marvel flicked through the tatty brown folder.

At the back of the file was a Polaroid of Anna Buck, the transcript of her interview, and an A5 envelope containing the drawings she had done.

She looked tired and washed out in the photo, but she was the only person Marvel had ever seen who looked better in a Polaroid than she did in the flesh. She was holding a plastic cup of water; the rim was just visible at the bottom of the frame. He had taken the picture himself, before Aguda brought in the tea. On a sudden whim, Marvel pinned the photo to the wall under the Mitzi bumper sticker he'd peeled off his car.

Then he found a photo online of Richard Latham — a screen-grab from a news bulletin — and printed that and pinned it beside the others.

The four pictures sat in uneasy proximity. Edie, Mitzi, Anna Buck and Richard Latham. He felt there was a link — some force of attraction between them — but he certainly couldn't see what it might be.

Marvel didn't believe in coincidence, but he did believe in a good hunch, and he felt better for having put all the photos on the wall together.

He tipped Anna's drawings out of the envelope. There were two small sketches — more doodles than drawings. The first was a window frame, with flowers beyond it and a weird perspective that showed no sky. Anna had drawn one of the flowers inside the bottom edge of the window — as if on the sill. All around the frame she had scribbled blackness. The second scrap of paper — torn from Marvel's own notebook — was a confusing sketch. He turned it around a few times to try to make sense of it. Eventually he held it vertically. A wide stand, a kinked shaft and a thick U-shaped bit at the top. It was the kind of thing Debbie would buy from Habitat and stick two candles in. On the widest part of the U was the number 88.

What's this? he'd said to her.

I don't know, she'd replied.

Marvel didn't know either. But he pinned the drawings to the wall as well.

The Anna Buck intervention in the Edie Evans case was just another shroud over a concealed truth. He almost resented that it had happened at all, but now that it had, it had to be treated as part of the whole, or he wouldn't be doing his job.

And his job — finding Edie Evans — had only become harder because of it.

He picked up the phone on his desk, called DCI Lloyd and asked him whether Anna Buck was nuts.

"She's lost her son," said Lloyd, after a small pause — as if that was an answer.

"But is she nuts?" insisted Marvel. "She came in here yesterday with a fake baby, claiming a photo was talking to her."

"Well," said Lloyd cautiously, "I'd say she's greatly disturbed."

"Nuts, you mean?"

"I'm not a doctor," said Lloyd.

Or much of a policeman, thought Marvel. Then he asked Lloyd to send over a photo of Daniel Buck, and hung up.

Somebody behind him said, "Sir?"

Emily Aguda had missed DCI Marvel at first because he was sitting in the far corner with his back to the murder-squad room, and with his feet on the desk. She only noticed him then because she spotted the Polaroid of Anna Buck on the wall over his desk. After that she recognized a photo of Edie Evans. There was also a picture of a middle-aged man in glasses, and a bright-pink bumper sticker pinned underneath them with the motto FIND MITZI!

So it *was* a real name!

"Sir?" she said politely.

"What?" said Marvel without turning round.

"I got that photo back from the lab."

Marvel used his feet to swivel his chair around enough to see who was talking to him. When he saw Emily, he scowled. "I didn't know you'd *sent* it to the lab."

"You told me to check it again, sir, and I wanted to get it right. They say the date on the rosette is correct and they can't see any evidence of tampering or manipulation, only a bit of damage caused by the water. So I called the show secretary and asked if they'd had any errors on the dates on their rosettes and she said no."

Marvel stared at her suspiciously for a moment, then said, "How did you get the photo back so fast? Usually it's like putting a message in a bloody bottle."

"I know Dean Frazzelli. He owed me a favour."

"What *kind* of favour?"

Emily had lent Dean Frazzelli her car to go on a blind date. It was a nice car — a neat little MR2 in candy-apple red. Apparently it had made quite an impression, because when he'd returned it, he'd told her he owed her one. And when she'd called and asked for his help analysing a photograph, he'd been happy to put it at the top of the pile.

"You still seeing that girl?" Emily had asked him.

"I am seeing a lot of her," Frazzelli had answered, with feeling.

"A. Whole. *Lot*." Then he'd offered to buy her car, and she'd said she would think about it.

"Just a favour," she shrugged. Marvel didn't need to know the fluff.

Marvel grunted. "Doesn't make sense."

"Sir?"

"It doesn't make any bloody *sense*." He slapped the desk, making her jump. "Even if she'd been kidnapped and brainwashed, or had run away and was living a new

198

life. She's at a *dog show*. With her *bicycle*. A bicycle that's been in the basement of this bloody building since January last year!"

He glared at Aguda as if she might confess that she'd made the whole thing up just to annoy him. But she said nothing.

"Frazzelli's an idiot," he concluded. "Because that photo is impossible."

He glared forcefully at Emily, but she didn't concede the point. She thought that Dean Frazzelli wouldn't last five minutes in his job if he were an idiot. She could feel the frustration coming off Marvel in waves, and understood his reaction, but wasn't going to be cowed in the face of it.

"Also, sir, I was thinking about what Mrs Buck said about her husband?"

Marvel glared at her, then said, "Go *on*, for Christ's sake! Just because you decide to put a question mark at the end of a statement doesn't mean I have to suddenly think of an answer to a question you haven't even bloody well asked."

Emily Aguda almost giggled. She was used to being demeaned because she was black and because she was a woman, and sometimes because she was gay, but she'd never been demeaned over her choice of punctuation before, and was surprised to find it a refreshing change.

She went on, "Mrs Buck said that she didn't trust her husband around children. It struck me as a strange thing for someone to say, sir."

Marvel nodded slowly. Then he said, "With children."

"Sorry, sir?"

"She said *with* children, not *around* children."

"Yes, sir." Emily was surprised that Marvel had picked up on it too — and so closely.

Marvel fixed her with a glare. "You know she's stark staring mad, right? The hysterics and the water and the fake baby. Anyone can see. Mad or a scammer. Pound to a pinch of dog shit."

Emily looked at his face to see whether he truly believed that. It was hard to tell.

"Perhaps," she said with what she hoped was a diplomatic note to her voice.

Marvel said nothing more, but he stopped scowling, so Emily pressed on. "I just thought it was interesting, sir. Given that Mrs Buck's son and Edie Evans disappeared within a couple of miles of each other. And given that — statistically — children are at greater risk of harm from a relative than they are from a stranger . . ."

Emily stopped herself saying more. She had a tendency to over-explain things and something told her it was a trait that DCI Marvel might not appreciate.

Marvel stared at Emily, but she could tell he wasn't thinking of her, so it didn't seem weird.

"James," said Marvel at last. "James Buck."

"Yes, sir," said Emily.

"OK," he said.

She started to go and he said *thank you* so softly that she wasn't sure she'd heard it. And when she turned to say *you're welcome*, he already had his back to her and his feet on the desk.

***

Aguda had gone, Marvel lowered his feet and logged on to his computer. He typed in James Buck's name and got nothing.

Marvel never trusted the computer when it said it couldn't find something. He always suspected laziness, rather than an absence of something to be found. But apparently James Buck of 148 Northborough Road had no previous convictions.

He sat and glared at the screen for a bit, not really seeing it, while his mind tested and discarded possibilities. His instincts were on the alert, just waiting for the right possibility to put its head above the parapet so that he could pounce on it. Mental whack-a-mole.

Marvel got up and went over to the big map on the wall near the door, which showed the South East murder-team patch. With one blunt finger he traced the roadway between Bromley, where Edie Evans came from, and Bickley, where James Buck lived.

It was two miles of suburbia — houses and little rows of shops and traffic lights and schools. Now and then a small patch of green — a cricket pitch, a football field, a strip of parkland or playground.

He saw nothing obvious. No reason why Edie Evans and James Buck might ever have been in the same place at the same time.

Marvel groaned inwardly. He was going to have to call Edie Evans's parents. He hated to do it. He knew that just hearing his voice would bring the pain back for

201

them, along with the adrenaline shot of instant dread or hope that she was dead or alive.

Right now, Edie was neither, and that was the hardest thing of all.

He reached for the phone, but before he could pick it up, Colin Brady pushed off hard from his desk, so that his chair rattled across the lino towards Marvel at speed, only slowing down a few feet from him.

"What did Abooba want?" he grinned.

Marvel was in no mood. "She had an interesting insight," he said coldly.

"Yeah?" leered Brady. "I bet it's interesting *insight* her knickers."

He laughed to encourage Marvel to get the joke, but Marvel said, "At least she *had* a bloody idea."

"Really?" said Brady.

"Really," said Marvel. "And I don't want to hear that name again, right?"

"What name?"

"Abooba."

Brady's expression said he suspected a joke, but he erred on the side of "Yes, sir."

"Tell the others."

"Yes, sir."

"Now fuck off."

"Yes, sir."

Brady slunk back to his desk as quietly as he could on castors, and Marvel picked up the phone. Whisky used to give him courage to do shit like this. Nowadays he had to rely on just not thinking about the consequences.

202

He called the Evans's number from memory. Mr Evans — Mark — answered the phone. Good.

"Mr Evans?" said Marvel.

There was the smallest hesitation, then, "Chief Inspector?" And the hope and the terror were right there in an instant.

"There's no news," Marvel said at once, and Mark Evans made a noise like someone undoing a radiator cap. The sound of tension leaving his lungs.

The next natural thing to ask would have been *How are you?* but Marvel had been in this job long enough to know that that only prolonged the agony. How was *anyone* when their child had been missing for over a year and they didn't know whether she was alive or dead?

Shit was a given, he always supposed.

So Marvel went straight to: "I wanted to ask you a question."

"Of course."

"Did Edie ever go to Beckenham to a dog show? On her bike?"

"*Beckenham?* No."

"You're sure? Or maybe just to a park or somewhere there might have been a dog show taking place?"

"No," said Mark Evans. "Definitely not."

"What about Bickley?"

Evans mused. "I know *Frankie* went to playschool over that way . . ."

"You remember the name of the playschool?"

"Ummmmm . . . Tiger something. I think."

"Tigger Time?"

"I think so. Hold on, I'll ask Carrie."

A little chill ran up Marvel's spine. Edie's brother had gone to the same playschool as Daniel Buck. Edie's *brother*. How had they missed it?

"Hello, John." Carrie Evans was trying to be bright, but he could hear the tremor in her voice.

"Hello, Mrs Evans." Marvel couldn't bear to use her first name, even though she always used his, and he didn't mind that. But calling her *Carrie* would have obliged him to make much more personal investment than he wanted to.

"Frankie went to the TiggerTime playschool. Why? Is it important?"

"I don't know," Marvel told her truthfully. For some reason, he had always been completely honest with the Evans family. He supposed it was because he had worked so hard on the case — so far above and beyond what might reasonably be expected of him — that there had never been anything to hide. He couldn't even hide the fact that he wanted Edie home almost as much as they did.

"Did Edie ever go with you to pick him up?"

"Yes. If it was nice we would walk, and Edie went on her bicycle. After a while she left her bike at home and we walked together."

Walking's for OLD people.

Marvel had never heard Edie Evans's voice, but he almost laughed out loud as the words popped into his head as clearly as if she was sitting beside him. Certainly, the Edie *he* knew would have wanted to ride her bike whenever possible.

204

It piqued his curiosity.

"Why did she stop riding?" he asked. "Did something happen?"

"I don't think so," said Carrie Evans. "Certainly nothing she told me. One day she just walked with me instead and she said it was so we could talk. I thought that was lovely. Before that she'd be racing on ahead and coming back to me, then racing off again — you know what I mean?"

"She didn't have a fall or knock into someone or get shouted at? Any kind of a fright?"

"Not that I know. Why is this important, John?"

"I really don't know whether it is, Mrs Evans. I'm just trying to work that out."

"OK," she said, and Marvel could almost feel the self-control it took for her to keep calm, keep answering his questions, not scream and tear out her hair.

"Did you or she ever speak to anyone, even just to say hello, on your way to or from the playschool?"

"No. Nodded at a few regulars, but that was all."

"But one day she just stopped riding her bike?"

"That's right."

"How long was that before she went missing?"

"Hmmmm," said Mrs Evans. "Maybe a month? I'm really not sure."

It felt relevant, although Marvel couldn't have said how. He almost pressed the point about the dog show, but he didn't want to reveal the photo at this point. Not until he was sure of exactly what it *was*.

One tenuous clue at a time, he thought wryly.

"Does Frankie still go to Tigger Time?" he asked.

"Oh no," she said hastily. "He'll be going to big school next year, so I thought it would be nicer to . . . you know . . . keep him at home . . ."

She gave a weak laugh. She was fooling nobody. But Marvel didn't blame her. She'd lost one child on her way to school, after all. She wasn't taking any chances with the other.

"Do you know the address of the playschool, Mrs Evans?"

"Sure," said Carrie. "One-five-two Northborough Road."

Marvel had a pen in his hand, but he didn't write it down. Instead he thanked her and said that he would call them if he ever had any news, good or bad.

The usual.

Then he hung up and got his notebook out of his drawer for the second time in half an hour. He flicked to the Anna Buck interview.

There it was, right at the front of the interview.

The man Anna Buck was married to — but still didn't trust with children — lived four doors away from the playschool.

CHAPTER
TWENTY-SEVEN

As James cut across the forecourt to work, he saw a stocky child with pigtails squatting beside the five footprints. He stopped beside her.

"Hello," he said.

"Hi."

"What are you doing?"

She glanced up at him, but lowered her head again before answering.

"Cleaning."

"Why?" he said.

"Just helping," she said.

He watched her pick tiny twigs and petals of blossom out of Daniel's footprints. Her hands were small and pink and she had a plastic ring on one forefinger, with a fake emerald in it. She had to keep stopping to adjust her school bag, which kept slipping from where it was slung across her back. She pushed it around patiently each time and carried on with her task.

"Do you know who made those footprints?" he said.

"Daniel," said the girl. "He got lost and this is all his mummy has left."

James felt unbalanced by hearing their lives summed up in a single bald sentence from a small girl he'd never seen before.

"She still has *me*," he said.

The child stared up at him. "Who are you?"

"I'm Daniel's daddy."

The girl looked away again, and carried on picking grit from the next print.

"You left the door open," she said.

All the breath left him as if he'd been punched.

He stared down at the back of the girl's head. Her shiny dark hair was parted in the middle all the way down to her nape and there were two hairclips holding the strands in place. Two little goldfish, smiling up at him, waving their fins.

Was she even real?

Was *any* of this real?

Was this how Anna felt when she had her visions? Shocked and sick and kicked in the belly?

"Yes," James said slowly. "I left the door open."

The little girl stood up and brushed her hands together, then wiped them on her thighs for good measure. She left dusty finger marks on her black uniform trousers.

She hitched her bag up on to her shoulder and looked up at James. "You must feel *terrible*," she said solemnly.

"Yes, I do."

"You didn't *mean* to do it though, did you?"

"No," he said huskily. "It was a mistake."

The girl looked down the road, pushed a strand of hair behind one ear and took a deep breath. "Miss Henderson says everybody makes mistakes, but it's what you do *after* the mistake that's important. Like, I pushed Bethany Court over because she called me fatty four-eyes, but then I said sorry, and she said sorry too, so it was OK."

James nodded and the girl hitched her bag up again and said, "I have to go to school now. Bye."

"Bye," said James.

They headed off in opposite directions.

Before he went into the garage, James looked down the street. The girl was still there, walking away.

She *was* real.

He watched her until she turned the corner, just to be sure. Then he went inside.

Marvel parked across the road.

Number 148 was next to a garage which had been built into a gap in the houses most likely caused by a wartime bomb.

Just a few doors down the same sooty terrace was 152 — TiggerTime playschool.

It might have been a coincidence. If Marvel had believed in them.

A tall man in dirty blue overalls leaned against the garage wall, smoking a black cigarette. Marvel took a photo of him — and of a Chinese kid with a broom who was sweeping the forecourt. Even through two lanes of traffic, Marvel could hear him singing. It was tuneless and yet with curious little lilts and curlicues that made it sound deliberately so.

The door of the flat opened and a slim, dark-haired young man in overalls and work boots emerged.

He presumed it was James Buck, and took three photos.

As Buck cut across the cement forecourt he stopped and chatted to a stout, bespectacled girl, who was squatting, playing some sort of game on the ground.

Marvel took another photo.

After a minute, the girl got up and, after exchanging a few more words with her, Buck walked slowly across the forecourt. He stopped briefly and looked back down the road, then disappeared inside the garage.

Some commute.

Marvel fiddled about until he found how to review the photos on the complicated digital SLR camera he'd checked out of work. One picture was of a blurred lorry. One was of the top of Buck's head. The third was his profile. The fourth was horribly over-exposed, even though the tech moron had assured him that the bloody thing was automatic. All he could see were Buck's legs, and the girl's, under a pale-blue haze. He'd have to use the profile shot. It wasn't great, but it was better than nothing.

He waited until the boy had finished sweeping the forecourt and gone back indoors. Then he got out of the car and crossed the road. On a whim, he took the camera with him.

There was a narrow alleyway between Number 148 and its neighbour, and Marvel went down it. It was a dank passageway, green with algae from gutters that must always be blocked and dripping.

The sound of the traffic muted behind him as he went, until his own footsteps were the loudest thing in his ears. It was so long since he'd been conscious of the sound of himself that it almost creeped him out.

He emerged behind the buildings into a slightly wider alleyway, and turned left. The rear of TiggerTime was easy to spot because the brick wall at the back of the tall Victorian house had been amateurishly painted in a Disneyesque nightmare. There was a spotted rat with a broken leg that he guessed was supposed to be Bambi, and a gurning axeman who looked like Richard Nixon. Marvel assumed it was one of the Seven Dwarfs, but only because there were six similar others — each armed with a different tool.

The back gate was locked, and there was a skip outside filled with playschool junk. Black bags overflowing with disposable nappies, broken toys and great sheaves of shite art. Finger paintings and sheets covered with thick black wax crayon. Marvel scraped at the black with a fingernail and — lo! — the colours underneath were exposed.

He smiled. He couldn't help it. He was a child again — and then, just for a moment, he was overwhelmed by the sense of the past and the future colliding. Right here, in his very own hands — the hands of the child he had been and the man he continued to be, existing simultaneously.

He heard Richard Latham in his head: *Your memory is my future.*

For a split second the understanding was huge and brilliant, exploding like a supernova in his head, illuminating *everything*.

Then the wonder of it slid through his fingers like silk, and he was left thinking stupidly of Lottery numbers.

Marvel sighed and dropped the papers back into the skip. He wondered if the mothers who cheerfully left their children at TiggerTime ever came round the back to look at the arse-end where all the crap was.

A door opened at the back of the playschool and Marvel withdrew quietly. He didn't want to make contact on any terms but his own.

He walked back down the potholed tarmac. Opposite the houses a tall metal fence ran above the steep drop down the embankment to the railway line. He stopped behind Number 148. There wasn't much to see. There was no garden, just a brick-walled yard. The downstairs windows had metal grilles across them.

He didn't know what he'd expected to find. Nothing, really. But it was always worth seeing things from every possible angle.

He went back down the alleyway, where a monster drip of water caught him right on the crown. When he put a hand up to wipe it away, he found what felt like the beginning of a bald spot.

Great. He'd peaked.

He went round the front of the building and knocked on the door of the flat.

Anna Buck opened the door, already looking suspicious — as if she'd seen him snooping, although he doubted she had.

"Hello, Mrs Buck," he said brusquely. "Can you spare a minute, please?"

She frowned. He could see she didn't want to say yes, but he *had* saved her life, and British people found it so hard to say no at the best of times.

A nation hogtied by its own social graces.

So, inevitably, Anna Buck said "OK," and opened the door.

The flat was a mess. A blue mess. Someone had thrown a lot of paint around. It was on the taps and the sink mostly, but there were drips across the floor too — through the living room and to a door that Marvel assumed was a bedroom.

There was a bucket filled with blue water next to the kitchen door. Anna Buck had been cleaning up.

"What happened here?" said Marvel.

"I spilled some paint."

"I see that," he said, but she didn't volunteer any more.

"Couldn't have a cup of tea, could I, Mrs Buck?"

She hesitated. She was desperate not to encourage him, he could tell, but she was the host and she had to be hospitable.

"I'll put the kettle on," she said neutrally.

"Thank you." He sat at the kitchen table. The chair was so cheap he felt it give a little under his arse.

He waited until she had made the tea, so that she couldn't stop halfway through and ask him to leave. Once he had the tea, the rules said he must be allowed to finish it.

She put it down in front of him, along with a bag of sugar, and he noticed her hands were blue too — right into the sleeves of her cardigan.

Marvel stirred two spoons of sugar slowly into his tea.

Anna Buck didn't sit down. She stood nervously by the sink.

"I noticed the playschool a few doors down," said Marvel. "Did Daniel go there?"

"TiggerTime? Yes."

"Nice place?"

"Yes," she said. "Why?"

"Edie Evans's little brother used to go there. Frankie. Bit older than Daniel."

Anna Buck gave a small frown and then said, "I don't think he was there when Daniel was. I don't remember a Frankie."

"No?" he said, and sipped his weak tea. She hadn't left the bag in long enough. Wanted him out of there.

"Did you take him there every morning, or did your husband?"

"I did. After James went to work."

"And you'd pick him up?"

"Yes."

"Daniel like it?"

"Loved it. He grew up so much." She smiled. Then she stepped to the fridge and slid two pictures from under a magnet. "These are his. He was always drawing and colouring in. His teacher said he was good."

214

Marvel stared down at the scribbles on the paper. Might have been a house, might have been a fish. Parents were delusional; teachers *must* know it.

"Very good," he said, because he needed her to want to help him. "Childcare's pricey nowadays, isn't it?"

"And how," she said. "I went back to work to pay for it. I mean, I loved having Daniel at home, but children need to socialize, don't they?"

"Yes," said Marvel, although he'd never felt much need for it himself.

"Do you have children?" she asked.

"No."

That wasn't true, but he didn't want to answer awkward questions. Names, ages.

Whereabouts.

So he said, "Where did you work?"

"I was a secretary at a little cosmetics firm in Penge. Part time, but it was enough."

"Nice," said Marvel, although he imagined it was shit. Typing, tea-making, slapping the boss's hand off her thigh. "And your husband? Where does he work?"

"Next door. At the garage."

"Mechanic, is he?"

"Yes."

"Good money?"

"No."

"That's a shame."

She shrugged. "Who makes good money nowadays?"

"Exactly," he agreed. Then he tapped the camera and said, "He doesn't know anything about photography, does he? I'm taking this to be fixed."

She shook her head, uninterested, and stared at his cup, as if willing him to drink up and get out.

Marvel changed tack. "Must have been hard on him when you lost Daniel." It wasn't the right time to ask the question, but sometimes that could *make* it the right time.

"I didn't lose Daniel," she snapped. "*He* did."

Jackpot.

"Really?" he said, trying to sound casual. "What happened?"

"James left the door open. Daniel ran outside."

It wasn't what Marvel had been hoping for. He'd wanted to hear that James Buck had never loved his son anyway, or that he'd been a discomfortingly strict disciplinarian. Even just the impression that there was a terrible secret . . . *Something* he could hang a motive on.

He suddenly felt a little sorry for James Buck. Leaving a door open didn't seem like much of a crime.

"I'm sure he feels terrible," he said.

"He should."

Marvel was taken aback by the chill in her voice. "He didn't do it deliberately, did he?"

Anna made a face. "Does it matter?"

"It would matter to me."

"Well, not to me," she said. "I miss Daniel too much for it not to *matter* —"

She stopped talking and Marvel could see the tears fizzing close to her surface.

He changed the subject. "Could I use the bathroom?"

216

She pointed through the living room and said, "You can't miss it."

Before he'd even left the kitchen she was filling a new bucket of warm water, ready for him to be gone.

Marvel stopped short of the bathroom, glanced behind him, and opened the door to what he assumed was a bedroom instead.

"Bloody *hell!*"

Four huge blue circles were scrawled across two walls. The rest of the room was spattered with paint. The doll thing was in a carry-cot on the single bed, but even the cot was splashed with blue. For some reason that disturbed Marvel almost as much as the walls, even though he knew now that it wasn't a real baby.

"I had to do them," Anna Buck said behind him.

He started to say he'd opened the wrong door, but she didn't seem to care that he was in here and not the bathroom. She sat on the bed with her hands upturned on her lap, and spoke just above a whisper. "It made a bit of a mess, but everything is circles, so I had to really."

Richard Latham's words popped back into Marvel's head: *Life's a circle and a circle never ends.*

Had Latham put her up to this too? First the photo, now the circles. Marvel couldn't see the angle, but there had to be a connection . . .

"What did Mr Latham tell you about the garden, Mrs Buck?"

"Mr who?"

"Richard Latham. The medium. From the church."

"Oh," she said, and immediately looked puzzled. "I didn't tell him about the garden, only about Daniel."

"No, I said, what did *he* tell *you?*"

She shook her head. "He said he couldn't help me," she said sadly. "He wouldn't even look at Daniel's photo."

She had misunderstood him — and Marvel didn't think it was deliberate. Richard Latham hadn't told her about the garden. Marvel was convinced of it now. He could see no chink in the woman, apart from the obvious madness. She seemed to have no interest in Richard Latham now that he couldn't — or wouldn't — help her. She had no interest in anything but her lost child.

She stared dully into the cot and said, "Sometimes I hear him cry, you know? Sometimes I wake up and run in here and it's like I can hear —"

She stopped talking and Marvel didn't start, and in the silence that ensued, Marvel became aware of the faint sound of traffic in the street, and of music seeping from somewhere. The garage, most likely.

Anna was looking at her blue hands now, as if she was seeing them for the first time. Marvel watched her open them out and turn them over, peering at the darker lines around her nails and in the folds of her knuckles.

Suddenly John Marvel felt like an intruder. If Anna Buck was crazy, she was crazy for all her own reasons. And they were reasons that were wholly understandable, and unbearably sad.

"I should go," he said.

"OK," she said.

"Thanks for the tea."

She nodded almost imperceptibly. She showed no signs of standing up or seeing him out. She didn't even watch him go — her eyes were fixed now on the four blue circles.

"Will you be OK?" he asked, and actually listened for the answer.

She turned and gave him a small, grateful smile. "When Daniel comes home, everything will be fine."

He stood there, not knowing how to answer her. Finally he simply said, "Yes."

As he left the room, she said, "Did you find the bell?"

"Excuse me?" Marvel stopped and turned to look at her again.

"The bicycle bell," said Anna dreamily, without turning her face towards him. "In the drawing I did of the garden. It's on the window-sill."

By the time he next had a cogent thought, Marvel was outside in his car and heading back to the station.

He wasn't even sure he'd said goodbye.

Edie Evans's bicycle was exactly where Marvel had last seen it a year ago — leaning against the back wall of the evidence room, at the end of a canyon of ceiling-high metal shelving packed with a vast array of items in clear bags and wire baskets.

He peeled back the plastic sheeting that covered the BMX and felt his chest knot up.

The back wheel was still buckled, the chain still drooped. The bike's only visitors in a year had been small spiders that had woven the wheels into delicate doilies.

The chrome handlebars were still pitted with rust and dusted with print powder.

Mr Evans had told him Edie never had a bell. He'd told Marvel it was an old bike and covered in scratches.

He was not lying — about the scratches, at least.

But these scratches — these *particular* scratches — were not old. Not as old as the other ones on the bike, anyway. They were an inch or so from the right handgrip, exactly where a bell would be, and some of the scratches were long and almost parallel, as if the clamp had been twisted back and forth on the bars. Some of them had actually cut through old pimples of rust, and trailed it minutely across the surface.

There was no bell on the bike.

But there was definitely a place where a bell had been.

CHAPTER
TWENTY-EIGHT

Edie Evans picked a lamppost and pedalled towards it as fast as she possibly could. Sometimes she would launch into space if only she got there fast enough — her front wheel lifting and people's eyes popping as they realized that what they had thought was a girl on a bicycle was actually a brave and skilled astronaut on an experimental one-man rocket. Other times she was winning the Tour de France. On a BMX! The crowds called her name and people lifted her on to their shoulders — and more cheering people lifted her little black-and-white bike on to *their* shoulders — and they were both carried through the streets of Paris under fountains of champagne.

Edie skidded to a juddering halt just beyond the lamppost, spun the bike around in an arc and pulled a little wheelie. Only a small one because she'd gone over backwards once and nearly knocked herself out, and that had been on grass, not pavement.

While she waited for her mother to catch up, she flipped up her visor and gave a TV interview in fluent French, even though the only French she knew was *Frère Jacques*.

"*Dormez vous*," she said with a dismissive wave, to show it had been barely an effort at all. And when the interviewer in a beret asked her how it felt to win the greatest cycle race in the world as a twelve-year-old girl, she gave a Gallic shrug and said, "*Sonnez les matines*" — and the crowd went wild.

Edie turned a half-circle and set off again slowly, and told Houston they needed to adjust the rocket boosters before she could make another attempt to launch.

As she navigated a series of potholes shaped like moon craters, a man fell into step beside her.

"Hello," he said.

"Hello," said Edie. She knew not to speak to strangers, but she was on a bicycle and there were loads of people around.

"For you," he said and held out a bicycle bell.

"Oh," she said uncertainly.

"Stop," he said, so she did, and twisted to look behind her for her mother. She could see her coming, pushing Frankie's buggy. Frankie was too big for a buggy really, but it was a long walk home for a four-year-old and he got stroppy when he was tired.

When Edie looked back, the man was using a screwdriver to attach the bell to her bicycle.

She didn't want a bell. A rocket ship didn't *have* a bell — especially not one with a picture of Mickey Mouse on it! Why was he putting a bell on her bike anyway?

But she said nothing.

He finished quickly, then rang the bell for her to show her how it worked. It was a coarse, rattling sound.

222

"Good?" he said.

It wasn't good; it was rubbish. But Edie had been brought up to say *please* and *thank you* almost as a reflex, and so she said "Thank you" and looked around again to see if there was any sign of Mum. She hoped so, because she wanted an excuse to ride on and not to have to speak to the man any more. He was friendly and full of smiles, but something about it was not right. She shouldn't have stopped; she shouldn't have said hello. If Mum saw, she would be cross that she'd spoken to a stranger.

Edie kept staring over her right shoulder as her mother approached with the three-wheeled buggy bumping easily over kerbs and pavement cracks, as her mind raced through all the explanations she was going to give — all the excuses — if her mother looked up and saw them.

And when she turned round again, the man had gone. She didn't even see where.

Edie sighed in relief.

"Hi, Edes," Mum smiled brightly. "Chain fall off?"

"No," said Edie. "I was just waiting for you."

"Aww, thanks sweetheart."

Edie rode the last fifty yards to TiggerTime slowly and close to Mum. It wasn't very daring, but she could be Neil Armstrong again tomorrow. Or next week.

Mum went to the Moon to get Frankie and Edie stayed outside, guarding the buggy, like Michael Collins. She kept looking around but the man was nowhere to be seen.

She slowly rang the bell.

223

All kinds of little jangly mechanical things clicked and clunked inside it, as if it was broken. It was more grinding than musical.

She rang it faster and it improved, but not much.

She wiggled it on the bar and it moved, so she wrenched it back and forth to see if she could dislodge it by force. Then Mum came out with Frankie.

She didn't touch the bell again, or Mum might notice it and ask where it had come from.

But Edie thought she should take it off before Dad came home.

CHAPTER
TWENTY-NINE

Mark Evans opened the door.

"Come in."

Marvel had called first to say he had no news, but there was still an air of nervous apprehension about the man.

Marvel and Brady followed him down the passageway to the kitchen. Breakfast was still on the table, and Frankie was still playing with it.

"Hello, John," said Carrie Evans. "Would you like a cup of tea?"

"No thanks, Mrs Evans."

"I'm sorry," she said to Brady. "I've forgotten your name."

"DS Brady, ma'am. Colin."

"Colin. Of course," she said, although Marvel could tell from her expression that she had not remembered Brady's name, nor cared to now. She was just being polite.

"Hi," said Frankie, and they both said hi back to him.

Then the four of them stood in the centre of the kitchen, held there by tension. The Evanses looked less haggard than the last time Marvel had seen them, but that expression of tense not-knowing put ten years on a face overnight, and Marvel had never seen it completely reversed, not even on those rare occasions when the result was a home win.

He took three photos from a card-backed envelope and laid them face-up on the counter. "Do you recognize any of these people?"

Mr and Mrs Evans looked down at them.

"Well, we remember Richard, of course," said Mark.

"From the case?"

"And the church," said Carrie. "I went a couple of times."

"Before or after Edie disappeared?"

"After," she said.

"I didn't realize that," said Marvel, wondering why that wasn't in the file.

"Yes," said Carrie. "It was me who suggested asking him for help."

That was why. DS Short had claimed it was her idea, but then it had backfired on her. Maybe that was why she'd gone off and got herself pregnant and stung the force for leave *and* pay. Still, it was a coincidence he should have picked up on at the time. Another one. If he hadn't been so keen to distance himself from all the psychic bullshit, he might have known about it back then. Back when there was still a chance, perhaps.

"I'm not really a believer," Carrie Evans went on, "but you're desperate, you know? You want to believe in *something*." She shrugged her narrow shoulders and looked out of the kitchen window.

"Did Mr Latham ever come to the house?"

226

"No," said Mark Evans, and when Marvel looked at his wife she also turned and shook her head.

"He wasn't a friend. Just a straw to clutch at."

Marvel nodded. "And you don't know these two?"

"I don't think so," said Mark.

"Take your time," Marvel said.

They did, while the kitchen clock ticked, and Frankie dribbled milk back into his Shredded Wheat.

"They're not the best pictures in the world," said Carrie Evans.

Marvel had taken them both. The Polaroid of Anna Buck and the profile shot of her husband.

Mark and Carrie Evans both shook their heads.

Then Marvel showed them the photo DCI Lloyd had sent over. Daniel Buck in a Transformers T-shirt, riding a Trafalgar Square lion.

"This is Daniel Buck. He attended TiggerTime too, and went missing in November."

The Evanses pored over the photo for far longer than it must have taken for them to know that they didn't recognize him. Marvel understood the desperation. That need to find a connection, almost *willing* the fragments of the mystery to come together and form a picture they could understand.

He knew they had nothing to tell him, long before they said they were sorry.

Marvel picked up all the photos and put them back in the card-backed envelope.

"How are they connected to Edie?" said Carrie suspiciously.

"I'm not sure they are," said Marvel. "But we are always alert to anything that might be."

"Thank you," said Carrie. "We appreciate it." She took her husband's arm and he nodded his agreement.

Marvel glanced at the kitchen ceiling. "Would you mind if we had a quick look in Edie's room?"

"Of course," said Carrie.

"Why?" said Mark.

"Just to refresh my memory," Marvel blocked. He wasn't going to tell Mark Evans why they were there. He told himself it was a precaution. After all, Mr Evans was the one who had said there was no bell, so he wasn't going to reveal right up front that they were interested in finding one.

Just in case.

He also wasn't going to confess that he'd been sent to find a bicycle bell seen in a vision by a certifiable nutcase.

He hadn't even told Brady that they were here because of Anna Buck.

"Of course," said Mark.

"Thank you," said Marvel. "We won't be long."

Mark nodded and sighed and gestured back towards the stairs. "Well," he said, "you know where it is."

Marvel did.

The bedroom was exactly as he remembered it.

He stood at the door and looked around while he wiggled his fingers into the powdered latex gloves.

The same posters and pictures, the same books on the shelves, the same mishmash of tomboy toys, the same mouse running circles in the same wheel.

He walked across the room towards the old-fashioned sash window.

"Where shall I start, sir?" said Brady, but Marvel didn't answer him.

About six feet from the window, a strange, tingling feeling came over John Marvel.

Weird.

The human brain was hard-wired to notice the slightest anomaly, the tiniest deviation from the norm. The scar on the face, the limp in the gait, the flaw speeding by on the factory conveyor belt.

But sometimes the brain caught a glimpse of something so *weird* that it had to take a second look to make sure.

He backed up a few paces, then reached into his pocket and took out the sketch that Anna Buck had done of the garden through the window. Then very slowly he walked forward again until his hips were almost against the window-sill.

"Sir?" said Brady again, still waiting for instructions. "Where shall I start?"

Marvel ignored him and very slowly bent his knees.

Too low.

He raised himself up, pressing the wall for support, half-squatting, thinking of the super and his wife and their piston joints, until he reached the perfect height.

The height of Edie Evans.

A cold shiver ran up his back.

"Sir?"

Marvel held the sketch out in front of him; from this height, the perspective matched perfectly. The old wooden window frame, the sweep of the flower beds. Even the dark, scribbled areas, which Marvel now saw were the walls at either side of the window, and the trees beyond the garden.

It was amateurish, but it was all absolutely *right*.

"Here," he said softly. "We start here."

The thing he had thought was a flower inside the room was on the right bottom corner of the window frame that Anna Buck had sketched. Now Marvel looked down at the right corner of the window-sill. It was old and broad, and had cracked along the grain. He pressed his fingers into the wood alongside the crack and it tilted downwards, opening a dark triangle in the sill.

Marvel blocked the light as he tried to peer into the space, so he reached in blind, hoping nothing bit him. His beefy fingers barely fit through the gap, but he managed to pinch something between two fingers and to lift it out, dangling like a prize from a seaside arcade machine, and drop it into his other hand.

It was a Mickey Mouse bicycle bell.

Was it possible? He was holding it in his hand, but still Marvel wasn't sure it was *possible*.

His mind was almost completely rational when he was sober, and he had been sober for a long time now, so he struggled with the irrationality of finding the bell exactly where Anna Buck had said it would be.

230

She must have been here; it was the only explanation. She must have seen the view from Edie Evans's bedroom window, and hidden the bell for them to find. Maybe Richard Latham *had* been here and told Anna Buck about it?

Or had somebody been in Edie's bedroom for even more criminal reasons?

But who? James Buck, who wasn't to be trusted with children? Mark Evans, who had insisted that the bell did not exist?

Marvel was suddenly bombarded with suspects and possibilities, when before he'd had none. It didn't matter. Rather too many suspects than too few. And any one of those explanations would have satisfied him; any one would have been something he could work with — follow up, write in a report, put to his super.

Live with.

The only other explanation was not rational, and Marvel shied away from it, even though it was what had led him here — to this dark crack and this shining bell.

That explanation was that Anna Buck had a psychic connection to Edie Evans, or to her killer. That she possessed mystical powers and had the secrets of the universe at her fingertips.

When she wasn't trying to jump in front of a train, of course.

Or breastfeeding a fucking *doll*.

"Oh," said Brady. "You found it." He sounded disappointed, as if tearing a twelve-year-old's bedroom apart had been top of his bucket list.

"Give me an evidence bag," said Marvel.

Brady opened the bag for him and he dropped the bell into it.

"How did you know where to look, sir?"

"Just a hunch," said Marvel.

CHAPTER
THIRTY

James Buck woke with his wife screaming beside him.

"Get it off me! Get it off!"

She was thrashing crazily, slapping at her own face and head, gripping great handfuls of hair and trying to tear it out by the roots.

"Anna!" he shouted. "*Anna! Wake up!*"

She didn't. Instead she started to punch and kick him, hysterical with terror.

James rolled out of bed, turned on the light and picked his spot.

He hit her.

Just once, but just right. An open-handed slap to the face that woke her and stopped her in the same instant.

She looked at him with wide, shocked eyes.

"Thank you," she said, and burst into tears.

He got back into bed beside her, and held her while she cried. It was the first time she'd let him hold her in five months. She'd lost so much weight! Everywhere James touched her, he could feel her bones through the thin, stretched skin. He hadn't noticed; he had hardly seen her naked in all that time, but touching her now, he felt a jagged edge of fear. He'd already been worried about her mental state — what with the church and the police and the blue circles — but her physical frailty was now obvious to his hands in brutal relief.

"What happened?" he said next to her ear, but she was crying too hard to tell him.

But she did allow him to hold her, to stroke her inflamed cheek, to spoon up behind her and soothe her like a baby, with soft "shushes" while she sobbed out her fear until she knew she was *here* and not *there*, and could speak again.

When she did, she spoke so softly that James had to lean even closer, putting his ear on her neck to hear her.

"There was an alien," she said.

James didn't laugh, she was too upset.

"It had this metal . . . *thing* — like a crown with wires — and it put it on my head . . ."

She ended in a small whining sound and touched her own head, as if she could still feel it there, and James touched her hair gently, reassuringly, in those same places.

"You're safe now," he said.

"I know."

"It was only a dream."

"I know," she said again. "But it felt so real."

He squeezed her, and she let him.

They lay together while the room grew light.

Anna was quiet for so long that James thought she had fallen asleep. He was close to dozing off himself when she whispered, "They want to know what I'm thinking."

CHAPTER
THIRTY-ONE

Marvel laid all his new evidence before Superintendent Robert Clyde and submitted an official request to be put back on the Edie Evans case.

"But John," said Clyde, "this isn't evidence. This is speculation based on the supernatural rantings of a mentally disturbed woman."

"What about the bicycle bell, sir?"

"What about it?" said Clyde. "Look, I'm not being facetious, but really, *what about it?*" It's a bell. From a bicycle. Granted, you found it under unusual circumstances, but even if I believed that this woman saw it in a crystal ball and led you to a big spot marked with an X . . . what does it tell us about what happened to Edie Evans? How does it *help?*"

"Sir, the garden, the other drawings, the bicycle bell — I'm not sure we can just ignore all these things. I'm not saying Anna Buck's not bonkers; I think she's as mad as a bucket of frogs. But maybe she's being used without understanding it. Maybe she has some involvement — some *knowledge* — and this is the only way she can reveal it. Maybe she knows much more about the Edie Evans case than even *she* knows. There may be other . . . insights she could offer. Other leads that might emerge from things she says that *will* prove to be useful. Maybe even vital."

Clyde got up and shut the window. It was Friday afternoon and the demand for kebabs started early.

"You know my feelings on psychics, Marvel."

A little alarm went off in Marvel's head. *Whatever happened to "John"?*

"I do, sir," he said. "And I share them, believe me. That's why I worked so hard to get Mitzi returned to Mrs Clyde as soon as possible. To avoid embarrassment for you, sir."

Marvel hoped the super knew that he meant more than just the embarrassment of a wife and a small fluffy dog. Had the man forgotten so soon that he had paid a thousand-pound reward, *no questions asked*, to some anonymous kid? How embarrassing would that have been for Clyde if it had got out?

Very.

The super owed him. Big time. Even if it was only for not revealing the humiliating details to the entire second floor. Owed him a bloody sight more than putting him back on the Edie Evans case! That should be just for *starters*.

Apparently Clyde didn't see things the same way.

"I don't think your suspicions hold water," said Clyde. "And I certainly don't feel that re-examining the Evans case on the basis of such tenuous evidence would be worthwhile."

Marvel could feel it slipping away from him.

"Superintendent Jeffries seemed to think it was worthwhile, sir."

"Well, maybe that's why Superintendent Jeffries is gone and I'm here," said Clyde sharply. "That case has been a bloody embarrassment to the force, to be frank. From beginning to bloody end." He sighed, then went on more kindly, "The trouble with the Evans case, John, is that you want it too much."

Marvel stared at him in mute wonder.

The fucking *idiot*.

How could you want to solve a murder *too much?* It would be like being too keen on world peace; too anti-cancer.

He suddenly knew he wasn't dealing with a reasoned argument, so he stopped and reassessed the situation.

Superintendent Clyde was a prick. A lamb-scented prick with a fat wife, a gay dog and a bull's cock on his living-room wall.

But Marvel wanted back on the Edie Evans case, and he still wanted that promotion. And he needed Clyde on his side on both counts.

The Mitzi strategy had gone wrong on him but there was still leverage in the matter of the reward — whatever Robert Clyde said. When the kid who'd brought the dog home finally came back for his money, Marvel would be all over him like acne. He'd show the super that when he was given a job to do, he *finished* it and got results.

So, although it churned him up inside to do it, he backed down. "Maybe you're right, sir."

Clyde looked somewhat mollified. "Good man," he said enthusiastically. "That's the spirit."

Arsehole, thought Marvel.

Screw Superintendent Clyde. If he couldn't close the Mitzi Clyde case with his superior's support, he'd do it alone. He'd ask some questions. Get some answers.

Be a bloody detective!

He couldn't wait to see Clyde's face when he unravelled the scam — and handed him back his thousand pounds for good measure. And when he'd done that — *then* they'd be back in business on the Edie Evans case.

Psychic or no bloody psychic.

CHAPTER
THIRTY-TWO

Ang was crying in the kitchen and putting all his worldly goods into a carrier bag.

"Hi," said James.

"Hi," Ang said through his tears. He cried in long, monotonous strings of sound, not unlike his singing.

"What's wrong?" said James.

"I's fired," he wept. "To China." He rolled up his mother's story cloth and tucked it carefully between half a pack of Penguin biscuits and his Goal aftershave.

"For peanuts?" said James cautiously. Maybe Brian Pigeon had changed his mind and decided to cut Ang in on the whole *getting fired* thing.

But Ang just shook his head and carried on keening.

James went to find Brian. It wasn't hard — he was standing under a VW Beetle, shouting at someone on the phone about the old pit and the new lift.

James laid out his tools and waited for him to finish.

When he had, Brian snapped his phone shut and shouted, "What?"

"Did you fire Ang?"

"No!" he yelled. "Jesus *Christ!*"

James ignored the yelling. It was Brian's default. Once you ignored it, it usually went away. "He thinks you fired him and he's going back to China."

Brian laughed and waggled his phone. "Well, I might have said I was calling Immigration."

James pursed his lips. He caught Pavel's eye and Pavel shrugged as if it didn't matter to him one way or the other.

"He's packing his stuff," said James.

"Let him! What a little drama queen."

"He's crying."

"Good!" said Brian. "*I'm* the one who should be crying. He bumped the bloody Alfa."

James glanced across the garage at Brian's green Alfa T-Spark. "Shit," he said.

Ang's first job every morning was to move the cars out of the garage and on to the forecourt, so there was space to work. But he had to sit on a cushion to see over the dashboard, and James knew he couldn't possibly have passed his test, given that he was an illegal immigrant. And Brian knew those things too, so James's sympathy was not with him, even though this was not the first car Ang had bumped, and was unlikely to be the last.

"Expensive?" he asked.

"Nah," said Brian. "It's a scrape. But I'm not *made* of bloody money and Nicole wants to go to Prague for Christmas."

"Very beautiful," said Pavel.

Brian looked at him. "You what?"

"Prague is very beautiful," shrugged Pavel. "But everybody steal."

"Oh, fucking great. Just what I need. More foreigners with their hands in my pockets."

"If it's just a scrape," said James irritably, "why scare the shit out of him over it?"

Brian rounded on him. "Don't *you* start! This is my garage, and if you don't like the way I run it you can piss off and find another job, and another place to live too!"

James didn't answer him. He just turned and headed back towards the kitchen to explain things to Ang.

"Don't you bloody mollycoddle him!" yelled Brian. "He's a grown man!"

CHAPTER
THIRTY-THREE

Officially, Marvel was back on the Tanzi Anderson case. He'd asked to review the file to bring himself up to speed, and did just that — while he sat in Jimmy the Fix's BMW and watched Robert Clyde's house.

It was three days before the boy who'd found Mitzi came back for his money.

He was a thin white boy, with neat brown hair. He was wearing jeans, big white trainers and a Spurs shirt. Marvel was a West Ham fan, but that wasn't the only reason his suspicions were aroused. The boy looked about thirteen or fourteen — certainly young enough to be accompanied by a parent in the matter of a thousand pounds, if he really had been denied a legitimate reward.

But this boy was alone.

He went up to the door and knocked on it and Marvel slid lower in his seat, although he was across a road that was cluttered and narrowed by parked cars.

Clyde himself opened the door. Even from here Marvel could hear Mitzi yapping.

The boy and Clyde talked briefly. The boy held out a piece of paper that Marvel assumed was the stopped cheque.

They talked, Clyde smiled and nodded, then replaced the cheque with what looked like another one. *Clyde himself* handed it over. Marvel wished he had brought that camera again. It would have served Clyde right. He had promised he'd be *very grateful* and he hadn't been. Fair enough, thought Marvel, if he'd done a bad job, but he hadn't; he'd done a good job, even though it wasn't one worth doing — let alone well. Now Marvel couldn't let go of the idea that he'd somehow been cheated out of the gratitude he'd been due, and therefore cheated out of his chance of a promotion.

If he had been cheated by this kid, Marvel wanted to know about it. And if there was a chance that he might still derive some advantage from the case of Mitzi Clyde, then Marvel wanted to know about that too.

Across the street the boy left, folding the cheque and putting it in his back pocket as he trotted down the garden steps and carefully closed the gate behind him. Before he turned away, he waved, and Clyde waved back and then shut the door.

Didn't even watch the kid go. Some bloody copper.

Marvel waited until the Spurs fan got to the end of the street and turned left before he pulled the BMW out of its space and followed him.

The boy walked like all kids did nowadays — like a gangsta with an *a*, and his underpants showing. That underpants thing never failed to get Marvel riled.

The boy passed the police station and went into the kebab shop. Five minutes later he came out and continued his journey, eating a huge doner, leaning well forward so the shredded lettuce and sauce didn't drop down his nice white Spurs shirt.

Marvel hadn't had a kebab for years. The smell of the super's office always put him off, but now he could see the food, he remembered the taste of pungent fat in his cheeks, and his mouth watered.

A thousand quid bought a lot of kebabs.

A thousand quid bought a lot of everything when you were fourteen.

The boy ate quickly, and when he'd finished, he balled up the wrapper — and then held on to it until he got to a litter bin.

Surprising.

His civic pride belied his underpants.

It made Marvel doubly suspicious when people didn't behave the way they should. Or at least, the way they *looked* as if they should. He was a firm believer in stereotypes. As far as he was concerned, stereotypes were there for a reason, and trying to ignore them for the purposes of objectivity was political correctness gone mad.

He continued the slow-motion pursuit with new interest. There was something about this kid he didn't like. More than just the Spurs shirt and his arse hanging out of his jeans.

Marvel's hackles rose even further when the boy slouched through the doors of Marks & Spencer — that bastion of the middle-aged and middle-class. Marvel pulled the BMW into a bus stop and hurried across the pavement to follow the boy inside. As his instincts had told him he would, the boy got on the escalator and went up to the second floor.

Straight to the café.

Marvel stood in the queue a few places behind him. He picked up a tray, for cover, and peered around the café's clientele.

There were the same well-to-do grey-haired customers and the same women in their monkey outfits, bustling between tables with trays and teacakes and toasted sandwiches.

There was nobody else in the café under the age of fifty. Marvel frowned. Had his instincts deserted him? He had been so sure he would see Richard Latham here. He looked down the line behind him, confused.

The boy up ahead stood out like a sore thumb. He'd picked up a tray but hadn't put anything on it. Yet.

Marvel swore to himself that if the kid bought a pot of tea and sat down and drank it alone, he'd hand in his resignation from the Metropolitan Police Force.

It was a close-run thing.

The boy got all the way to the till before he ordered something.

Then he pulled out a few coins and his green loyalty card — and the cheque. If Marvel hadn't seen him tuck the cheque away at the super's house, he would never have spotted it now, folded neatly under the card.

The woman behind the till didn't miss a beat. She put the money in the till; she stamped the card; she pocketed the cheque.

The boy picked up his coffee, put it on his tray — and left them both on the table nearest the door on his way out.

Marvel was momentarily torn over whether or not to go after him, but quickly decided to stay with the money. He reached the till himself and asked for a coffee. The generic middle-aged woman with the fez was as chatty as a chimp. "Anything to eat with that, sir? Do you have a loyalty card, sir? Do you want one? Every ten coffees you get one free . . ."

When she opened the till for his change, he looked at her big bosom and read her name tag.

Denise.

No thanks, Denise. The teacake will be fine for now.

This was the woman who had come over and made a lame joke about Richard Latham. She'd patted his shoulder. They knew each other. And she had just received a thousand pounds in reward money for finding a lost dog that Latham had promised would "be home soon".

Jackpot.

When Denise handed Marvel his change, he snapped a handcuff on her wrist and told her she was under arrest for extortion — for starters.

She said "What?" then burst into loud tears while her colleagues rushed over from all corners of the café, screeching and chattering their confusion and outrage.

Marvel left M&S with Denise trailing reluctantly behind him, feeling like an extremely smug organ-grinder.

246

The moment they opened the door to Denise Granger's home, Marvel could smell the dogs.

There were four of them in a back bedroom, all pedigrees and each in a wire cage, turning circles in its own shit. Marvel thought of Denise giving him his change, and wished he could wash his hands.

"I *knew* he was hiding something," Marvel told the super — but Clyde said nothing.

One of the cages was empty.

"Must've been where she kept Mitzi," Marvel went on.

Superintendent Clyde only grunted. Marvel had never seen anybody less happy to get a thousand pounds back.

Eventually he spoke — staring at a miniature Schnauzer. "Has she confessed?"

"Like the fucking pope!" Marvel said gleefully. He handed Clyde the same flyer that had lured Anna Buck out of the house. "Nice little business. Kid steals the dogs, Granger looks after them. Then they drop church leaflets through a few doors in the area where the dogs were nicked. TV psychic, blah blah blah. Depending on what the owner does, they either sell the dog on for cash, or Latham keeps the owner on the hook for a while for donations and then they collect the reward."

No questions asked. The words hung in the air so loudly that even Marvel didn't think there was any mileage in repeating them.

Clyde stared at the dogs for a moment, then said, "I'm Catholic, Chief Inspector," and walked out of the bedroom and down the stairs.

Marvel rolled his eyes at his crappy luck and followed him downstairs to the hallway of the small terraced house.

Through the open door into the lounge he could see three lanky teenagers crammed together on the sofa — two girls and a boy. Despite their mother's arrest and the police in the house and the stolen dogs upstairs, all he saw in their eyes was the reflection of the TV screen.

Clyde spoke without looking at Marvel. "She's implicated Latham by name?"

"Yes, sir. And the kid's the grandson of a neighbour. Bloody Spurs fans." He stopped quickly in case the super was a Catholic *and* a Spurs fan, but if he was, he didn't say so.

"So," Marvel counted charges off on his fingers. "We've got theft of property, extortion, misrepresentation, obtaining pecuniary advantage by deception, conspiracy to defraud." He paused, then added, "Obstruction of justice . . ."

The super gave him a chilly stare. "I'll tell you what you've got, Marvel. Three defendants, one of them a minor, another one a mother of three who works at M and bloody S, and an old man who was once paid two thousand pounds by this very department to talk to the dead. Workload — huge; chance of convictions — maybe five per cent. Sentences — a slap on the wrist all round if we're lucky. Publicity — bloody terrible. All over a lost dog that you promised to find quickly and discreetly as a *personal fucking favour.*"

The super's voice had increased in intensity to the point where even the teenagers were staring at him now, like three wise monkeys on a sofa. The one with the remote had even hit Mute, in order to hear him better.

The super glanced round, then leaned into the room and pulled the door shut on them. "You couldn't let it go, could you?" he hissed. "Even after I *told* you."

Marvel understood the super's anger. Clyde's transgression was not big, but it was potentially very damaging. Any half-smart lawyer would point out his failure to carry out a proper investigation at any trial, to try to discredit the department, and it *was* a discredit. At Clyde's rank — at his time of life — a black mark on his record would put the brakes on any further progress he'd hoped to make.

"There's still time to stop this," said the super.

Marvel hesitated. There *was* still time, and he knew it. All he had to do was give Denise Granger a caution, scare the kid, give Latham notice to cease and desist, and return the dogs. That would keep Clyde happy, the whole thing out of court, and he'd be on easy street — cherry-picking his cases and almost certain of that promotion, whether he deserved it or not.

But he'd lose any leverage he'd ever have on Richard Latham regarding the Edie Evans case.

Marvel sighed deeply. He'd always rubbed people up the wrong way; he was a throwback whose face didn't fit the new, modern police force peopled by short men with degrees, and vegetarian lesbians. He hadn't always made the right friends, said the right things, kissed the right arses.

Now Clyde was offering him a chance to change all that, and all he had to do was . . . *nothing*.

He didn't really have a choice.

"I'm arresting him," he shrugged.

Superintendent Clyde stared at him in disbelief, then glanced at the door to the living room. "This isn't about stolen dogs and you know it! It's about your obsession with Edie Evans."

Marvel couldn't even deny it. "Latham knows more about her than he's told us."

"If he knew any more, he'd have told you when you were *paying* him to tell you."

"Not if *he* killed her."

"What do you mean?"

Marvel wasn't sure what he meant. The words had fallen out of his mouth before his brain had even engaged. But now that they were out there, they started to make sense to him. And something — *anything* — making sense right now felt like a breath of fresh air.

He looked over his shoulder at the living-room door and lowered his voice. "Look what he did with Mitzi. Kidnapped her and made money off the back of it. Not just reward money, but people coming into the church every week, paying for private consultations, making donations to that bloody roof until — lo and behold — the dog is returned, just as he said it would be. And all of it stroking his ego. Building his reputation as a psychic. Earning him money."

"So?" Clyde looked unimpressed.

"So," said Marvel, "think about Edie Evans. What if he kidnapped her, only so that he could *find* her?"

Clyde blinked in surprise and Marvel hurried on. "All of a sudden he's on TV, being a big shot. The numbers at the church go into orbit. His ego goes into orbit. All he has to do is waffle about gardens and rolling white wheels for a while and then lead us to her and he's got it made. A bigger church; a TV series; books, videos, movies, the lot. After that he's always going to be the psychic who found Edie Evans."

"So what went wrong?" said Clyde.

"I don't know! But *something*. Maybe something beyond his control. Maybe an accident. She fell, she choked . . ." Marvel took a deep breath. "Or maybe he just snapped and killed her."

Clyde was silent. The sound of *Family Fortunes* seeped through the living-room door. The coarse *Uh-oh* of a wrong answer.

Marvel said urgently, "But we'll never know if we don't have *this* to hold over his head. I need him in a room, under pressure, distracted by the immediate threat of prosecution, and with his eye off the bigger ball. Make him slip up on one thing when he's concentrating on hiding the other."

"So let me get this right," said Clyde slowly. "You'd throw me under the bus on the off-chance of getting some tiny scrap of information you don't even know would be useful — from a *psychic*."

Marvel said nothing and Clyde's lips tightened bitterly. "You know, you can arrest a hundred people for a thousand stupid little things, and it will never change the fact that *you're* the one who failed Edie Evans."

Marvel bumped the super's shoulder hard as he brushed past him on his way to the front door. As he reached for the handle, Clyde hissed, "You're opening a *whole can* of worms, Marvel."

Marvel yanked the door open and said, "I hope so."

CHAPTER
THIRTY-FOUR

"This is a bit beneath you, isn't it, Chief Inspector?"

"I'm not proud," said Marvel. "I'll talk to anyone, me."

"Not me," said Richard Latham. "I'll wait for my solicitor, if you don't mind."

Latham didn't look half as cocky without a toasted teacake in front of him, but he was still putting on a good show in Interview Three.

"Suit yourself," said Marvel, but he sat down anyway and added, "Mrs Granger didn't wait for *her* solicitor."

"I'm sorry?"

He'd heard him. But Marvel said it again anyway. "Mrs Granger didn't wait for her solicitor."

"I don't think I know a Mrs Granger."

"I'm sorry?"

"I don't —" Latham stopped and Marvel grinned at him. Latham leaned back in his chair and folded his arms.

Marvel could barely hide his self-satisfaction. Then he decided he couldn't be bothered to. "I *knew* you were hiding something, Latham. Didn't I say so, Brady?"

DS Brady nodded at the psychic. "He said you were hiding something."

"Turns out it was nothing special after all. Nothing clever. Nothing *supernatural*. Just common or garden theft." Marvel gave an exaggerated sigh. "Mrs Granger is the lady who looked after all those dogs you pretended to find, Mr Latham."

"I don't know who you're talking about," said Latham. "So I'd prefer to wait for my solicitor before getting this matter cleared up, thank you."

"Of course," said Marvel. "It shouldn't take long once we get going; Mrs Granger's given us chapter and verse."

Latham pursed his lips. He didn't answer immediately. Instead he stared at the ceiling for a bit. Then he said, "Chapter and verse. That's an interesting turn of phrase."

Marvel ignored the invitation to ask *why*. He sipped the tea he'd brought in with him and looked at his watch.

"One Corinthians," Latham went on. "Fifteen twenty-six. *The last enemy to be destroyed is death.*"

"What's your point?" said Marvel.

"Are you a religious man, Chief Inspector?"

"No."

"Aaah," sighed Latham, "you will be one day. Everybody gets there in the end."

Marvel snorted. "Are you a betting man?"

"No."

"Lucky for you," said Marvel. "I'd win."

"Even as you lost," said Latham sadly.

254

Marvel yawned. "How long did your solicitor say he'd be?"

"About an hour."

"From when?"

"About an hour ago."

"Good," said Marvel, and opened the case file.

Marvel would have felt naked walking into an interview without a case file, so he'd hastily put one together on Mitzi Clyde, although it consisted of little more than a few photos and the recovered cheque, so it was necessarily thin.

Latham laughed, but it sounded short and hollow in this small, featureless room. "I see you have *lots* of evidence against me, Mr Marvel."

Marvel liked the fact that Latham had been concerned enough to check, so he smiled back.

"Enough is all I need," he said. And it was true. Cases could stand or fall on a single hair or a solitary thumbprint. Sometimes a boxful of paperwork was only evidence of how confusing a case was — or how confused the investigating officer was.

"So," said Marvel. "Mrs Granger — Denise. Are you two . . ." Marvel left the words hanging but made a small twisty motion with two fingers.

"Don't be distasteful, Mr Marvel."

"What?" said Marvel. "I thought you didn't know her. She could look like Julia Roberts for all you claim to know."

Latham pushed his glasses up his nose and glanced at his watch.

"So it was just a business relationship?" said Marvel.

"I'm waiting for my solicitor," said Latham.

"It was just about the money," mused Marvel. "That's very you, isn't it, Richard?"

"I hope Mr Proctor gets here soon," said Latham, looking at the door. "No offence, Chief Inspector, but you're a very boring man to be stuck in a small room with."

They all stopped talking.

Marvel finished his tea.

Brady folded a page from his notebook into a paper plane and flew it into the clock.

Latham sat.

"Tell me about your church," Marvel said to his own surprise; he hadn't known he was going to ask.

Latham looked at him suspiciously.

"I'm serious," said Marvel. "While we're waiting. Might as well."

Latham shrugged. "Well," he started, "it's small —"

"With a big roof," said Marvel.

Latham looked at him like a headmaster. "Do you want to hear about it, Marvel, or do you just want to poke fun?"

Marvel locked his lips and threw away the key. Brady laughed.

Latham ignored them and went on. "We've only got about fifty members now. And only twenty or so come regularly."

"What about when you were on TV?"

"Ah. That was a different story. We had hundreds sometimes. Standing room only."

"So what went wrong?"

Latham shook his head. "You know what went wrong, Mr Marvel."

"You mean after you screwed up on Edie Evans, people realized you were a fake."

Brady laughed, but Latham's throat and ears started to go red, like some exotic lizard.

"Everybody laughs," he said. "Everybody thinks it's a big joke. It's not a joke, Chief Inspector, it's a *gift*."

"A gift you expect people to pay for."

Latham fixed Marvel with his one good eye while his other kept a lookout. "Why not? People pay for rubbish they don't even need. Milkshakes and porn mags and Botox. Why *shouldn't* people pay for my gift? It's something I've worked at, something incredible — this skill, this *magic*."

"I did pay for it, remember?" said Marvel cheerfully. "But now I want a refund."

Brady laughed again, but when Latham spoke next, there was an angry tremor in his voice. "A hundred years from now, you'll see. People like me will be paid our due. We'll be on the front page of every newspaper, received by presidents and kings. We'll live in stately homes, like idiot footballers do now. Mansions and palaces, Marvel. Mansions and palaces!" He slapped the table, making them both flinch, then jabbed his finger at their faces. "People like *you*, and *you*, will look like the Flat Earth Society, while the psychics and the seers and the shut eyes rule the world. You'll see, Marvel. In the future we'll be heroes. In the future we'll be gods!"

"Maybe," said Marvel with a dismissive shrug. "But until then you can always make a few bob nicking dogs."

"Shut up," snapped Latham.

Marvel didn't shut up. Instead he pressed his forefingers to his temples and gazed up at the strip lighting. "I can see Rover, Mrs Jones. And I predict that he will be miraculously returned to you. I also predict that will happen very soon now, when I get sick of cleaning shit off the bedroom carpet. Don't give up hope, Mrs Jones, and that'll be fifty quid for the church roof, please."

"Shut your fucking *mouth*."

Brady and Marvel stopped laughing and stared at Richard Latham.

The man was shaking with fury, his fists gripped the edges of the table so hard that his knuckles were white, and there was spittle on his lips.

"You shut your fucking *mouth*."

Suddenly Marvel felt uneasy being this close to Latham. Even here in the police station, with Colin Brady by his side. There was something off-kilter about the man that he'd never noticed before. Not just his eye, not just the marionette bounce.

Something else.

Something that made him want this to end.

"All right," he said, "all right. Let's all just calm —"

"Fuck you, Marvel! You think you're the only one who wanted to find Edie Evans? It was just another case to you. But it was my future on the line. My career. My whole reputation!"

Marvel looked at him coldly. "If your reputation depends on a lie, how much is it worth?"

"It's not a *lie!*" Latham shoved his chair back hard as he got to his feet and leaned over the table. "It never *was* a lie!"

"Sit down, Mr Latham," said Marvel coldly, and when he didn't, he and Brady got up too, exchanging wary glances. But Richard Latham didn't come at them. He leaned on the table, punching it with his knuckles and poking the air for emphasis.

"I know things!" said Latham. "I see things! I see *you* and I see *you*! I see you both! *Your* wife is pregnant. And *you're* burning up in the ice and snow, with all the questions and none of the answers!"

Marvel tutted. "Typical."

"These things are true!" shouted Latham. "These things are *real*! *These things are not a lie!* Oh my God! My *God!*"

He stopped suddenly to draw wheezing breath, leaning on his fists, red in the face; his glasses had slid so far down his nose they were held only by the fleshy tip. Then he slid slowly back into his chair.

The silence pulsed off the walls of the little room, making its own pressure, which Marvel could feel like a heartbeat under his eyes.

"If you were a shut eye you'd have told me where Edie Evans was. You'd have been able to tell me what had happened to her, at the very least. But you couldn't. And you still can't." Marvel looked at him coldly. "Because you're not psychic, Richard. You're not

259

special. You're nothing but a liar and a fraud and a common thief."

Latham started to say something, but his voice caught in his throat. He cleared it and tried again in a hoarse whisper.

"I did find her."

"No you didn't."

"Yes I did," said Latham.

The man spoke with none of his previous fire, and yet Marvel felt his balls shrink into his body in a primal response.

Latham unclenched his fists and took off his glasses and sighed. He looked and sounded exhausted. He rubbed his red face and looked up into John Marvel's eyes. "I found her the very first time I looked for her. The very first time I was shown her photograph."

"Where?" said Marvel.

Latham looked at his hands and shook his head. Marvel leaned down and shouted in his face, "*Where was she?*"

Richard Latham started to cry.

"She was already dead."

CHAPTER
THIRTY-FIVE

For the first time since she'd been taken, Edie Evans was really scared that somebody might hurt her.

She'd been woken by a strange, persistent warbling noise unlike anything she'd heard since her abduction — or before it.

She sat up in bed and stared at Neil Armstrong on the back of the door. Neil wouldn't be scared. Neil would be calm.

Edie tried to be calm, and it worked. A bit.

Then the bolt on the door squeaked and she tensed up again as the warbling noise grew louder.

The door squealed open and the alien came in, holding a wire lampshade and a plate of Mr Kipling Bakewell tarts.

Edie was confused by the lampshade. The light in the room wasn't the kind that needed a shade. It was a long strip of light right up high on the ceiling. This contraption was like a wok, with dozens of spokes fanning out from the middle and bent down sharply at the ends. There were electrical wires running from them, with multiple little knots and lumps in a complex and dangerous-looking web. "What's that?" she said warily, but he didn't answer her.

Instead he tried to put it on her head.

Edie pushed it aside and scrambled off the bed.

Her mind raced and her heart beat so fast she could feel it against her T-shirt. She knew that aliens did experiments on humans when they took them off in spaceships. They drilled into their teeth and took away their babies, and read their minds.

They read their minds.

Even as Edie had the thought, he came at her again, still making a high-pitched, wavering sound, and raising the wire helmet over her head.

"No!"

This time she knocked it out of his hands and it fell to the floor with a clatter.

The alien dropped the Bakewell tarts and they rolled across the floor like little white wheels with cherry hubs. He bent to pick up the machine, holding his arms out to protect it from her. He stopped singing and shouted furiously in his alien language.

Edie didn't care. She'd had enough. She wasn't going to let anybody read her mind. Her mind was *hers* and it was *private* and she was the only one who could say who was allowed in there, not this stranger who'd given her a bicycle bell and some soft Ritz crackers, and now seemed to think that she owed him her *thoughts*. Her head was the only place she had to hide now — the only place where she could be the old Edie the way she was before — and she didn't want to share it.

It was *her* mind.

Edie pushed him aside and stomped on the wire thing. He shoved her away, but she was frightened and furious, and those two things gave her strength and courage. She pushed back and reached around him and kicked and stamped until the mind-reading machine was a useless mass of spikes and wires, broken on the floor.

The alien knelt to retrieve it — to *save* it — and Edie ran for the door.

It opened on the room she'd been in before — with the dark ceiling and all the pipes.

"Help me!" she shrieked. "Help me!"

His arm snaked around her neck and dragged her back inside. He wasn't big, but it was scary to realize how much stronger he was than she could ever hope to be.

The door slammed shut.

He let her go, turned her round and slapped her face.

Edie stumbled backwards and sat down heavily on the bed, holding her cheek in shock, while the masked man that she could no longer pretend was an alien stood over her, shaking the wire mess in front of her, showing her what she had done.

"You break my hat!" he shouted. "You break my hat!"

CHAPTER
THIRTY-SIX

Ang Nu had left home by accident.

Four years earlier — at the age of twelve — he had followed his third brother, Suav, out of their home in the dead of night, just to see where he was going.

It was only when Suav spotted him a mile away that he'd found out his brother wasn't going back. A girl had rejected Suav's *zij* gift and everybody was laughing at his shame.

Ang couldn't pretend it wasn't true.

"Go home," Suav had told him angrily, so at first Ang had kept following him, just to be annoying.

But the first time they'd stopped to sleep, he'd discovered that Suav had taken his mother's story cloth, and the spirit mask his father had given her for *zij*.

Ang had been shocked. Taking the story cloth was bad enough, but the ancestors resided in the spirit mask, and stealing it was sacrilege.

"I'll sell them for food," Suav had boasted. "Then they'll be sorry."

They had fought in the dirt and Suav had beaten him soundly. "Go home," he'd shouted again.

But Ang knew he could never go home now. Who in Padong would believe that he wasn't a thief?

He could never face the shame.

And so Ang had kept an uneasy alliance with his brother through a journey of many months. Through forests, across rivers, in cities, working when they could, going hungry when they couldn't, as they headed for their goal of England, where Suav claimed money was easy to come by.

Over a year later they arrived in Folkestone — balanced precariously on the axle of a flatbed lorry.

They were cold and wet but that was nothing new. What was new was the excited smile on Suav's face.

The first time the lorry stopped at lights, Ang asked for something to eat. He was hungry, and Suav had the bagged rice and the chocolate.

Suav took one hand off the chassis and reached into his shirt. The lorry started with a jerk, and Suav toppled backwards and disappeared.

Ang didn't even have time to call his brother's name.

The next time the lorry stopped, Ang slid from his hiding place and dropped on to the wet tarmac of a foreign land. Praying fervently to the ancestors, he walked all the way back to the docks.

He never found Suav, or even the chocolate.

But it was not until two years later, when he was getting married, that Ang Nu felt truly alone.

He was barely fifteen but two of his brothers had been married, so he knew what to do. He had saved up the bride price. He had chosen his bride. He had given her a gift and she had accepted it. He had followed her home . . .

Then — as the Hmong tradition of *zij* dictated — he had kidnapped her.

Hmong girls understood *zij*. They understood that they would be kidnapped and stay at the groom's home while his father and brothers negotiated a bride price with her parents. After three days — if they did not come to take her home — then the wedding would proceed, with singing and dancing and so much food that Ang still dreamed about it.

Hmong girls understood *zij*.

Edie Evans apparently did not.

On a dim January morning, he had stopped Edie to tell her to get into the car, but instead of doing what he'd told her, she had pedalled away from him — as if she had forgotten all about the Mickey Mouse bell!

Ang had been confused. His bride had accepted the gift; now she must submit to the *zij*, not run away! It was embarrassing, and he'd been flustered, and he had put his foot on the throttle and gone after her.

But Mr Knight's car was big and powerful, and Ang could barely see over the dashboard. He was only used to moving cars about on the forecourt — not driving on roads and going into second gear.

He had hit her. Not hard, but hard enough to knock her off her bicycle and on to the grassy area alongside the pavement.

Ang had got out and manhandled the unconscious Edie into the passenger seat. Then he'd carried her bike to the bushes and thrown it away. The wheel was bent and it was no good to anyone. The Mickey Mouse bell had fallen off. He looked about for it because it had cost him four pounds and was a symbol of their love, the way the spirit mask had been his father's *zij* gift to his mother. But he couldn't find it, and only looked briefly before losing his nerve and driving the car back to the garage with adrenaline throbbing through his veins and panic clouding his mind.

For the first time since leaving Padong village on China's endless south-western border, Ang Nu was truly lost. For the first time he knew that he hadn't only left his home and the fields and his parents and brothers — he had left a world he understood, and which understood him.

His bride had tried to escape the *zij*. Whatever might happen next? Would she reject him when she found out that he was completely without family? When she found out that he had no father to negotiate the bride price for him? No mother to prepare the feast? No uncles to perform the ceremony of welcome in her new home?

In desperation, Ang had tried to explain *zij* to James and Mikey, who were the closest thing he had to a family now, but his English was so bad that even *he* got confused.

But although he was only a boy, Ang Nu had not survived a journey through *Dab Teb* without a man's backbone.

So he'd made another plan.

He would have to be father, brother, uncle and — when the wedding came — mother to himself.

Maybe Edie wouldn't guess until after they were married that he was all alone in the world. And after they were married, she would see that he was a hard worker and a good husband and by then it wouldn't matter.

So Ang had donned the spirit mask to perform the welcoming ceremony — fixing it atop his head and draping himself with a long black cloth, in the way of the shamen. Then he had taken the bride price to Edie's home himself. He had put all the money he had saved — one hundred pounds — in an envelope he'd found in Brian's desk. He'd posted it through the door before dawn and run away before anyone could see his shame — that he did not have a family to negotiate for him. On the envelope, he'd let Edie's family know where she was, as was required. He wrote the details of where they could find her in his most ornate Hmong script, so they could see he had been to school and was worthy of their daughter.

Now it was their turn to act.

Edie's father must come and get his daughter within three days.

If he did not, Edie was his.

This was Hmong.

While they'd both waited nervously, Ang had treated Edie with great respect. He had brought her food every day, and water in a heavy glass jug. Even crayons from the bottom of the skip behind the nursery school, with which she had started to decorate their home. That had made him happy. She was not Hmong and yet she was making something like her own story cloth already! He had chosen well. His mother and father might never see her, but he hoped the ancestors would be proud.

Edie's father never came for her.

So Ang made a marriage hat.

He used mechanic's wire from the stockroom and copper wire from old flexes on toasters and microwaves he found in skips. Wire was very Hmong, and Ang and his brothers had always made their own toys. Now he put every bit of skill he had learned into the marriage hat.

The frame was made of dozens of straight wires, twisted together at a central point and fanning out evenly like bicycle spokes in a spectacular symmetrical round. Each wire turned down sharply at the end to make a stiff metal fringe. Once he was sure that the frame was firm, he started to decorate it with the copper wire. He remembered the toys of his childhood and recreated them in miniature from the fine, beautiful red wire. Each twist, each turn, was lovingly wrought, each loop of copper was a conduit for an array of meaningful symbols and intricate charms. Some were copied from the story cloth, some remembered from his mother's own marriage hat, which had had pride of place on the only shelf in the hut they called a house. Other charms told his own story — his and Suav's — since leaving home. Little copper flying fishes; the bowl he had bought in the market — before they'd learned that a bowl just delayed food on its way to your mouth; the key to the garage, which gave Ang the freedom to come and go as he pleased, with nobody knowing or caring what he did as long as he kept the garage and forecourt spotlessly clean.

When Ang had finished the hat, he wished his father could see it. He wished his mother could. He was not a boastful boy, but the hat was the most beautiful thing he had ever held in his own two hands. Not every part of the *zij* and wedding had been or could be so Hmong, but the hat made up for all of it.

Three weeks after Edie stopped belonging to her father and became his property, Ang had washed his clothes and his hair and gone to the shop and bought brand-new cakes. They were the first food he'd paid for since coming to England, and each had white icing on top and a lucky red button in the middle.

He'd rolled up the story cloth and tucked it into his waistband; it would become Edie's after that day.

As would he.

Then Ang Nu had said a prayer to the ancestors, and had gone to claim his bride.

CHAPTER
THIRTY-SEVEN

DCI Marvel had left his body.

He watched Richard Latham's head, cradled on his arms, and felt very far away from the thinning patch on top of the shiny pink scalp.

A million miles. A billion. A light year from himself.

He was a murder detective. They'd found blood at the scene. They'd always been looking for a body and a killer.

And yet Marvel had never truly believed that Edie Evans was dead.

He only admitted this to himself here, now, as he watched Richard Latham weep into the elbows of his jumper, with his spectacles on the table beside him.

In Marvel's head Edie had always been alive, and just waiting to be found.

By him.

"You're a liar," he heard himself choke.

The coming bald patch twisted slowly from side to side in denial.

"You don't know," said Marvel. "You can't *know*."

Latham raised his head briefly and said, "I know."

Then he put his head back down on his arms and gave a sigh so deep that it ended in a shiver.

The hairs on Marvel's forearms prickled. He had seen a thousand confessions and most of them ended like this — with a cavernous sigh, as if the body was relieved to be finally rid of the burden the mind had forced it to bear.

Marvel's own mind whirred with connections and possibilities.

If he discounted the mystical, Richard Latham might have been a suspect all along. He'd known of Edie Evans through her mother, who had been to Bickley Spiritualist Church; his home was a bare mile from the Evans's home. And, most damning of all, Latham had lied to police during a murder investigation.

At best, he had misled them by failing to disclose that Edie was already dead when he came on to the case.

At worst, he had killed her.

Marvel glanced at the recorder to make sure it was working. "What are you trying to tell me, Richard?"

"ImmosheMED!"

"What?" said Marvel impatiently. "You have to take your face out of your jumper."

He did. "I know she's dead!"

"Who killed her?" said Marvel.

He shook his head. "Nobody."

Marvel frowned. "Was it an accident?"

Latham hesitated. "I . . . I don't think so. But I couldn't see."

"So you know she's dead, but you won't say who killed her or how she died?"

"I can't," he insisted.

272

"Sounds pretty suspicious, doesn't it, Richard?"

"I'm just telling you what I know."

"Well, if you knew she was dead and you had nothing to do with it, why didn't you just tell us at the time?"

"How could I? How could I say so? How could I tell those poor people?"

"That's bullshit. You didn't have to tell her family anything. You only had to tell *us*."

Latham started to cry again. "But what if I was *wrong*? What if people stopped looking for her and I was *wrong*?" He shook his bowed head. "I couldn't tell anybody. I wasn't sure."

"So instead you were forced to take our money and string everybody along," said Marvel. "How convenient."

"What else could I do?" said Latham, pushing his glasses up his damp nose. "It was already too late." He wiped his nose on his jumper and sniffed up what he'd missed. He looked at Marvel pleadingly, his cheeks shining. "It nearly destroyed me," he said. "Every day she haunts me. That's why I don't look for missing children. I could never go through that again."

"Of course," said Marvel. "Poor you."

"That's not what I —" Latham stopped and shook his head. "Meant," he finished. "That's not what I meant."

"Well," said Marvel, "it's a good story."

"It's the truth," said Latham.

"Maybe it is," said Marvel. "Maybe a jury would believe it."

"What do you mean?"

"Maybe they'd only convict on the lesser charges — the obstruction of justice and the fraud."

Panic started to creep across Latham's face. "What do you mean, *lesser charges?*"

"Maybe they would consider the case for murder too circumstantial —"

"*Murder?*"

"But that's not up to me. It's up to the CPS to decide on the charges. It's just my job to present them with the evidence."

"What evidence?" said Latham. "There *is* no evidence."

"Well, there are close parallels, Richard, you have to admit."

"What parallels?"

"Between nicking dogs and then finding them to boost your reputation as a so-called psychic, and kidnapping a child to do the same."

"*What?*" Latham looked stunned. Then he started to cry again. Harder this time.

"All that publicity. All that TV exposure. All that *money.*"

"That's not . . . what . . . happened."

Marvel shrugged. "Maybe you didn't mean to hurt her. Maybe you were going to keep her for a bit and then return her, just like with the dogs. Maybe something went wrong."

"No!" cried Latham. "Nothing went wrong! I didn't take her and I didn't hurt her! I'd never even heard her name before the police called and asked for my help! I didn't even know she was missing!" His weeping now

274

was unrestrained and noisy, with streamers of clear snot looping off his nose and chin. "When I found her it nearly *destroyed* me!" he bawled. "It nearly killed me! You don't understand what it's like! You're *there*. You feel what she *feels*! Never again! That's why I wouldn't help that woman with the picture of her son."

He stopped talking and took off his glasses so he could wipe his eyes.

Marvel sat back in his chair and watched Latham through narrowed eyes. Brady was shooting looks at him, but knew better than to interrupt him at a critical point. Or at any point.

Marvel made a face, as if he was finding it all very hard to believe. "So what you're telling me, Richard," he said carefully, "is that you kidnapping the dogs has nothing *whatsoever* to do with the kidnap and murder of Edie Evans."

"*Nothing*," said Latham fervently. Then his eager look faded as he realized what he'd done, and his lips turned down yet again.

With grim pleasure, Marvel knew that — if he played this right — he might get everything he wanted and needed out of Richard Latham. With the leverage of that one-word confession, he might solve the Edie Evans case *and* let Superintendent Clyde off the hook. A double-whammy of promotion-worthy proportions.

With perfect timing, the door of the interview room opened and Dale Proctor strode in. He dropped his tatty old briefcase on to the table with a great puffing out of cheeks to indicate that he'd been moving Heaven and Earth to get there as fast as he could.

"Say nothing," he barked at Latham.

"Why is my client crying?" he demanded of Marvel.

Marvel ignored him and leaned across the table to look deep into Latham's eye. "I *might* be able to get you a deal, Richard."

"My client has done nothing wrong," declared Proctor. "So why would he make a deal?"

But Latham glanced up. He reached forward slowly and picked up his glasses, then put them on so he could see Marvel properly. "What kind of deal?"

"*Hey!*" said Proctor irritably. "We're not making deals. Dale Proctor is not in the deal-making business!"

Marvel looked at the lawyer. "Your client just admitted his involvement in a plot to steal dogs and to extort money from their owners."

Proctor rounded on Latham. "Jesus! You didn't, did you?"

Marvel went on: "And those owners include the wife of a senior Metropolitan police officer."

"Nobody's supposed to speak to my client until I *get* here!"

"That's what *he* kept saying," grinned Marvel. "You can hear it on the tape if you wind it back. Along with his confession to theft, fraud, deception and extortion."

They both looked at Latham, whose ruddy, tearful face acknowledged that all of it was true.

"Bollocks," said Proctor. He slumped down into the chair next to Latham.

"Sorry," said Latham.

"Hey," shrugged Proctor, "it's your neck."

"What about the deal?" said Latham.

276

Proctor made a long-suffering face. "All right," he said grumpily. "Let's hear it."

"I'm not promising anything. I need to tell you that right up front. But I *might* be able to make this dog thing go away." Marvel spoke with caution; people never wanted something you were too keen to give them.

"Yeah?" said Proctor. "Tell me more."

"Your client gives us complete cooperation on the Edie Evans case."

"Who's Edie Evans?" said Proctor.

"She's a twelve-year-old girl who disappeared just over a year ago. Mr Latham here was employed by us in his capacity as a psychic, but she was never found."

"Is my client a suspect in that case?"

"No," lied Marvel. "But he admits he's withholding information that might be vital."

Proctor exchanged a brief glance with Latham, who did not deny it.

"And what would that cooperation involve?"

"Not much. Just look at some pictures and use his . . . gift. We have new information he hasn't worked with before. See if he can get anything from it that might be helpful to us. If he can't, he can't — but right now he's not even prepared to try. That's all I ask — that he tries."

"Shit," said Brady.

Proctor laughed and nodded at him. "Even DS Brady thinks it sounds too good to be true! What's the catch?"

"The only catch is, the deal's so bloody good the super might not go for it."

The super would bite his hand off up to the elbow. Marvel couldn't believe his own genius. It was the perfect solution. He would be able to offload the Mitzi Clyde millstone *and* reopen the Edie Evans case in one easy step. At best, Latham might incriminate himself while revisiting it. At the very least, he could shed valuable light on the one case that still had the power to keep John Marvel awake at night, blinking up at the charcoal ceiling while Debbie slept the sleep of the ignorant beside him and Buster snored on his feet.

Proctor turned to Latham and asked, "What do you think?"

Latham shrugged. "I don't know . . ."

He was playing hard to get. Let him, thought Marvel. Let him play the innocent who wanted his day in court. They all knew different, but if Latham wanted to be dragged kicking and screaming to the deal by his lawyer to keep up the pretence, then *let him*. Marvel wanted Latham to suffer, but he wanted to know what had happened to Edie Evans more; it was as simple as that.

He got up. "How about I run this past the super so we know exactly where we stand? There's no point in me offering it if he's not going to go for it."

"Right," said Proctor.

Marvel left the room.

He walked to the machine and got a cup of soup and put two sugars in it.

He stood there until the soup had gone cool, then he dropped it into the bin marked NO LIQUIDS, and went back to Interview Three.

"Took some doing," he said. "But the deal's on the table."

Proctor — whom Marvel noticed was now noticeably red in the face — said tightly, "My client has decided to decline your offer."

"What?"

Marvel looked at Latham. Unlike his lawyer, he looked pale and sick.

"I don't want to do it," he said.

The look that Marvel and Proctor exchanged was brief, but so transparent that they each knew in an instant what the other was thinking.

Nobody would turn down that offer but a fool or a guilty man.

Even Clyde got it.

"Is he an idiot?" he asked Marvel as they sat in his greasy mint office an hour later.

"He's *being* an idiot," said Marvel. "But no, sir, I don't think he *is* one."

"Then he killed her," said Clyde firmly. "Or knows who did."

Marvel nodded. "That's my thinking too."

"But we have no evidence against him?"

"Only his own claims that she is dead. Seen in psychic visions. And if he's willing to take the drop for the dognapping thing rather than talk about it again, then where's our leverage?"

Clyde sighed and shook his head with a pained expression on his face. "The CPS'll never go for that. They'd laugh us out of court. *Shit!* What a bloody mess you've made of this, Marvel. You only wanted to get Latham for the dog thing because you couldn't get him on this other case.

"And now, when you try to cut him loose and make everything better, he won't *be* cut loose because either he really did kill the girl — which he's *never* going to tell you — or because you've scared him so shitless that he thinks you're trying to fit him up for murder! Now *he's* screwed and *I'm* screwed and the only person who isn't screwed is *you!*"

But Marvel *felt* screwed. Screwed by whoever really had stolen Edie Evans and really had killed her — whether by accident or design.

He had to try to salvage *something* from this mess.

"I can go over Edie's file again, sir —"

"No," said Clyde.

Marvel adjusted his sights in an instant. "In my spare time. It's still open. I could look at it right from the start with Latham at the middle. Alibis and witness statements —"

"*I said no.*"

Marvel stopped talking and looked at Clyde's face. It was oddly patient, despite his angry words. As if he knew what was coming, and it was worth waiting for.

And suddenly Marvel knew too. His heart dropped into the pit of his queasy stomach as he realized what had happened. That Edie Evans had made a chink in him that was too big to fill or hide. And that he had

280

spent so much of his life looking for weakness in others that he'd forgotten to disguise his own vulnerability. It was a mistake he would never make again, but he had made it now — and his boss was going to punish him for it.

He understood the rules of the game.

He'd just never thought they applied to *him*.

"Please . . ." he started, and then stopped and finished the rest of the sentence in his head. *Please don't do this to her*.

If Superintendent Robert Clyde read those words in John Marvel's eyes, he ignored them.

"I'm closing the Edie Evans case."

CHAPTER
THIRTY-EIGHT

Edie stared at the door.

Her wonky Neil Armstrong stared back at her.

She had been sitting like this — not moving, cross-legged on her camp bed — for three hours, although she had no way of knowing that. Cross-legged in quivery stillness, her ears vibrating with the strain of listening for the man to return.

She also had no way of knowing that it was now eighteen hours since she had broken his hat, and he had stormed out and bolted the door behind him.

In her dry mouth, it felt like more.

Still he didn't come.

Edie licked her lips, but her tongue was dry too.

And bigger. It felt bigger than before.

She got up slowly to check the jug again. Another dribble had collected in the bottom, but this time it was barely a few drops. The glass jug was heavy, but she held it tipped against her lips until her arms got tired.

Swallowing was difficult. It was like there was a lump of cotton wool in her throat. She had to gulp two or three times just to feel her swallow was still working.

Her legs ached. Even after she had stretched them, they ached.

She stretched them again anyway, and banged on the door. The sound was dead, like her shout had been that first time.

She shouted again anyway, but now her mouth was so dry that the sound that came out was shockingly small, even in this shockingly small room.

There were still four of the Bakewell tarts left, but although she was hungry again, she was wary of eating one. They cried out for a cup of tea.

Tea.

Her mother made good tea.

Her mother made good everything.

Edie's face tingled with approaching tears, and when they rose on her lower lids, she collected them on her finger and swallowed them greedily, painfully.

But they brought no relief — only the faint taste of salt.

She returned to the big glass jug and ran a finger around the inside walls.

It came away shiny with moisture and Edie licked it off, again and again and again.

How could she have forgotten the water on the sides of the jug? How could she have wasted it? All this time those few precious drops had been evaporating.

She winced at a sudden cramp in her stomach. It went on and on, and left her breathless.

She lowered herself on to her bed and lay on her side with her knees drawn up.

She waited it out.

She waited for everything. For the door to open; for the man to return. For more water. For more water. More water.

She waited so long that she fell asleep, and dreamed of ice cubes clinking softly in a glass.

The first sip was heaven.

The liquid gushed over long-dry lips like a flash flood across a cracked and dusty riverbed.

The tongue fizzed in gratitude.

The palate swelled in relief.

The throat opened to welcome it home like the prodigal son.

Before the mouth was even full, the rest of the body was tingling and alert to the onrushing paradise.

Heaven on Earth.

Marvel put down the pint of bitter and felt that he had found his way home.

CHAPTER
THIRTY-NINE

Anna was putting the baby to bed when somebody knocked. At first she didn't even know where the sound came from. They rarely had visitors now, and never bought anything that required delivery.

She frowned and went into the kitchen.

The knock came again and she went warily down the stairs to the front door.

It was DCI Marvel. The shoulders of his coat were damp, even though it was no longer raining. It made her wonder how long he'd been out, or how far he had walked.

"Mrs Buck," he said, "I need to speak to you."

He was drunk. Not *rolling* drunk, but she could tell.

Anna stared at him. He looked unwell. His face was pale and his eyes were red and tired, although that might have been from the cigarette smoke that curled up into them on this damp, windless night.

But there was something else in his eyes that told her that refusing him entry was not going to work.

"James will be home soon," she said cautiously.

"That's OK." He shrugged and stepped forward, so she stepped backwards, and all of a sudden he was in the house.

"I won't be long," he said, and looked up the stairs as if to remind her where they were supposed to be going.

"Can you take your shoes off, please?"

"Really?" he said. "I'm on official police business."

"Really," she said, and he took off his shoes.

She gestured for him to go first. On the way up the stairs she noticed that his right sock had a hole in one heel.

"In here?" he said at the kitchen.

"If you like," she said.

He sat at the table and she put down a saucer for his ash.

"You've cleaned up the paint."

"Yes," said Anna. "It took a while."

He looked around and said nothing. Anna knew she should offer him a cup of tea, but she didn't want to encourage him.

"So," she said bluntly, "what do you want?"

He sat for a moment, silent, eyes narrowed by smoke.

"Earlier today, Richard Latham told me Edie Evans has been dead from the start." He turned up his palms. "I mean, I don't believe any of this psychic bullshit. But . . ."

He stopped.

Anna didn't know what he wanted her to say, so she said, "I'm sorry."

He nodded slowly, and said *thank you*, and Anna realized with surprise that he felt he deserved that sympathy.

286

Which somehow made him deserving of it.

"Would you like a cup of tea?" she asked.

"Please."

She put the kettle on and the little kitchen with the black windows was suffused with the subliminal thrum of water.

They didn't speak again until she put two mugs on the table and sat down opposite Marvel.

"What made you think she *wasn't* dead?"

Marvel shook his head. He flushed. He was embarrassed, she could see.

"Just hope," he said. "But it felt more . . . *substantial* than that. More rational." He sipped his tea and cupped his hands loosely around the mug. "Now it just seems a bit stupid."

Anna suddenly felt very close to DCI Marvel.

He went on, slow and measured, "Latham said she died a month or so after being taken. That means that all the time I've spent looking for her and thinking about her and wondering where she is and how she is — fifteen months! — has been a waste of time. Because she's fucking *dead*!" He threw up a hand and jolted tea out of his mug on to the table. "Sorry," he said.

Anna got a cloth and wiped up the spill. "Your time wasn't wasted," she said.

"You don't think so?"

She looked into her tea. "I think about Daniel all the time. I wonder how he is, what he's doing, whether he's thinking about me, how he's changing, how tall he is now, whether his clothes still fit him or whether someone has bought him new ones . . ."

She caught her voice before it could break and gave a tremulous smile at the bittersweet pleasure of her own imagination.

"Thinking about him keeps him alive for me," she said. "It gives me hope, and hope keeps *me* alive for *him*."

Marvel stared at her. He lit another cigarette. He used matches, not a lighter, and the delicious, dangerous smell of sulphur hung over them for a moment, before the dull and dirty smoke took over.

He clamped the cigarette between his lips and leaned sideways so he could take something from the inside pocket of his coat.

Anna averted her eyes. She knew what it would be. "Please don't ask me to look at her picture," she said in a rush.

"Why not?"

"It hurts."

"How can it hurt?"

"I don't know, but it does. *Here*." She cupped her belly.

"Latham wouldn't look at it either," said Marvel. "Even after I offered him a deal."

"But if you don't believe in psychic powers, what was the point of asking him to look at it?"

"I don't know," said Marvel irritably. "*I don't know!* Shit!"

He sighed and leaned back in his chair, which creaked precariously. Then, after a moment, he said, "I *do* know. Latham's a lying son of a bitch, but he said

288

something that stuck in my head. He said *Everybody gets there in the end.*"

"Gets where?" said Anna.

"I think he was talking about God."

"What does it mean?"

"I suppose it means that people want to believe in *something* — God or Santa Claus or some bloody thing — even if it's just because they're scared and desperate."

Marvel deliberately put the curled photo of the dog show down on the table in front of Anna. He half laughed, but there was no pleasure in it. "Well, now I'm desperate," he said. "I can't go another day not knowing what happened to Edie Evans, and if *you* don't understand that, then nobody can."

Anna looked at him with fierce calm. "You *can* go another day, Mr Marvel, and you *will*. Whether I help you or not. Whether *anybody* helps you or not. For as long as you live, you will go on. Because the only alternative is *not* to."

The night on Bickley Bridge hung between them.

Then Marvel said, "Let me tell you something about this photo before you say no."

She nodded. "OK."

"This photo was taken last September. Eight months *after* Edie went missing."

Anna frowned, then looked suddenly hopeful. "But that's *good*! That means Edie might be —"

"No, it doesn't," said Marvel. "Because you see this here?"

He pointed and Anna glanced down obliquely. "This is Edie's BMX bicycle. Which we found at the crime scene, and which has been in the basement of Lewisham police station since January last year."

Anna frowned. "But that's impossible."

Marvel shrugged. "No, that's just improbable. You haven't heard the impossible bit yet." He took a breath. "Before I came here tonight, I went to see Sandra Clyde. I wanted to pick up the negative or digital file or whatever, so we could enlarge the photo in the lab. Get the best image to work with. Maybe identify other people in the picture. Something to go on, you know?"

Anna nodded.

Marvel leaned forward. Then he stopped and sat up straight again, and looked around the room as if he'd forgotten what he was going to say.

Anna watched him closely. He looked more than drunk; he looked old. He looked confused.

He looked scared.

She felt fear trickle down her own spine.

"What?" she said. "What is it?"

Marvel looked at her and shook his head. "Edie's not *in* the original photograph."

"I don't understand," said Anna.

He went on: "And she's not in any of the other copies."

"What do you mean?"

Marvel's eyes met hers, and he spoke carefully. "Your photograph is the only one Edie's in."

Anna's scalp prickled. "I . . . I don't . . . has it been . . ."

"Doctored? Tampered with? Manipulated?" Marvel shrugged. "Our lab says no."

"Then how?" she said. "How can that be?"

Marvel slowly stubbed out his cigarette in the saucer. "*That's* the impossible bit."

Anna's hand made an involuntary movement towards the photo, but she stopped herself.

She had to see, but she didn't want to look.

Marvel spoke again, choosing his words carefully. "But it made me think of something else Latham said to me . . . He said the dead are in control. He said the *dead* choose what they show. And who they show it to. And *that* made me think . . . Maybe Edie wanted to show these things to *you*. Maybe she knew *you* would be the best person to see what she wanted to show you. Because of Daniel. Maybe that's why she knew you would pay attention. And maybe that's even why I stopped you jumping off Bickley Bridge. Shit, I don't know. It's crazy and I'm drunk, and all I know for *sure* is that they're closing the case and abandoning Edie, and so *now* . . . Now I'm ready to believe in something. In anything . . ."

Anna flinched as Marvel took her hand and she thought of Latham doing the same that night at the church, when *she* was the one doing the begging.

He spoke in a desperate rush. "*Please*, Mrs Buck. If she's dead, I want to know. But if she's alive . . . If she's alive I *have* to find her. And you're my only hope. *Please*."

They sat at opposite sides of the small kitchen table, the impossible photograph between them, while the clock on the oven ticked quietly and a bus pulled away from the stop outside.

Finally, in a very small voice, Anna said, "Can you get me a glass of water, please?"

James was rolling drunk, so he might have fallen over anyway.

He took two strides into the kitchen in his socks and skidded over backwards with his feet in the air.

The hand he put out to break his fall splashed down beside him like a belly flop from a high board.

The kitchen was swimming in water.

"Shit!" he said, as he lay on his back with his hair all cold and wet.

He could hear water running from somewhere, so he stayed there, taking a moment to examine the ceiling for leaks, but it seemed to be fine.

He wallowed about on his side and his elbows and his knees, before finally getting back to his feet.

The kitchen tap had been left open so far that the recoil was splashing the walls and the window. The plug wasn't in the sink, but despite that, the plughole and the overflow had had no chance of coping with the sheer volume of water pounding down into it.

"Fuck!" he said angrily and paddled across the floor and turned off the tap.

Then he looked around.

Nothing else seemed to be wrong. The kitchen was otherwise as clean and tidy as it always was.

"Anna!" he shouted.

He crossed to the living room. So had the water, and the carpet was like a sponge.

"*Anna!* Jesus Christ. *Anna!*"

She was asleep in their bed, curled on her side with her knees drawn up.

James tugged the covers off her. She was fully clothed and soaking wet.

"Anna! What the bloody hell happened in the kitchen?"

Anna woke slowly with a vacant look in her eyes. "What?" she said thickly.

"What happened? In the kitchen?"

Anna looked at the bedroom doorway as if to remind herself where the kitchen was. "The police came," she told him, still not fully awake. "They wanted to read my mind."

CHAPTER
FORTY

Edie thought about taps.

In particular she thought about the garden tap. The one that leaked every summer when Dad put the hosepipe on it.

Every summer was the same. Once the rain had stopped for long enough for the garden to need watering, Dad got the hose out of the shed and fixed it to the tap.

Then every summer he remembered he hadn't fixed the tap. As soon as he turned it on, some water went in the hosepipe, but some water also came out of the handle where you turned the tap on.

Every summer Dad said, "Washer's gone. I'll have to fix that."

Edie was twelve and she could remember that happening when she was eight *at least*. So that was four years. Four summers. Four summers when water that should have been going down the hosepipe and to the flowers was instead bubbling out of the gaps in the metal and dribbling on to the concrete next to the house.

Wasted.

Curled up on the camp bed, Edie thought of that tap all the time. She thought of kneeling beside it and turning the handle and watching the water squeeze through the gaps. She thought of touching her tongue to the cold metal and feeling the tiny pressure of the flow on her tongue. She thought of waiting until her mouth was half full and then opening her throat to allow the water to trickle gently down her gullet and into her stomach. She imagined the way it would feel spreading through her whole dry, wasting body, making her plump and strong and happy with water.

Happy with water.

She checked the jug again.

It was dry.

Her tummy cramped in want, and she dropped the jug and it broke into icy shards.

Dry icy shards.

When she wasn't thinking about taps, Edie thought about Peter. She thought about her mouse often now. She thought that as soon as she was back home, she would set him free. She'd only been here for a few weeks. Or maybe months, it was hard to tell — but Peter had spent his whole life in a cage.

He coped well with it. In many ways Edie thought he would have made a better astronaut than she was. He ran in his wheel and he hid in his cardboard tubes and climbed his little ladders. He cleaned his whiskers and rubbed his tiny pink hands over his eyes in that way that made him look so cute and human. He burrowed into the clean shavings and made a nest, and chose the sunflower seeds first from his food bowl, before eating the pellets and then those weird yellow flakes.

Peter kept himself busy.

Edie raised her head a little and looked around the spartan room. A bed, a poo bucket, a strip light, in a room that was barely bigger than a cupboard. Even Peter would have a hard time making much of it.

She got off her bed and nearly fell. She was a lot more tired than the last time she had left it.

She knelt and pulled the carrier bags from under the bed. There were great handfuls of black and brown and dark blue; the few reds and yellows were long gone, and Edie sifted through the rest, searching for the last stubs of maroon or purple.

The sound of the crayons was comforting — a soft, hypnotic clicking as they rolled off her palms and tumbled back into the bags.

For a while she just sat and did that, not really thinking about anything but the sound and the dull feel of the wax sticks falling through her cupped hands.

Space isn't all it's cracked up to be.

The thought caught in the back of Edie's throat and made her feel like crying.

Then another much better thought popped into her head and she giggled out loud with the fun of it, although the giggle came out all dry and soundless.

She picked up one of the bags and walked unsteadily to the wall opposite the bed, where she had drawn her bookshelf and Captain Kirk. She selected a dark-blue crayon that was almost complete and stood for a moment, judging the space and the approach. Where to start? How to proceed? There was no going back really — even on these smooth cement walls, it took ages to scrape mistakes off with a thumbnail.

Edie's tongue poked out a little from between her lips, the way it always did when she was thinking really hard. She was thinking so hard that she had forgotten how dry she was.

She didn't take long to decide; when it came, the idea was so perfect that she really only needed to step forward and reach out her arm and press the blunt point of the blue crayon against the wall.

Then, with one big, satisfying loop that sent a little thrill up the back of her neck, Edie Evans started to draw herself an escape hatch.

CHAPTER
FORTY-ONE

James couldn't remember the last time he had been this angry. He leaned hard on the heavy glass door to the police station and looked around, spoiling for a fight. There was a little window in one wall, like a Tube station ticket office, and behind the window was a police officer.

"I want to make a complaint," he said.

"Yes, sir," said the woman. "What about?"

"About some copper who's been bothering my wife."

"OK," said the officer, pulling a pad of plain paper towards her. "Can you give me your name, please?"

James told her his name, and his age and address. And the name of his wife.

The officer tapped her pen on the paper for a moment. "And do you know the name of the officer involved, sir?"

"Marvel," said James.

She wrote it down. Very slowly.

"And what is the nature of your complaint, sir?"

"This arsehole has been coming round my flat and forcing my wife to help him on a case. She's already stressed. My son is missing and she's mentally not so great, you know? The last thing she needs is this . . .

298

prick coming round and making her do stuff that's making her worse!"

The officer nodded up at him. "I understand, sir, but please could you watch your language? There's no call for it."

"I'm sorry," said James. "I'm sorry. But I got home on Saturday night and my kitchen was flooded because my wife didn't know what she was doing, because this idiot had come round and upset her so much."

"I understand, sir," nodded the woman.

"*I'm* upset too," said James. "My wife's very fragile. She just doesn't need it. We don't need it, and I want something done. I don't want this man coming round again. I want him to leave us alone."

"Absolutely, sir," she said, and James felt the tension starting to leave his body. The officer was very soothing, and now that he was calmer, he looked at her properly for the first time. She was young and attractive, with big, intelligent eyes that made him instinctively trust that she would do the right thing.

"You take a seat, sir, and I'll see how I can help you with this, OK?"

"Thank you," he said. "Do you want me to fill in a form or something?"

"No, sir," she said. "You have a seat."

There *was* a form to fill in, but Emily Aguda didn't give it to James Buck.

She still might. Procedurally speaking, it was the right thing to do and so she wasn't ruling it out. But she didn't want to do anything that couldn't be reversed.

She got up from her desk at the window, met eyes with Sergeant Caxton, who would relieve her for five minutes, and left the office behind the window.

She didn't go far. After going through the double doors into the corridor that led to the cells and the cafeteria, Aguda leaned against the wall and thought about everything she knew about Anna Buck and James Buck and the Edie Evans case.

There wasn't a lot, but she figured every detail was important in the decision she had to make.

For a start, Anna Buck was crazy. *Mentally fragile* was as kind as you could be about it, so Aguda reasoned from that that James Buck was kind and loved his wife. And a man who loved his wife, even though she was crazy, couldn't be all bad, could he? Couldn't be a killer of children, surely? Certainly, she had gone to see Marvel about her suspicions over James Buck, but now that she had met him — albeit briefly — she thought those suspicions were probably wrong. After all, if Anna Buck's idea of a baby was that hideous thing with a battery heart, then her concerns over her husband's childcare skills were probably similarly skewed. James Buck could be Father of the Year for all Aguda knew.

But if he were a dangerous man, Aguda couldn't see how it would help the Edie Evans case or Anna Buck's lost son if the first official police contact with James Buck was in the form of a complaint. That would complicate everything — especially as Aguda had a feeling that it was a complaint that would be upheld. She had no doubt that Marvel had been round to James Buck's flat and had bothered the hell out of his wife. No doubt whatsoever. However good the reason, that was pretty outrageous behaviour, and Aguda seriously doubted that Buck's complaint would be the first one that had ever been made against DCI Marvel. The man was too abrasive, too rude, too much of a *prick* to have escaped previous brushes with the disciplinary system.

Thanks to her role as a glorified force mascot, Aguda recognized that her opinion on all these scores was less scientific deduction and more feminine intuition. It wasn't something she was about to write up in a report, but it felt like common sense.

And that was her favourite of *all* the senses . . .

So she opened the door to the foyer and beckoned James Buck off the bench. She led him up to the second floor, past the drinks machine, through the Jenga and to the desk in the far corner, and introduced him to a surprised-looking DCI John Marvel.

Then she left.

As her mother used to say, *Let nature run its course.*

Marvel and James Buck both looked a little embarrassed.

Aguda had merely introduced one to the other and walked away, but she might as well have made them shake hands and told them to play nice.

In awkward silence, they watched her leave.

Then Buck said, "If you're Marvel, I came here to complain about you."

"Yeah?" said Marvel. He was angry with Aguda for bringing the man right to him, when his instinct was always to keep trouble as far away from himself as was humanly possible. Maybe she hadn't understood that this man had wanted to make a complaint *about* him, not *to* him. Idiot.

But James Buck was here now, looking sullen, and Marvel would have to make the best of a bad job. He gestured to the empty chair at the next desk. "Have a seat," he said, "and complain away."

Buck sat down angrily. "You came round my house and upset my wife."

"I'm investigating a murder," said Marvel. "I'm allowed to do stuff like that."

"Yeah?" said James. "At nine o'clock on a Saturday night? Don't tell me that's official!"

Marvel shrugged. "Justice never sleeps."

"Maybe, but Justice flooded my bloody kitchen."

Marvel frowned. "I didn't flood your kitchen."

"I get home and my wife's soaking wet in bed and the flat's ankle-deep in bloody water!"

"I don't know anything about that," said Marvel. He decided not to tell James Buck about the several glasses of water he'd fetched for his wife. Or about how he'd left her still gulping greedily from the kitchen tap. "All I know is that I went round there to ask for her help on a very serious matter —"

"What matter?"

"The kidnap and possible murder of a child."

"What would she know about that? Just because we lost our son doesn't make us bloody CSI Bickley."

Marvel shifted uncomfortably in his chair. He didn't want to look like a fool, but he also didn't want this bozo taking his complaint any further. "Mr Buck," he said, "are you aware that your wife claims to have some psychic power?"

"Yeah." To Marvel's relief, Buck looked as uncomfortable as he himself felt about it, now that he was sober.

"Do you believe it?" he asked.

"Course not," said Buck. "It's mental. Like something out of Harry Potter."

"Exactly," said Marvel. "*Exactly.*"

For a second they were on the same page.

It was a shame Marvel had to turn it.

"Except . . ." he said, and opened his hands at James Buck, hoping the young man would jump at the opportunity to admit he secretly believed it after all.

"Except what?" said Buck suspiciously.

So Marvel sighed and told him about the photo of Edie Evans, and about the garden and the bicycle bell.

James Buck stared at him as if he were mental too. Which he'd started to wonder himself lately. "You saying you think she *is* psychic?"

"I'm just saying maybe — even subconsciously — she heard something from someone who knows something about the case . . ." He tailed off; it sounded so lame.

Buck looked at his hands. Then he gazed around the squad room until his eyes settled on the wall behind Marvel's head.

"Why have you got a photo of me up there?"

Shit.

"Where?" said Marvel, even though he knew exactly where James Buck was looking. His Edie Evans montage.

Buck stood up and leaned across the desk. "There," he said. "One of me and one of Anna! What's that all about? Are we under suspicion or something?"

"No, no," said Marvel quickly. "Those are just people who might be helpful on the case I'm investigating. Which is why I'm glad you've come in today, Mr Buck."

Marvel was proud of the segue. It was pretty smooth.

Not smooth enough. Buck peered more closely at the photos. "They're not good pictures even."

Everyone was a bloody critic.

Buck pointed at Richard Latham. "Who's that?"

Marvel hesitated. He still had no hard evidence that Richard Latham was anything more than a fraud, and he was unlikely to find anything else, now that Edie's case had been officially closed. It didn't mean he wouldn't try — even if it meant doing it in his own time. He would have to re-examine every bit of evidence by the light of Richard Latham. He'd have to comb through his interview in the file for inexplicable knowledge of Edie or her home — particularly her bedroom. But right now, all he knew for sure was that the man claimed that Edie was dead, and that he didn't want to talk about it.

"He's a psychic who was called in when the girl first went missing."

"Another loon," snorted James, and sat down.

Marvel laughed and the tension relaxed a little.

"Did Anna help you . . . that way then?"

Marvel hesitated.

Had she?

Had the horror that had unfolded at Anna Buck's kitchen table helped him? Or had he been witness to madness? The kind of madness that — in another time — would have seen her in a straitjacket.

Still might.

He'd been drunk, of course, but it had all seemed so *real*. Watching Anna Buck go away into another place, another time.

Maybe even another person.

Begging for water through cracked lips, clawing at the walls as if she could pass through solid brick. Curling into a foetal position of arid pain.

All he had asked was how Edie had died.

After she'd showed him, Marvel had left Anna Buck's home and reeled out of the flat and vomited on to the garage forecourt. Dropping to all fours so he wouldn't splash his trousers, he had vomited and spat and vomited again, his knees wet and his hair plastered to his forehead with sweat that had made him shudder all over . . .

But he *had* been drunk.

Not so drunk that anyone else would notice. Not *rolling*.

But drunk, after what felt like years of being dry . . .

So he was careful in his reply to James Buck. "I don't know," he said. "This kind of thing is hard to quantify."

"Because it's bollocks, right?"

"Because it's bollocks," said Marvel.

"And what about me?" said James Buck warily, nodding at the photo on the wall. "How can *I* be helpful?"

"I don't know," said Marvel. "Yet."

Buck looked at Edie on her bicycle. "Is that the girl?"

"Yes," said Marvel. "That's Edie Evans."

Buck looked at the picture for a good long minute, then said softly, "Poor kid."

"Yes," said Marvel and got up. "You want a coffee or something?" he said.

"Yeah, OK," said James Buck. "Two sugars, please."

Marvel went to the machine. While he waited for it to rip him off in liquid form, he watched James Buck from across the room.

Despite his own suspicious nature, nothing about the man made him suspicious. He just seemed like a bloke who'd come in to defend his wife, even though he thought she was a loon. It was almost endearing.

Endearing-cum-stupid.

Marvel wouldn't have done it. If Debbie had come home from work and told him she'd been talking to dead people, Marvel would have asked her to turn in her key.

Not so James Buck.

But he was glad now that Aguda had brought Buck up here, even if it had been by mistake. At least Marvel was pretty sure he wouldn't be filing a complaint now. He was almost as sure that James Buck couldn't be helpful to him in any way whatsoever.

He carried the two cups back to his desk.

"What about our boy then?" said Buck. "It's all very well us helping you with your case, but what about Daniel?"

"Ah . . ." Marvel reached into his top drawer and took out the photo of Daniel on the lion. He pinned it on the wall next to the others. "I took this out on a job with me," he said. "Nobody's forgotten about Daniel, Mr Buck."

"Thanks," said Buck, and the mood in the room palpably relaxed.

"Did Anna do those?" Buck nodded at the drawings pinned between the photographs.

"Yes," said Marvel. "She said they were visions."

Buck sipped his coffee. "Can I see them?"

"Sure." Marvel unpinned the two pieces of lined paper and laid them on the desk between them.

The garden through the window, and the weird candelabra thing with "88" on it.

"She saw the garden first," he explained. "And it turns out to be very like the view from Edie Evans's bedroom window."

"Yeah?" said James Buck.

"And this thing here that I thought was a flower . . . Anna said it was a bicycle bell, and we found it right there, hidden under the window-sill."

"Yeah?" Buck seemed more interested this time. "She painted huge circles on the walls of Daniel's room too. Huge blue circles. Made a right mess."

Marvel nodded; he thought it best not to admit that he knew. "Did she say what they might be?"

James Buck shook his head and frowned into his paper cup. "There are noodles in this coffee."

"Yeah," said Marvel. "Sometimes they mix up the soup with the other things."

"Oh," said Buck. "OK." And he went on drinking it. "What's this?"

"I don't know what that one is either," said Marvel. "It looks like a candlestick or something. With the number '88' on it."

Buck picked the drawing up and held it as he sipped his soup. A splayed bottom, a long kinked stem, branching out into a thick top with two things that could well have held candles.

He turned it sideways.

He turned it upside-down.

He looked at Marvel in surprise. "I know what this is!"

Marvel put down his cup. "What?"

Buck frowned at the paper. "But how the hell would she know?"

"Know what? What is it?"

James looked at him, clear eyed with confidence. "It's the exhaust system on Mr Knight's Audi TT."

CHAPTER
FORTY-TWO

"There's vomit on the bloody forecourt!" Brian Pigeon slammed the door of the Alfa and sought out Ang, who was skulking across the workshop with his broom.

"There's vomit on the forecourt!" he shouted again. "I nearly drove right through it!"

"Yes," said Ang, although he looked confused.

For a start, he worked from the inside out every morning, and he hadn't seen the vomit yet.

Also, he'd never heard the word "vomit".

"Well, don't just stand there! Get a bucket!"

"Yes," said Ang. "I know."

He looked around but he didn't move.

Brian Pigeon took out his phone and shook it at him. "Jesus, Ang! Are you going to clean up that mess outside or am I going to call Immigration?"

He hit the Dial key.

"Shit, no," said Ang and hurried towards the door with his broom.

"Not a *broom*! A *bucket*!"

Someone answered the phone and Brian Pigeon said, "Hello? Immigration?"

Ang ran back to the kitchen for a bucket so fast that Brian Pigeon almost choked laughing.

"Hello? Hi, yes — sorry about that. Brian Pigeon in Bickley here. Listen, Autolifts should be delivering this week. Are you ready to roll when I call —"

He stopped as Ang passed him with a bucket and a roll of polishing cloth that cost four quid a metre.

"*What are you doing?* Jesus Christ. What a complete moron . . . Sorry, not you. I'll call you back."

He tossed the phone down on the workbench and steamed towards Ang Nu, who didn't know what he'd done wrong this time.

Marvel studied Anna Buck's drawings as they drove to the garage. Of course, now that he thought the candlestick was actually an exhaust system, it was obvious. The splayed bottom was the engine manifold, combining smoothly into one pipe and running almost straight to the big square silencer at the back of the car. The bits he had thought were candle-holders were exhaust pipes.

The number 88 was apparently the letters BB. Buck said they stood for the makers of the custom exhaust — Billy Boat.

And the four circles must be an Audi logo.

It all made sense now.

In a nonsensical kind of way.

DS Brady drove. He'd been nervous about coming at first because of the case having been closed, but when Marvel had shown him the drawing and explained the new lead, he'd been too excited to say no.

Now Marvel twisted the rear-view mirror away from Brady so he didn't have to turn around to speak to James Buck. "Do you know this Mr Knight?"

"Only from the garage. He's rich. Bit of a dick."

"And you don't know where he lives? We could go straight there."

Buck shook his head and stared out of the rain-spattered window at row after row of small, cheap shops selling dusty cake tins, second-hand furniture and other people's jewellery.

"Not around here," he snorted.

James had caught the bus to the police station, but the ride home was a lot quicker.

That was good. He needed to speak to Anna about the drawing. He was sure he was right; he had admired that exhaust as it hung over his head on the lift in the workshop. Mikey had called him over to have a look at it because the whole thing was chromed and was the cleanest thing James had ever seen under a car. Billy Boat made exhausts for a range of top-line cars — each distinct from the other — and James remembered thinking that this single exhaust unit probably cost more than he could have earned in two months. So he was sure he was right, even without the BB insignia that confirmed that Anna hadn't just drawn a weird, coincidental shape.

How could she know what Mr Knight's exhaust looked like from underneath the car? She sat outside the garage all the time, but she didn't come in.

He needed to speak to her.

He would be able to soon. The shops became their local shops — the newsagent, the playschool, the florist . . .

The car stopped across the road from the garage. James could see Ang scrubbing the forecourt in the drizzle. For a moment he thought he was cleaning the five footprints, but then realized he was a few yards from there.

"Wait here a minute," said Marvel and got out with the sergeant.

James had no choice; the back doors were locked.

He watched Marvel and Brady stride purposefully across the road, their coats flapping around them in the bitter wind.

"Oi," one of them said — James couldn't see who, and the sound was too muffled to tell from inside the car with the windows up.

Ang looked up at the two men bearing down on him, and even from fifteen yards away, James could see the expression on his face turn from mild interest to fear as he scrambled to his feet, holding the bucket, and started to back away.

"*Shit!*" James yanked at the locked door again and then dived over the front seats in a desperate scramble to get out.

Even as he opened the door, James saw Ang hurl the bucket at Marvel.

Then he turned and ran.

If he hadn't run, they wouldn't have chased him.

312

Marvel and Brady had no *reason* to chase Ang Nu, other than getting a bucket of something thrown at them. They weren't there officially and they weren't there for him, and if Brady hadn't been there too — hurtling after the kid like he was storming Goose Green — Marvel would have given up before they even reached the garage door.

But Ang Nu did run, and Brady *was* there.

Brady chased the kid and Marvel chased Brady — at a distance — through the garage, between cars with their bonnets open and under cars with their wheels off, past a tall, skinny man who observed them with unsurprised eyes, and a tubby man, yelling, "What the *hell* is going on! I'm calling the fucking police!"

"We *are* the police!" shouted Marvel.

"I didn't call you!" the man shouted furiously, looking around. "Where's my fucking *phone?*"

A radio blared pop as Marvel ran into a dead end where there was nothing but an inspection pit filled with junk and an old mattress.

"Shit!" He turned round and shouted into the face of a pale-skinned man with white hair and eyelashes. "Where's the back door?"

The man took his own sweet time pointing, and Marvel jabbed a finger at him and said, "I'll be back for you, Whitey," like he was a Terminator, not an out-of-shape forty-five-year-old, panting and blowing.

"You'll have a fucking heart attack first, Fatty!" shouted the man as Marvel banged his way through the back door and into the alleyway behind Northborough Road.

Brady and the kid where nowhere to be seen.

Thank Christ.

Marvel slowed to a brisk walk and headed past the back of Anna Buck's flat. Walled yards on one side, high railway railings on the other.

Marvel stopped and leaned on the wall, and pressed a hand into his side to stave off a stitch. His head pounded and his mouth was dry in a way that reminded him of Anna last night, curled on the floor . . .

He should really lose some weight. Debbie was killing him with culinary kindness. He should walk the dog. Get fit.

His breathing slowed.

His heart rate steadied.

His side stopped aching.

A small electronic beep made Marvel turn his head.

The Chinese kid was clambering out of the skip behind Tigger-Time. While he still had one leg over the edge, Marvel rushed him.

He nearly got him.

At the last moment, the boy saw him coming and hurled himself backwards, away from Marvel and out of the other side of the skip. He hit the ground with a grunt but was up like lightning, and by the time Marvel had crossed the four paces between them, he was off and running again.

This time Marvel had to run fast. There was nobody else to rely on. He did his best to keep his arms moving and breath passing in and out of his lungs.

It was agony.

314

He could see that the alleyway ended fifty yards ahead. A merciful dead end created by the rising wall of Bickley Bridge, where he'd first met Anna Buck.

It's all circles.

The boy reached the wall and stopped and turned to see how close Marvel was.

"Hold it right there!" shouted Marvel, and for one second he could see in the kid's eyes that he just might do that.

Then Brady shouted and burst out of a yard somewhere behind Marvel, and the boy hurled himself at the steel railway fence and started to climb.

Marvel got there just in time to grab his foot, but the boy kicked out at him so hard that his phone fell from his pocket and his shoe came off in Marvel's hand. Then he toppled over the top of the fence and dropped into the grass and brambles and litter on the other side. For a second their eyes met through the railings.

"So sorry!" panted the boy, pleading. "So sorry!"

Then Brady hit the fence beside Marvel with a rattle, and went over it, and the boy turned and ran again — this time along the steep bank beside the tracks.

Marvel got a bad feeling, a sudden dread. "Stop!" he yelled. "Brady! Stop!"

Brady did, and so did the boy — he stopped and half turned to see what was happening.

Pivoted on one toe.

The overflow of momentum took him back a step.

The drop was steep, and when he put his foot down behind him, the ground wasn't where it should have been.

One minute he was standing, looking at them, arms still swinging around his body with the energy of the chase.

The next, he had tumbled backwards down the bank and out of sight.

"*Shit!*"

Marvel waited for the sound of a train to complete the horror, but there was nothing. He tested the railings in his fists and — with a deep grunt — pulled himself up and over them. Sweat sprung up on his face at the unaccustomed effort. He got his coat snagged at the top and half jumped, half fell on to the other side, accompanied by a loud ripping noise.

He got to his feet unsteadily.

"Where is he?" he yelled at Brady.

Brady turned towards him and pointed down the bank. "There."

A few feet from the fence, the ground fell away steeply, so Marvel approached cautiously.

Ang Nu had not had that luxury.

At the foot of the embankment, abutting the brickwork of the bridge, was a wrought-iron fan of Victorian railings, made to keep children and the homeless out of the short tunnel.

Today its sharp points had broken a homeless child's fall.

One had speared Ang Nu's buttock; another protruded from his chest.

A third had gone straight through his skull and right eye.

The smell of old death rose up to meet them — as if Ang Nu's life had already ended here, a long, long time ago.

Marvel said nothing and neither did Brady.

There was too much not to say.

CHAPTER
FORTY-THREE

Brady boosted Marvel back over the fence. His coat caught again on the top, but it was already torn. It smelled of vomit too, which made him remember the bucket the kid had chucked at him, and how hard he'd tried not to throw up on himself after leaving Anna Buck's flat last night. He shouldn't have bothered; it had got him in the end.

He turned the boy's shoe over with his toe, and picked up the phone. The shoe was an Adidas knock-off with a hole in the heel; the phone was quite new.

Marvel left Brady at the embankment to keep rubberneckers at bay and walked slowly back to the garage, like a kid reluctant to go home for a hiding.

They weren't even supposed to be here. Clyde had closed the case. He was supposed to be charging Richard Latham for dognapping or arresting some other bastard for shooting Tanzi Anderson.

Anything but this. Here. Now.

He was in deep shit.

By the time he got back to the garage, the tall skinny mechanic and the short white curly one had both vanished.

"Where's Ang?" said James Buck.

"What's his name?"

"Ang Nu."

"Why'd he fucking *run?*" Marvel complained, making the victim into the culprit with a single short question.

"You scared him. He thought you were Immigration."

"He's not legal then?" Marvel was slightly cheered. That was good news. The kid was an illegal immigrant. Chasing down a guilty man was a whole different matter. A *guilty* man was fair game. Why he was guilty was beside the point.

Marvel looked around. "Where did the other two go?"

"I don't know."

"*They* legal?"

Buck reddened and his eyes flickered towards the tubby man whose slicked-back hair and blue overalls made him look like Chairman Mao.

"You the boss?" said Marvel.

"Yes."

"What's your name?"

"Brian Pigeon."

"Well you're in deep shit, Mr Pigeon." It was nice to pass it on. The man in the overalls didn't even bother asking why. Just looked worried.

"Where's Ang?" James Buck insisted.

"Little shit took my phone," said Pigeon. "Right here off the bench!"

"Ang's dead," said Marvel.

"*Dead?*" said James. He and Pigeon exchanged stunned looks. "What *happened?*"

"He fell."

"What? *How?*"

Marvel sighed and answered him out of courtesy for his help and for not making a complaint.

Yet.

"Look, your colleague fell while trying to evade arrest, and sadly is deceased. The important thing now is to take care of matters in an appropriate manner. Did he have family here?"

Buck shook his head, looking sick, and Brian Pigeon answered, "No. Nobody."

More music to Marvel's ears. Nobody was going to make a fuss about Ang Nu. Nobody was going to cry to the newspapers. Nobody was going to call for his head or sue the Met.

"Where did he live?" he asked.

Buck glanced at Brian Pigeon, who said, "Here. He lived here. He couldn't afford rent so I let him stay here."

"Anything to do with the fact that you're employing a bunch of illegal immigrants?"

Pigeon said nothing more.

Marvel pointed a firm finger at him. "You're under arrest," he said. "Don't go anywhere."

The next several hours were a blur of ambulances, flapping crime-scene tape, news crews, Transport Police, Railtrack PR suits, and scenes of crime officers in white jumpsuits. Clyde himself made an appearance

320

and gave a statement to TV reporters on the garage forecourt, before telling Marvel to go home.

"But this is my case," Marvel had said defiantly.

"This isn't your case," Clyde had replied coldly. "You don't *have* a case. As of right now, you don't even have a job."

When Marvel had looked blank, he'd added, "You're suspended."

Later, as Marvel got as drunk as he possibly could in the warm embrace of the King's Arms, he watched the story play out on the TV over the bar.

Behind Clyde's fake sorrow for Ang Nu, he could see Brian Pigeon being led away from the garage in handcuffs.

And beyond that was what looked like a small blue tent pitched on the edge of the forecourt. He thought the SOCOs might have erected it over the place where he'd vomited the night before. Then — just before the shot cut to the railway embankment — the little tent moved and he realized it was a person sitting there in a big blue nylon *something*.

When it moved he saw it was Anna Buck. A skinny blur, head bowed, legs like sticks.

Marvel suddenly realized the irony of seeking help on a missing-persons case from someone who couldn't even find her own bloody kid.

He ordered another Jameson.

Another double.

Marvel finally got home a little after midnight, bloodshot and exhausted, to find that the coffee table had gone.

So had the Habitat sofa.

"Debbie!" he shouted.

So had Debbie.

"Buster!" he said loudly. "Buster?"

There was no clatter of tiny feet.

There was an envelope with his name on it taped to the TV screen with something that left a mark when he ripped it off.

He knelt and scratched at the gummy mess until he woke up with his forehead pressed against the dark screen and drool on his chin.

The sofa may have gone but luckily the rug was still there, so he lay down on it.

It was only as he fell into the wonderful, dreamless sleep of the hopelessly drunk that John Marvel remembered that the exhaust system on the Audi TT had not yet been checked.

But by then, it didn't seem that important.

Edie Evans cried without tears. She made the face and a tiny humming sound. She hoped her body's own memory might muster some moisture to ease the gritty blinking of her lids. When it didn't, she closed her eyes instead to keep them from turning to little husks in their sockets.

Her bed floated in the dark.

322

The escape hatch that had invited her through the wall and into the blackness had repeated and widened in inexorable circles as she passed slowly into the beyond, until the walls were dark with escape.

There was nothing left now of Edie's bedroom and books and Peter the mouse, and there was nothing left of the crayons but what was under her nails. Every last sliver of brown-blue-black wax had been pressed against the cement with her thumb; every bumpy smear had obliterated her life, and opened her eyes to other possibilities.

The view of the garden had been the last thing to go.

She missed it.

She *missed* it.

Now, as Edie lay curled and crisping on the bed, her hand flinched with independent desire to reach up and scratch away the dark wax and to uncover that memory once more.

She tightened her fist to keep it by her side.

Her past was gone, and trying to find it again would only make this harder.

Now Edie prepared to accept her future.

CHAPTER
FORTY-FOUR

Anna and James Buck had breakfast together the next morning for the first time since Daniel had disappeared.

Neither of them ate, although Anna made toast, but they sat at the table with mugs of tea and sipped them together, bonded by a tragedy that was even more immediate than the loss of their son.

"What will you do today?" said Anna.

James shrugged. "As much as I can, I suppose. Brian's sure to be back soon. His wife will bail him out."

She nodded. "Poor Ang," she said.

James nodded. "I wish I knew where to send his stuff."

Ang's possessions lay on the table between them. The story cloth, a wire horse in the making, a carved wooden mask with small mouth, big teeth and wide eyes. The bottle of Goal.

Anna slowly unwound the cloth.

"He told me his mother made that," said James.

Anna ran her finger over the raised stitching, tracing the whorls of petals and the spiral shells of snails. She bit her lip and said, "Now she'll never know what happened to him."

James reached out and touched the back of Anna's hand.

After a moment, she turned it over so he could hold it.

DCI John Marvel (susp.) woke with a mouth like an old sock.

He was still on the rug in front of the TV, and that gummy mark was still on the screen.

Debbie had known it would infuriate him. That's why she'd done it, of course.

He smelled vomit and turned his head to look at the rug on either side of him, then realized it was him. He was still wearing his coat.

He rolled on to his side with the intention of rising, and winced as something in his pocket dug hard into his left buttock. He got unsteadily to all fours and, from there, to his knees.

His head was a medicine ball full of bees.

He needed a drink.

He put his hand in his pocket and found Ang Nu's phone.

Bollocks. He'd have to call Brady now to come and take it in for evidence.

Suspended. *Shit*.

He'd never even come close before. He'd had a few run-ins with arseholes in senior positions, but nothing like this.

Never chased someone to their death.

In his other pocket he found his cigarettes and his lighter. Without rising from his knees, he lit one and felt a bit better. By the time he was halfway done, he thought he might be able to make it to the chair.

It wasn't a comfortable chair, but it was all there was and it wasn't the floor, so Marvel shuffled over to it on his knees with his big head lolling and buzzing. He hauled himself up on to the seat like a man who's been tipped out of his wheelchair, then sat there for a moment, getting his breath back around the cigarette.

He took the phone out of his pocket again and stared at the little screen. He fiddled idly until he found the contacts list, but it was empty.

He put it down on the side table, but it fell on the floor, which was when he realized Debbie had taken the side tables too.

He sighed and stubbed his cigarette out on the arm of the chair, then lit another one.

He thought of Ang Nu, draped over the fan of spikes like a magic-show illusion. He thought of the moment before that, when he'd grabbed his warm ankle as he went up the fence. If he hadn't stopped in the alleyway to press a hand into his stitch, he'd have run straight past Ang Nu, just the way Brady had. The boy would have slithered over the lip of the skip behind him and run out on to Northborough Road.

Disappeared.

Survived.

It would have been annoying, but it would have been better than this.

Suspended.

326

Dumped.

Debbie had dumped *him*. He hadn't seen that one coming. Although now he thought about it, he wondered if he should have.

The envelope with his name on it was still there, unopened, on the floor next to the TV. He didn't think he'd bother reading it. He had no interest in a litany of his shortcomings.

Marvel smoked for a bit and brooded. Then he remembered the small beeping noise that had alerted him to Ang Nu's presence in the skip yesterday.

He leaned out of the chair and fumbled around on the floor for the phone.

He pressed the Dial key. That was the beep he'd heard.

He pressed the Stop key. It was the same sound.

Marvel took a long drag on his cigarette and thought about things.

Ang Nu had called somebody. While he was crouched in a skip filled with toys and crayons and old powder paints, being chased by the police, the boy had made a phone call. All Marvel had heard was him pressing the key to end it.

Who the hell did he call? He had no family. And if he'd had friends, Marvel imagined he'd have been living with them instead of in that tiny shithole of a workshop kitchen.

Who would someone like Ang Nu call in his hour of need? A solicitor? A taxi? A hit man?

He pressed the Dial key again and peered at the screen to read the last number dialled. Marvel had to hold the phone further away and pull his head back on his shoulders to read the landline number, but it meant nothing to him.

He hit Dial once more and winced his eyes closed while he listened to the great clanging of the ringtone.

"Blue Circle Cement. Can I help you?"

Marvel hung up.

He stared at the phone. The cigarette burned down until his fingers got hot.

He stared at the phone.

Blue circles on the wall of Anna Buck's bedroom.

The sound of the radio seeping through the walls.

What was it she'd said? *Sometimes I hear him crying.*

Chasing Brady chasing Ang through the garage. Almost falling into the inspection pit . . .

From where a person would have the perfect view of a Billy Boat exhaust on an Audi TT.

Marvel was so drunk, he drove.

And as he drove he hit Dial again.

"Blue Circle Ce —"

"This is Detective Chief Inspector Marvel from Lewisham police. Have you got a job booked at Pigeon's garage in Bickley?"

There was a pause while someone decided whether it was a prank call. Then she said, "Yes. Why?"

"What is it?"

"Ummmm . . . filling in an inspection pit."

"When?"

There was a suspicious beat. "Can I ask what this is about, please?"

"No you bloody can't!" he shouted. "*When is the job? WHEN?*"

An offended silence.

And then the woman said, "Now."

CHAPTER
FORTY-FIVE

Open the door.

Open the door.

Edie watched the door through the smallest of slits in her eyelids.

Even that hurt.

Everything hurt. Her empty tummy, her ripped fingernails, her raw, swollen lips and tongue and throat.

She had stopped trying to swallow when one got stuck halfway like a lump of coal, and only slowly, slowly relaxed. Next time she might not be so lucky.

Her lips had stuck together and she didn't try to tear them apart. Her nostrils were so dry they bled now and then, but she barely noticed any more.

She drifted between sleep and this, whatever this was. She hoped it wasn't death, because death should be better than this. All she knew was, it was always a blow to wake up and find herself still in this tiny room.

Open the door.

Open the door.

She saw it happening. A thousand times she heard the bolt click; she saw the door swing open on to the black velvet sky, and the diamond pinpricks of other worlds guiding her home.

Edie Evans hoped she was in space.
Otherwise, dying seemed like such a waste.

CHAPTER
FORTY-SIX

Anna put the toast in the bin and washed the mugs.

As she dried them, she looked out of the kitchen window and her heart clenched painfully.

Daniel.

She dropped the mug. It smashed silently at her feet.

There was a cement lorry parked on the garage forecourt.

Just as there had been on 5 November.

The smell of fireworks and the dull, white light of the coming winter. James's arms slipping around her from behind, and the little chocolate frog that kept hopping in and out of Daniel's lunchbox.

The horror of hindsight unfolding once more outside her kitchen window.

A man in overalls, boots and gloves was laying broad white corrugated piping up the forecourt and through the open garage doors.

As Anna watched, he went back to the cab of his lorry and, somewhere deep in her guts, she felt the machinery thrum into life as the giant drum on the back of the vehicle slowly rotated, mixing the cement and the stone into concrete.

And every time it turned, there was a big blue circle.

It was only when she began to feel faint that Anna realized she had stopped breathing some time ago. When she started again the air dried her mouth so fast that it hurt.

She reached for the tap. Then stopped.

No time, she thought. *No time for water.*

She went downstairs and opened the front door. A bitter wind slashed at her body.

No time for a coat.

She crossed her arms for warmth and stepped outside.

By the time she reached the lorry she was almost running and almost crying.

She didn't know why. She didn't know what she was doing and she didn't know what she would do when she got there.

"Hello!" she shouted and banged on the driver's door. "Hello!"

She reached up and yanked it open. The driver wasn't there.

Her stomach cramped and she doubled over and cried out. People looked at her, then looked away. She ran across the forecourt, past the five footprints and into the garage.

The radio wasn't on. Nobody was there.

"Stop!" she shouted — panic making her voice small and squeaky. "Stop!"

She followed the juddering pipe across the floor, under a car on a lift, and to the back of the garage.

Too late.

It was too late.

The white pipe was draped over the lip of the old inspection pit, and thick grey concrete sprayed from the end in great juddering pulses.

Something hit the steel door.

It shuddered and bumped. Was the key turning? Were the hinges about to squeal? Who was out there?

What was out there?

And what was coming in?

Sssh! Sssh!

The door vibrated and the noise was like a million stones hitting it all in a rush.

BUH-BUH-BUH-buh-buh-buhbuhbuhbuhbuhbuh . . .

"Hey. *Hey!*" The words fell dead to the ground like autumn leaves — too small to make a sound.

But the apprehension was *huge*.

Something amazing was about to happen! Something terrifying! Better get ready!

The rumbling got louder and louder and the note of it against the door changed to something deep and underwater.

Whatever was outside, it was getting . . .

. . . *more*.

Edie's in the pit. Edie's in the pit. Edie's in the pit.

The bees in John Marvel's head were like Spitfires.

He could hardly hear the responses from the woman at Blue Circle over the buzzing and the roar of the BMW. But that wasn't important. What was important was that *she* heard *him*.

"You stop it!" he shouted. "Call him and stop it!"

"Szzshwwzzzszzshwss," said the woman.

"If he hasn't got a phone, call the garage. Tell them to stop pouring!"

"Ssshwzzzsshwwzzzshsssh," said the woman.

"Right now! You understand me? This is a matter of life and death! *Call him right now or I'll fucking arrest the shit out of you!*"

Then he hurled Ang Nu's phone on to the seat beside him, and crashed into a bench.

The bees swarmed away, leaving a single boy soprano holding a top C in his head.

Laaaaaaaaaaaaaaaaaaaaaaaaaah . . .

Somebody tapped on his window and he got a flash of déjà vu. Something that had happened — or was yet to come. Then he pushed open the door and stumbled out.

"You all right, mate?"

The man was wearing an England football shirt and had a swastika tattoo on his neck.

Marvel surveyed Jimmy the Fix's steaming, dripping car as if from a distance, and saw that it was a write-off.

The garage wasn't far though.

He started walking.

"He's drunk!" said his mother, or somebody just like her.

"Hold on, mate," said the man with the tatt. "You can't just walk away!"

Marvel realized he was right.

He started to jog.

CHAPTER
FORTY-SEVEN

"Stop!" Anna shouted. "Stop it!"

The driver was there. Was it the same one as last time? The man who had run up and down, showing people how tall Daniel was with a hand at his hip? Anna didn't know and didn't care. She bent and hugged the big pipe and tried to pull it away from the edge, but the driver grabbed her arm.

"Hey!" he said. "Hey!"

"Stop it!" she shouted hoarsely. "James! James!"

"Hold on!" said the man. "That stuff'll burn you and blind you!"

"You have to stop it!" said Anna. "Please!"

"Who are you?" said the man.

James ran out of the office and said, "What's going on?"

Anna gripped his wrist so hard that he winced.

"James," she croaked. "Open the door."

"What door?"

"She's trying to stop the pour!" said the driver.

"It's OK, Anna," said James. "It's where the new lift's going to go."

"No!" Anna dropped slowly to her knees, as if she'd been shot in the back in an old Western movie, and

336

James looked down into her pale face. She was not the woman he'd left at home twenty minutes earlier. Her eyes were huge and bruised, her lips were dry and cracked. She pointed at the old mattress propped against the far wall of the pit and her voice was so papery he had to lean down to hear her.

"James," she whispered. "*You have to open the door.*"

James Buck's wife was crazy. Anyone could see.

Except . . .

DCI Marvel's voice rang in his head like a bicycle bell.

Except . . .

Except there *was* a door. Behind the dirty old mattress. A door to the tiny tool room that meant you didn't have to climb out every time you needed a fourteen-mill socket. But it didn't *lead* anywhere. It just —

Anna's eyes closed and her grip on his wrist loosened as she slid to the ground.

James jumped into the pit.

Somewhere behind him, the driver shouted "*Shit!*" and then he heard nothing else.

The concrete was like hot stone porridge. It was up to his knees and every step took a lifetime. It clung and it squeezed and he could feel the catalytic heat through his overalls. He hadn't expected it to be hot! He had to fight panic and keep moving towards the mattress.

So slowly . . .

337

James fixed his eyes on the mattress as he twisted and lifted his heavy, hot legs.

Two more agonizing steps.

He reached too early and stumbled . . .

He scared himself upright, his heart thumping with the near miss. If he fell in this stuff he was dead. He calmed his breathing and made himself take a more careful step.

He grasped the mattress and hauled it aside. It flopped awkwardly, half in his way; he had to wade around it now to grip the knob on the bolt.

He drew it back and pulled, but the rising tide of concrete kept the door shut.

With only the bolt to hold on to, he strained to open it even an inch and, when he did, the concrete slid through the gap in a vicious, viscous eddy. Trying to beat him to the prize — whatever that might be. Squeezing ahead of him, seeking out what was rightfully his.

"No!" he shouted. "No no *no!*"

He got his fingers around the crack in the door and strained.

Another two inches.

Not enough! He was just making it easier for the greedy grey sludge.

It wouldn't beat him. It *mustn't!* Anna had told him to open the door and he was going to do it or die trying.

James gripped the door with both hands, braced his right foot against the wall and leaned perilously backwards.

Slowly, slowly, the door edged open, until James could see into the room.

The child was sitting on the bed, cross-legged and wearing a helmet with a tinted visor, as if waiting to be launched into space.

"Daddy!" he shouted, and held out his arms.

CHAPTER
FORTY-EIGHT

"Daddy!"

Ang Nu looked up and saw Daniel Buck running across the fresh cement with a piece of paper in his hand.

"Daddy, look!"

"*Hey!*" Ang reached and grabbed the boy's arm. He yanked him off his feet and into the air. "James!" he shouted. "James!"

"Ow!" said Daniel, but Ang held him tight.

Ang looked down and made a strangled sound that was half fury, half misery. There were five little footprints in the cement. Mr Pigeon would be angry. With *him*.

"You bad!" He shook Daniel hard — and the boy's drawing tore.

Two goldfish in a blue pond.

Daniel looked down at it with wide eyes. "My fishes!" he said.

"Ssssh!" said Ang.

But Daniel didn't shush. Daniel started to cry.

"*Sssh*," said Ang.

"Daddy!" wailed Daniel. "Ang bad!"

"*Sssh!*" hissed Ang. "*You* bad. You daddy angry! Sssh!"

The noise of the cement truck drowned the sound of Daniel from the street, but in the garage his crying bounced off the walls. Ang dangled him through the garage in a panic. Holding his arms too tight, he knew. Hurting him out of fear. He didn't call for James again. He didn't want James to come. Not now. Not while Daniel was crying.

It wasn't his fault. It was Daniel's fault. But all the crying and kicking made it *look* like his fault.

"*Sssh-sssh-sssh.*"

"Daddy!" howled Daniel. "Daddy!"

But James didn't come. James didn't see. Nobody saw.

Ang lowered Daniel into the pit.

Just until he stopped crying.

"*Sssh!*"

He jumped in after him. He pulled aside the mattress. He bolted the door.

The sound of crying became like the mewing of a small kitten.

Ang pressed his damp forehead against the cold steel.

"Be quiet," he sobbed against the door.

"Be quiet. Be good. Go home."

Home,
  home,
  home.
The cement was ruined

and he'd get the blame.
He'd held Daniel too hard,
and there would be bruises.
He'd torn his picture
and he'd started to cry
Ang bad! Ang bad!
When Daniel stopped crying,
he'd let him go.
In a minute.
An hour.
A day, a week, a month.
Home,
home,
home.
Each time he meant it. Each time he lied.
Daniel could never go home.
Because of the shame.
He would tell them about the room in the pit,
and they would know everything . . .
Too hard.
Too horrible.
Ang could never go home.
Home,
home.
And when Immigration finally came for him, there
was only one way to hide his shame.
For ever.
Blue Circle.
Ang turned a final somersault and landed on the
spikes.

★ ★ ★

The post-mortem would show that death was instantaneous.

But that was just his lucky body.

For as he shuddered on the iron palings, Ang Nu — who was not a grown man, and never would be — knew that nothing could be hidden from the waiting ancestors.

And that the greatest shame of all was yet to come.

CHAPTER
FORTY-NINE

James waded slowly from the dark little room with his son in his arms. His eyes sought out Anna, kneeling at the edge of the pit.

I found him! he said in his head. *We found him!* But his throat was too clogged with exertion and emotion to make words.

Instead he raised his son up and gave him back to his mother, who said, "*Daniel,*" so soft and unsurprised that he might have been gone for five minutes, not a lifetime. She tipped back the helmet and stared in mute wonder at her son's new face.

As he stood there, knee-deep in burning concrete, with his arms still raised and as stone as a statue, James Buck heard the door in his head click gently closed behind them all.

CHAPTER
FIFTY

Marvel got there as an ambulance pulled away.

There was a cement truck on the forecourt, and a thick pipe running from it through the front doors. A man in fishing waders was rolling a broad hosepipe on to a reel, and a sopping wet Anna Buck stood nearby, holding a child who was really too big to be carried.

Marvel splashed through the streams of grey water running across the forecourt.

"Where is she?" he shouted at Anna. "Is she in there?"

He didn't wait for an answer but ran past them all into the garage.

The concrete in the bottom of the pit was a few feet deep.

The door to the tool room stood ajar — held open by the flat grey sea.

Marvel started down the ladder.

"Oi!" The man in the waders was striding towards him. "You go in there and I'll call the police!"

"I *am* the police," said Marvel. "What happened here?"

"Christ knows," said the man. "All *I* know is, I'm doing my job, as requested, and this bloke jumps in the pit and opens the door and finds a bloody *kid* in there!"

"Edie? A girl?"

"Nah, a boy. He's outside."

"Fuck!" said Marvel. "I have to search that room."

"Oh no you don't," said the man. "Already got one bloke gone to hospital with alkali burns, and Health and Safety on their way to kick my arse."

"There's somebody else in that room," said Marvel. "Give me your waders."

The cement was drying fast, but Marvel still left a trail of footprints to the open door.

A couple of times he hit a softer spot and his foot went in up to the shin, but the waders were slick and not too hard to tug free.

He had to turn sideways and duck his head to get through the shortened doorway, and when he turned to face the room he felt every hair on his body stand on end.

"My God," he said. "*My God.*"

The deep concrete had made the ceiling so low that his head almost touched it, and had covered anything that might have been on the floor. All that was left was the strip light overhead and the walls, which were solid blue-black.

Except in one place, where a window opened on to another world.

Even through a veil of bitty black, Marvel could see the curve of the lawn, the coloured-in flowers, the trees at the bottom of the garden.

The view from Edie Evans's bedroom window.

And on the sill, the bicycle bell, somehow revealed.

346

Marvel held his breath and touched the bell. It felt greasy under his fingertips.

Just as he had done to the pictures he'd found in the skip, Marvel reached out and scratched at the black wax near the window, and watched the colours emerge magically under his nails.

He was a child again, his past overlapping his future here, in this moment.

It *was* all circles.

Marvel pulled off the waders and walked out of the garage and on to Northborough Road.

Numb.

A lost boy found. A dramatic rescue. There should have been mayhem outside. There should have been fire trucks and ambulances and police cars parked from here to the bridge. There should have been TV crews and flapping tape and top brass arriving to take credit for all the stuff they hadn't done.

Marvel would have called them all, except he wouldn't have known what to tell them.

He didn't know what to tell himself.

Anna Buck had disappeared, so all there was to show for the drama was the driver smoking a fretful cigarette next to his lorry.

Blue Circle.

Marvel stared at it, too dazed to think about whether or not he believed in coincidences any more. He was too dazed to think about anything; he just stood there on the garage forecourt, while commuters split around him. People walked fast, with their heads down, their ears plugged with white cables; a woman in turquoise lycra jogged slowly past; a man walked two Dachshunds, and children on bicycles wove their way between the pedestrians, cheeks rosy and hair ruffled by the sharp wind.

Marvel didn't know what to do or where to go. Something had ended, but it was as though he was the only one who had seen its passing.

"You're standing on the feet."

"Hmm?"

A small girl with brown pigtails glared up at him through thick glasses.

"You're standing on the feet." She pointed at the ground and Marvel looked down to see he was standing on one of five small footprints made in the cement. He stepped off it and said "Sorry," and the child said "That's OK," and walked away.

As she did, he noticed that the clips in her plaits were shaped like little stars.

CHAPTER
FIFTY-ONE

When Anna Buck opened the door of the flat, Marvel already had his shoes in his hand.

"She isn't there," he said, and burst into tears.

She led him upstairs and made him some tea.

Marvel couldn't remember the last time he had cried. He hadn't cried in front of anybody since he'd fallen off a swing when he was six. Now he wept like a child, while an even smaller boy with straggly blond hair and dirty fingernails worked his way through slices of toast, dripping with butter, at the opposite side of the kitchen table.

Anna sipped her own tea and kept touching the boy's head, kept leaning in to smell him, kiss him, hug him.

"This is Daniel," she said huskily, when Marvel finally stopped weeping.

Marvel had so many questions that he didn't know what to say, so he just said "Hello," but the boy only fixed him with steady blue eyes.

The three of them sat there making small sounds. Daniel chewing. Anna sipping. Marvel sniffing now and then.

"Have you called DCI Lloyd?" he finally asked.

"Not yet," said Anna.

"You need to call him," he said.

"I will," she said. "There's plenty of time."

Marvel knew that, for Anna, there was.

Plenty of time.

A great calm seemed to have descended on her.

There was no rush. Not any more. No rush to call the police; no rush to find out what had happened; no rush to do anything but touch her son and feed him round after round of hot buttered toast.

That all started to seem very sensible to Marvel.

All very sane.

He clung to the sanity; it was a nice change.

He wondered whether the blue circles were still on the bedroom wall, and that made him think of the day when Anna Buck had told him that sometimes she heard Daniel crying.

That seemed logical now too. Everything could be explained away if you just thought logically.

"You must have heard him crying through the walls," he said.

"Maybe," said Anna.

"Subconsciously, maybe you knew he was there all along."

"Maybe."

She was humouring him. She didn't believe that for a second, and neither did he. Everything could be explained, but that didn't mean it made sense.

Anna sipped her tea and stroked her son.

He hesitated, then told her, "The window was on the wall, just the way you saw it."

She nodded, and Marvel looked at Daniel's buttery hands. He could see that the dirt under every ragged nail was made of blue-black wax, like his own were now.

Months of scratching at the dark walls.

He stared into the bottom of his mug. "But the cement had covered everything else. If she was in there . . ." He trailed off and shrugged.

"Was there a girl in the little room with you, Daniel?" said Anna gently.

The boy shook his head and went on chewing.

"Never?" said Marvel.

Daniel shook his head again.

"What I don't understand . . ." Marvel started, then stopped because there was *so much* he didn't understand that he should really try to put it in some sort of order.

"If she showed you all those things, Anna. If she left all those clues so you could find her . . ."

Anna nodded.

"Then where *is* she?" he said.

Anna stroked Daniel's hair and shook her head sadly. "I don't know," she sighed. "We found Daniel. That's all I know for sure. Daniel is home."

Then she hugged Daniel so hard that he squirmed.

Marvel phoned for a cab.

"We must go too," said Anna. "Go and get you checked out and see Daddy in the hospital, mustn't we?"

Daniel nodded soberly.

"Is James OK?" asked Marvel.

"He has burns on his legs, but the driver got a lot of water on him really fast and apparently water's really important . . ."

She stopped, then shrugged.

"Yes," said Marvel. "Yes."

Even though it was out of his way, Marvel got his cab to drop them both off at the hospital.

Anna held Daniel's hand tight as she got out, then turned and thanked him.

And although he was suspended, Marvel offered to tell DCI Lloyd that Daniel had been found.

"I'll do it," she assured him. "I promise I will, but . . ." She looked at Daniel, then went on, "I just want a couple of days first. Being a family. Being normal. Being sane."

Marvel hesitated, then nodded. "I suppose it'll wait a couple of days," he said. "The important thing is that you have your son back."

"I know," she smiled. "Thank you."

Then she leaned into the cab and kissed his cheek.

CHAPTER
FIFTY-TWO

It was a hot day in late summer and Superintendent Clyde had foolishly opened his window. The fumes of fatted lamb gambolled up from the Happy Kebabby and made Marvel's stomach roll.

"So you're off," said Clyde.

"Yes," said Marvel. He had his box on his lap. There wasn't much in it — his ashtray shaped like lungs, his *Reservoir Dogs* poster, and the photo of Edie Evans.

With her space face.

"Taunton, eh?" said Clyde, clapping his hands together like a vicar. "Fresh start. Lovely part of the world. We used to go walking there. Quantocks. Exmoor. Beautiful."

Marvel said nothing. He had passed a sign for Taunton on the motorway once. Middle of fucking nowhere. Mile upon mile of grass and cow shit, peopled by bumpkins swigging cider and riding pigs to market.

Bizarrely, Taunton had been the only DCI transfer he could get in the whole country. He could have stepped back down to detective inspector and gone somewhere else in the Met, but he'd rather have died first. And he had no future here now at Lewisham. He didn't need a psychic to tell him that.

There'd been several DCI posts in London and other major cities on the transfer lists, but by the time he'd made contact they'd all gone. Filled internally, he'd been told again and again.

And again.

After the fourth time, he'd called the recruitment officer at the West Midlands force and asked him what the hell was going on. In an accent that had made the rejection easier to bear, the officer had confirmed that the post had been filled internally. Then, at the end of their brief conversation, he'd asked Marvel to give his best to Robert Clyde.

That's when Marvel had realized that leverage worked both ways, and that Clyde was calling in favours and pulling strings to herd him out of the city and into the sticks, just as surely as a sheep.

Finally, Marvel had felt a grudging respect for his superintendent.

Too late, of course.

"Brady finished up the dog thing," said Clyde.

"Yeah?" Marvel no longer had any inclination to call him *sir*.

"Yes," said Clyde, apparently unperturbed by the omission. "He cautioned Latham and Denise Granger and spoke to the boy's parents. He really didn't feel there was a need for anything more."

He left Brady's supposed opinion hanging there, almost inviting disagreement, but Marvel disagreed via the medium of silence.

"He's gunning for inspector," Clyde said.

Marvel mused. "Everybody's moving up."

"That's right," said Clyde impassively. "Everybody's moving up."

"You might want to give Aguda a chance," Marvel said. "She's too good for the desk."

Clyde made a *maybe* face. He scribbled a blunt note with a sharp pencil, and Marvel wished he'd said something earlier, when his opinion might still have carried a bit of weight.

"Brady should do OK," he added, over-generously.

"Maybe," said Clyde. "If he's not too distracted."

"By what?" said Marvel.

"The baby," said Clyde. "His wife's pregnant, you know?"

Marvel's belly flip-flopped with memory.

Your wife is pregnant.

And you're burning up in the ice and snow.

"No," he managed faintly. "I didn't know."

Clyde got up and moved around him to the door, and after a long, paralysed moment, Marvel got slowly to his feet and walked out in a daze.

Across the squad room. Down in the lift. Through the foyer with his cardboard box.

If anybody else said goodbye to him, he didn't hear them.

There was scaffolding on the roof of the Bickley Spiritualist Church.

Marvel parked his rental car and walked back to the grubby little church hall next to the King's Arms.

He stood for several minutes, staring up at the new roof and wondering what percentage of it belonged to the Metropolitan Police.

The yellowing lights were on inside, although they were wan and watery through the filthy windows, and there was a soggy paper sign pinned to the split and peeling plywood noticeboard: THE DEAD ARE WAITING TO SPEAK TO YOU.

What bollocks, thought Marvel, as he opened the door.

Inside the hall was tired and dingy, and there was a damp patch on the ceiling that looked like Africa.

Marvel put a tenner in a wooden bowl overseen by two frail old women, who panicked over it until someone came in behind him and they could make change.

He saw Richard Latham. The man was surrounded by a coterie of misfits and old folk, all gazing adoringly up into his face, or nodding like toys, listening in rapt attention to some story he was telling.

Marvel studied him. The medium was wearing a brown jumper with the label sticking out of the neck, beige slacks and scuffed black shoes.

If it *was* all about the money, Latham was hiding it well.

The man reached the climax of his story and his voice rose just enough so that Marvel could share it.

"So I said, '*Come on, Marilyn! You're dead!*'" Latham reached out a helping hand and his acolytes parted hurriedly, as if they'd been standing on Marilyn without even knowing it. "And then I —"

Richard Latham froze as he met Marvel's eyes across the blue-rinsed room. He stopped talking, lowered his arm and excused himself. Then he poked his glasses up

356

on his nose, and left the knot of parishioners in the middle of the afterlife-and-death battle.

"I never expected to see you here, Mr Marvel." The man's forehead shone with nervous sweat, but — as usual — he was putting on a good show.

Marvel had been about to say something cutting about money and TV and dogs, but even as he opened his mouth he realized there was no point.

He had lost, and Latham had won, and both of those things were too insignificant to squabble over.

So he just shrugged and said, "I never expected to be here."

Relief dawned on Latham's face and, to his surprise, Marvel didn't even regret putting it there.

"I see you got your roof," he said.

"Yes," said Latham. Then, after an awkward pause, he said, "Want to buy a bucket?"

Marvel snorted. He looked around at the threadbare carpet, the plastic flowers and the dusty crucifix. "Just thought I'd come in and see what all the fuss was about," he said.

"That's nice," said Latham sincerely. "You're very welcome, Mr Marvel."

Marvel nodded slowly. "Well," he said, "I've seen it."

"You're not staying for the open circle?"

"Nah," said Marvel. "Ghosts are not my thing." He waved a vague hand in the direction of Africa.

"Not your thing?" Latham said gently. "After everything that's happened?"

Marvel laughed and shook his head. "*Especially* after that!" It was a knee-jerk response. If Marvel had thought about it, he might have said something different. Something more . . . measured. Although he had no idea what that might have been. Whether it would have been about everything that happened.

Or everything that *might* . . .

"I don't even know why I came in," he said a little angrily, feeling foolish in the face of his enemy.

But Latham opened his hands generously. "Everybody goes everywhere eventually. Does everything. We all go round in circles, Mr Marvel. Maybe you'll come again."

Marvel gave him a wry look. "Maybe I've been before."

"Ha!" said Latham. "Very good!"

Marvel headed for the door.

"Remember, Chief Inspector . . ."

Marvel turned.

"A circle never ends," said Richard Latham. "Even yours."

Marvel walked out of the church and stood on the pavement opposite the brick parapet of Bickley Bridge.

The sun had set but the days were still long, and the twilit clouds had formed spectacular banks of fire and smoke against the fading blue.

Marvel couldn't remember the last time he had looked at the sky.

He looked at it now, and felt better for it.

Maybe Taunton wouldn't be so bad after all. He'd be a big fish in a small pool. Show the yokels a thing or two. And maybe they'd have some good murders there.

Something he could get his teeth into. Maybe he could advance the forensics of pitchforks and slurry.

He snorted and turned towards his second church of the night, where the lights were already shining to guide the faithful home.

As he did, his eye was caught by a family walking towards him. It was Anna and James Buck, with Daniel.

Anna still had hold of Daniel's hand, while James pushed the baby buggy.

Marvel watched them. He wouldn't have said anything, but Anna saw him and waved, so he crossed the road.

They met at the spot where they had first met six months before, on that bitter night — both Valentine's cheats, flirting with drink and death.

Anna kissed his cheek again, and James shook his hand, and Daniel hid behind Anna and watched him from there.

Marvel ignored the buggy. It was just too weird.

He asked after James's legs. They were healing up well; he'd have scars, but that's why God invented trousers. He asked how Daniel was settling in and Anna must have told him, but he couldn't remember any of it, because she was so *different*. Everything about her was so filled with life and joy that he could barely believe that this person had been inside her all along, just hidden by pain and loss.

He remembered how the orange light had fallen on her bare, goosebumpy arm on that frigid February night — right here on this bridge — and wondered whether she was thinking about it too.

She didn't look as if she ever thought about it, and that made Marvel oddly happy.

Anna Buck was beautiful — anyone could see.

She was still talking, and he was still not quite hearing, when she bent over the buggy and pushed back the hood.

With a sense of dread, Marvel looked down at a bag of cement.

"We got Blue Circle," said James. "For old times' sake."

They all laughed then, and Marvel caught up with the fact that they were on their way to fill in the five footprints.

"Danny's going to do it, aren't you, Dan? He made 'em, he's going to fix 'em!"

Daniel poked his head out from behind Anna just long enough to nod happily at his father. He was holding a toy car in one hand — made out of wire.

"Better get off before it gets dark, then," said Marvel.

They said goodbye and the little family carried on down Northborough Road. Marvel went to cross over to the King's Arms.

"Edie's in space!"

Marvel's heart pumped a jolt of pure electricity. He turned to look at Daniel.

The boy was still holding Anna's hand, but had stopped at arm's length to stare back at him with a fathomless blue gaze.

"*What?*" Marvel choked, even though they had all heard it. "*What?*"

360

Daniel only ducked shyly against Anna's leg, hiding his face.

"*Daniel* —?" Anna started, but Marvel held up a hand to stop her.

Suddenly, he didn't want to hear any more than he already had.

Couldn't live with a different truth.

Edie was in space.

That was all he wanted to know.

Acknowledgements

The character of Richard Latham is named for the *real* Richard Latham, who won that dubious right in an auction to raise funds for Clic Sargent — a charity which cares for young people with cancer, and their families. Any similarity between Richard and my character ends with the use of his name.

The Shut Eye was inspired by humanearth.net — a campaign to raise awareness of human trafficking between Vietnam and China.

Many thanks to Vang Neng Thao for his help with the Hmong language.